BLOOD CASINO

"Blood Casino is nothing like I've read before. Nina Walker takes vampires to a whole new level in this first installment of Vampires and Vices that will have you reading all the way through the book in one sitting! With intrigue, suspense, and sprinkles of romance, you can't go wrong with this series!" —Heather Renee, USA Today Bestselling Author of The Broken Court Series and the Shadow Veil Academy Series

"Fans of TrueBlood rejoice, your new Eric Northman is here! Walker's intriguing new vampire novel takes a dark spin on the mythical creatures we know and love. In the words of the main character: there are no sparkly vampires here. And I'm all in for it." —G.K. DeRosa, USA Today Bestselling Author of the Darkblood Academy Series

BLOOD CASINO
VAMPIRES & VICES NO. 1

Copyright © 2020 by Nina Walker

Published by Addison & Gray Press, LLC.

This book is a work of fiction. Any references to historical events, real people, or real places are used fictitiously. Other names, characters, places and events are products of the author's imagination, and any resemblances to actual events or places or persons, living or dead, is entirely coincidental.

Cover Design by Clarissa Yeo of YOCLA BOOK COVER DESIGNS
Interior Formatting by WE GOT YOU COVERED BOOK DESIGN

Ebook ISBN: 978-1-950093-19-9
Paperback ISBN: 978-1-950093-20-5
Hardcover ISBN: 978-1-950093-21-2

BLOOD CASINO

VAMPIRES & VICES NO. 1

NINA WALKER

ADDISON & GRAY PRESS
WWW.NINAWALKERBOOKS.COM

This book is dedicated to the healthcare workers who've fought so valiantly to get us through a global pandemic.

Thank you.

ONE

Only two types of people frequent the blood casino: gamblers and their children. Standing outside on the steps of The Alabaster Heart, I can safely say that hate isn't a strong enough word to describe how I feel about this place. And okay, maybe there aren't that many of my peers trying to drag their parents out of here, but I've seen plenty over the last few years. Enough to know that once gambling sucks someone in, it's pretty much impossible to get them to stop.

New Orleans Canal Street traffic bustles by in a cacophony of irate drivers. They honk at the slow-moving tourists, who, like slugs on pavement, are too stifled by the humidity to care. The famous street cuts the city in half. On one side is the well-known French Quarter and on the other is the post-colonial builds. I prefer the newer part, even though the older is far more beautiful. Something about the newness feels safer to me, like maybe it's not crawling with centuries-old evil. That's probably wishful thinking.

Guess which side of the street the casino is on?

I clench my hands into fists and sigh. I should be used to going in there by now, but I can't help the nerves from firing in my belly. Out of habit, I check to make sure I'm wearing my crucifix necklace. The dainty thing rests against the hollow in my throat, warm from the sunlight. It's superstitious, I know, but it helps me breathe. In this city, it's better to be superstitious than sorry.

I force myself to ascend the steps. The hotel and casino's late 1800s architecture mirrors many of the buildings down here by the French Quarter with towering white columns, weathered red brick, and ornate metalwork. Since it's the only land casino in the area that has gaming tables, I know my mom will be saddled up to one of them. She's never been keen on the slot machines. "They favor the house," she always says, "doubling down at the tables is the only way to make any real money."

Yeah, like money is the biggest worry in a vampire-run casino.

I wipe my sweaty palms on my jean shorts and open the door. I have to pass through two vestibules to get inside. It's the vamps way of keeping the light out. It could be worse, though. Mom could be on the riverboat casino again. It runs weekend nights and once someone gets on, they can't get off until it docks in the early morning hours. I'm not old enough to step foot on that thing so I hate when she does. I hate feeling helpless. It's something I've experienced a lot lately.

The stale odor of old cigarette smoke hits me like a wall. I blink as my eyes adjust and then I begin weaving through the rows of flashing slot machines. I swear those things are programmed to attract toddlers. *Ding, ding, ding! Winner every hour! Jackpot!*

That's casino speak for, *Give me your money.*

So far I'm under the radar, but my heart rate only skyrockets as I edge closer to the gaming tables. No matter how many times I save her from herself, she always comes back for one more bet . . .

It's not all about money.

It's the game. The addiction.

The thumping roll of the dice, the chance of a win, the dopamine release with each turn of the cards. It's the euphoric feeling of chips being pushed her way. It's taking those chips to the cashier at the end of the night and trading them in for cold hard cash she can slip into her purse, making her feel invincible. Valuable. Loved.

It's too good and it sucks her in every single time.

And I always follow, ready to pull her away when her body can't take another drop. I don't trust *them* to care, even though it's the law. They promise not to bring the gamblers to the brink, but they have ways of covering their tracks. I am not my mother's daughter in that way, I can't handle those odds.

I find her at the Texas Hold'em table, her drug of choice.

It's only four o'clock on a Tuesday and all the seats are filled. Gamblers are cozied up together, talking shop like war heroes. They may look different—different sizes, ages, ethnicities—but their eyes each have the same glossy sheen, their movements the same practiced calm.

"Mom." I approach her from behind, talking low in her ear. "It's time to go."

She doesn't respond right away, but her bony shoulders still. The middle-aged human dealer shoots me an aloof glance. He deals the hands from the deck, the sound of redemption to these people. I look away. I don't want to be carded. The staff won't get too fussy if I'm in and out fast, but at only eighteen years old, they can boot me in a heartbeat. It happens all the time to those of us under twenty-one who are constantly trying to rescue our parents. Not that the age will stay twenty-one much longer. The vampires are lobbying hard to lower it to eighteen. It's all over the news.

I wait for the hand to finish. Mom drags a pile of winnings toward her and straightens triumphantly, like a fisherman with a tugging line. I cringe. This will only make it harder to get her out of here. She thinks she's the one reeling them in, but really, it's the other way around. "Mom," I try again, "please, let's go. You've played enough."

"Shh–none of that, Evangeline. I'm on a winning streak," she says, brushing me away as she leans over her cards, the IV in her hand tugging at the vein.

My heart drops, but the dealer is quick to push more cards at the players, so I step back again. The cards are thick and gold and shiny, with the swirly heart pattern embossed on the back. The casino's logo. I look away, focusing on the metal drip stand next to us. The plastic bag hangs heavy with blood. I can practically smell the metallic stench of it. She's been playing far too long but the more it fills up, the more chips the house gives her to keep her going. We don't have a lot of money to our name so this is Mom's way of increasing her odds. Another thing she always says, "You have to play big to win big." That and, "The bigger the risk, the bigger the reward." I hate all her little gambling ramblings because the reverse is also true. I study the other five players: two of them have a blood bag slowly filling drip by drip as well, but none are as full as Mom's. Hers is practically bursting at the seams. She needs to stop.

Panic is a beast of claws and teeth, ripping me open and spilling fear out right there on the ugly swirl-patterned carpet. Finally the hand is over, and once again, more chips come clanking toward her. "See, baby," she says, turning to face me, "I'm on a roll." She's as bright as Sunday morning, despite the blood loss. It won't last. Underneath her immaculate makeup, a ghost smiles back at me.

"Nice," I try again, sweet as honey this time. "Let's cash out while you're up, huh? Go shopping or something."

When she turns back to lay yet another bet, I nearly scream. This is ridiculous. I should just leave her and let her deal with her own consequences. I twist my foot into the carpet, readying to go. But instead of leaving, I remind myself that this isn't entirely her fault. The vampires are to blame, too. They're feeding on her addiction, and I have no doubt, compelling her to come back at the soonest opportunity.

I glare at the dealer. Sure, he's human, but he's still part of the problem. The guy is the definition of forgettable. He has a bulbous red face and beady little eyes. One look and I know he won't help me. They don't call him a "dealer" for nothing. He's a mouse enslaved to the serpent. Speaking of—the pit boss glides toward us. I tell myself it's the casino's air conditioning that causes a chill to run down the back of my neck, not the presence of a vampire.

He comes to stand behind the dealer, observing as gamblers move chips forward like they mean nothing, like they don't amount to mortgages and bills and food in their children's bellies. Everything about this vamp lacks empathy. His humanity is nothing but a relic of an abandoned past. His eyes flash cold when he catches my hard gaze. When he tilts his head, his white-blond hair shines under the neon casino lights.

He whispers something to the dealer and stands back.

"Can I see your ID, please?" the dealer asks, looking up at me grim-faced. The whole table turns to stare now, and anger fills me up.

"I'm not playing."

"There's no loitering allowed around tables if you're under twenty-one."

Right, like we haven't all seen the news talking about how the vampires are lobbying hard to get the gambling age lowered to eighteen. It will be another in a long line of laws changed to get humans addicted young.

"We were just leaving." I tug on mom's shoulder. It really is time to go.

"You go'on out and wait for me, okay, Evangeline?" Mom says, "I'm just going to play a few more hands, then I'll go find the nurse and turn this thing in." She motions to her blood bag.

I don't move. We're both staring at it now. It's *stupid* full. If a fly landed on it, I swear it would pop. My hands are still clenched into fists and begin to sting as my fingernails bite into my palms. Why haven't they cut her off? Of course she thinks she can last a little longer, she always thinks that. I know better. At only five-foot-one and barely a hundred pounds, she can't handle this much blood loss. She's a tiny woman. Simply getting the needle taken out of her hand will exhaust her, and that's if we leave *now*.

I glare at the pit boss, meeting his hollow gaze eye-for-eye.

My brain is not fully developed, so we both know I'm too young to be influenced by his vampiric compulsion. He raises an eyebrow as if to warn, *Not much longer, little girl.*

"She's going to pass out," I growl between gritted teeth, leaning over Mom to talk directly to the vampire. Immaculately groomed, he looks to be in his mid-thirties. He's more than likely much older than that. "If you don't cut her off before that happens, you'll break the law." I add, "And I'm here to witness it."

He gives me a sickly smile, fangs extended, and actually sniffs the air. My stomach churns. "She smells fine to me."

"Yeah, well, I know her better than you. She's not fine."

Meanwhile, the dealer has started another hand. The *slap, slap, slap* of cards is followed by Mom pushing out several hundred dollars in chips. In the space of time it takes for me to follow what she's doing, she doubles down.

I swallow a gasp and step back. All in. Fifteen hundred dollars. The exact amount I know we have to turn in to Mrs. Maybee tomorrow for our rent. Whatever she's earned from her blood donation, whatever she's brought along with her, whatever she's won on her streak—she's just bet it all.

"You had enough, already," I hiss. "Why did you do that?"

"I have three aces, Angel." Mom turns to me with a chastized whisper, swiping her auburn curls out of her brown eyes. Her complexion is even worse than it was minutes ago. The longer she plays, the longer she's hooked up to that stupid life-draining thing, the closer she gets to an accident. Drip, by drip, by drip, she plays her game and they collect their blood and the risks grow.

When the dealer flips over his cards, we're as still as the eye of a storm. A straight flush. Everyone around the table deflates, Mom the most.

She lost.

"I can win it back," she mutters as she reaches for the zipper of the purse strung over her bone-thin arm. Enough. I yank her up, and she squeals. Shame prickles through me as I pull her away, the drip stand rolling right along with us. But it's no use, Mom's knees buckle and she collapses in my arms. Not much bigger than she is, I'm only able to hold her weight for a moment. Falling to my knees, I lay her on the floor. The drip stand falls and the blood bag bounces against the carpet. It's a miracle it didn't break. Mom's brown eyes lose focus and flutter closed.

Oh, hell no!

"I told you she would pass out," I yell at the pit boss. "Now what, huh? Should I call the police?"

He seems unaffected, still back behind his table, but I know better. This is a fireable offense. This is the kind of thing that will get him in trouble with the vampires higher up in their royal hierarchy. There are treaties, laws, and rules for a reason.

A team of nurses swoop in moments later. I won't leave Mom. I shift back onto my butt and watch her carefully as they get to work. "She's lost a lot of blood," one of them says. "Virginia's lost a lot before," another adds, "she'll be okay." The fact that the nurses know my mom by name makes me even madder. And they're probably right, she'll probably be okay, but I'm about ready to burn this place to the ground anyway.

The pit boss jumps over the table, the players, and the crowd of gawkers, landing softly to survey the scene. He practically flew, he moved so fast. Maybe he did fly. I've heard some of the suckers can do that. I roll my eyes, unimpressed.

The laws on this kind of thing are clear. Vampires are not allowed to take "donations" to the point that a human passes out and absolutely no bleeding anyone dry. For as much as they need our blood, they need us alive, more.

Vampires use blood bags because feeding directly on human flesh isn't allowed unless there is written consent from the human *and* permission from vamp royalty, which as far as I know, never *ever* happens. The bloodsuckers have chosen to keep that kind of feeding to a minimum for their own secretive reasons, thank heavens. And when I say secretive, I mean *secretive*. I've done a ton of research on this subject and haven't found a plausible reason as to why they don't feed directly from us. Sure, there are a zillion theories floating around out there, but the vampires won't confirm anything.

So it's blood bags for feedings, and those nasty creatures like to bite into them when they're as fresh and warm as puppies. Casinos are one of the best places vampires can use human vices against us, and they own them all. So take a seat, but first, you'd better stick out your arm and open a vein. The chance of winning money is too enticing for some people, add that to a nice dose of compulsion layered on each visit to "come again soon," and voila, you have yourself a herd of willing blood donors.

The whole thing makes me sick.

Luckily, I'm not twenty-five, the age that compulsion begins to work. My brain is still developing, which means my prefrontal cortex doesn't rule my decision making, so the vamps can't get inside there quite yet. Note to self, get away from here before the big day. When that happens, I don't want to be anywhere near vampires. Too bad they're in every urban city now and I never pictured myself living in the sticks. I hate bugs and I love fresh sushi. What's a girl to do?

Eyes watering, I lean forward to brush the hair from Mom's forehead. The nurses have been quick to administer their treatment. They must sense the anger still roaring in me because they don't ask me to move.

I can't wait to report this.

"Adrian has requested to speak with you. He wishes to apologize in person," someone is saying. I look up to meet the dealer's beady little eyes. The pit boss is behind him, talking on a cellphone; his voice is muffled and calm, but his expression is mighty strained.

Hello consequences, meet vampire, I hope you two get to know each other very well...

"Who's Adrian?" I ask the dealer, confused why someone would think for a second that I'd be willing to stick around. I'm getting Mom out of here at the first possible second and then we're filing a police report. That alone almost makes the fact that we can't make rent worth what happened. Almost.

At the end of the day, we still can't make rent, and Mrs. Maybee isn't the nicest landlady. We've been late too many times in the past. She'll only give us three days this time. That's it. And then what? Go to a shelter? Those places are cesspools for evil to prey on the weak. The world isn't what it used to be. Ever since the vampires crawled out of the shadows seventeen years ago, nobody is safe anymore. I've never known a world without them. I was a chubby little one year old when it all went down.

"Adrian runs this place," the dealer explains in a rush. "We'll make sure your mom is okay. But trust me, you'd better go, Adrian is not someone you want to say no to."

"And why's that?" I grumble, my mind already out of here and onto the next thing I'm going to have to do to clean up this mess. Maybe I can ask my boss for an advance? *Ugh, that's not going to work.* I just started at Pops and they're a place of *business*, not a charity.

Mom's eyes flutter open. I sink farther into the ground with a sigh. One of the nurses has switched her IV to fluids and she's already starting to look alive again. "You're going to keep a meticulous record of how much she donated, right?" I press the nurse. "So she doesn't donate again before she's safe?"

"Of course," the nurse replies as if that's a given, but I don't know if I believe her. She's human but she still works for *them*.

The dealer waves his hand in my face. "Hey, I'm still talking to you. This is important."

I roll my eyes at him. "What?"

"You really don't know who Adrian is?" The dealer frowns at me like I'm a complete idiot, like I should know everything that goes on in this casino, including who this Adrian guy is.

"Whatever, I'm only eighteen." I shake my head. The fact that I'm even here is total crap, and I blame it on the vamps. They were buying up places like this for decades before they ever went public, all part of their master plan. Places where they could convince humans to trade blood for addiction. And it's as easy as it sounds.

The dealer squats down next to me, getting right up in my face. He stinks of cigarette smoke just as bad as the carpet does. It makes my eyes burn. Another vice, cigarettes. I don't care what it is, if it's an addiction, I don't want any part. "Adrian's one of the North American princes. He doesn't just run The Alabaster Heart, he runs New Orleans and most of the southern United States."

"A prince, you say?" I snort. The idea of this Adrian character is a spark that settles into me, an answer to a problem. I decide to pour gasoline on that idea. Yes, this vampire has the kind of power that could squash me. Yes, he could murder me in a second if he chose. But I'm the one in the power position here. I'm the girl he needs to convince to shut up. My idea started as a spark but it's a full-on inferno now. Will it work?

I only have to strike a deal with the devil to find out.

TWO

My sparkly white flip-flops smack on the pearlescent marble tile as I follow the pit boss out of the noxious gaming area and into the attached hotel lobby. Being in The Alabaster Heart is like walking through a time capsule. It's all reflective golden surfaces and polished white accents and deep, dark black everywhere in between. Magnificent crystal chandeliers hang from the ceilings and tufted black and emerald green furniture litter the space. The stunning art deco style is something my interior design-obsessed best friend Ayla would salivate over, but it does nothing but twists me into tight little knots.

"Kelli will help you." The pit boss steps aside, motioning toward a receptionist stand, and strides away. I wish I could follow and go back to mom. I hated leaving her back there, but the nurses insisted she wasn't ready to get up anyway.

A bright-eyed secretary slips me a demure smile. This must

be Kelli. She's a California-looking bleached-blonde with big roller-curled hair and high cheekbones. She looks like she would've had glowing tan skin in her previous life but her deadness spoiled that. I catch sight of her gleaming white teeth and try not to stare. At least she has the decency not to extend her fangs. Her beauty is vampiric and unnatural and it sets me on edge. She looks me over and grimaces, as if judging me in two seconds flat and deciding I'm not worth her time or attention.

"Hi," I say, the greeting slipping out of me.

"Adrianos Teresi will see you now," she purrs in response. She nods toward a private elevator and I walk inside, more than happy to put distance between us. I'm surrounded by reflective gold on all sides in the elevator box. Gold ceiling, gold floor, gold walls—super weird. Even weirder is that fact that there are no buttons. I've never been in an elevator without buttons and I can't say I like it. As it rises, inertia settles low in my belly. I suddenly notice the lack of silver in the design. Nowhere in the entire hotel is anything silver. Makes sense, I guess. Vampires hate silver.

When the doors slide open, I'm directly facing a large office.

"First thing you need to know," I announce, stepping inside, "is it's going to take a lot of money to make me go away."

The office itself is a monochromatic cocoon of polished oak. The design is mid-century modern, like that TV show Mom used to watch obsessively, Mad Men. Everything about it screams masculinity and power. A twenty-something man stands before a vast, darkly-tinted window overlooking the Mississippi river. His hands are tucked together behind a crisp gray suit jacket. He's tall, thin, and stoic, with golden-blond wavy hair that's longer on top and cut close to his scalp on the sides. His suit contrasts perfectly against his pale skin like inky night and golden day. When he turns, an undertow of curiosity surfaces within me. It's his eyes. They demand my attention with their glacial blue, biting to my center.

He tilts his head to the side and runs those arrow-eyes down my body. I break out into a sweat. "You want money." His gaze narrows and he sounds almost disappointed. "That's all?"

"Yes, that's right." I steel myself. His people hurt my mother. He owes me. "I want our money back and then some."

"Asking for money is so uninspired, don't you think?"

"That's easy to say coming from someone who has it. Try living without money and you won't be so quick to judge me."

Rubbing his angular chin with his long pale fingers, he slowly walks toward his desk and flicks a hand at the open chair across from it. A businessman in his lair, he smiles wickedly. "Why don't you have a seat?"

"I'd rather stand."

He stops. His jaw clicks, and something that's either lust or thirst crosses his expression. "I'm sure you would."

Something tightens in my stomach. Is he toying with me?

"You're not what I thought you would be," he says. The

slightest of Mediterranean accents alerts my basest instincts that he's different. If I had to guess, I'd say the tumbling melody of his tone, his light coloring, and last name Teresi, suggest that he's of Greek descent. He's certainly beautiful enough to have been the muse for those Greek sculptures. How old is he? Any accent he would have had is now watered down, likely through centuries of travel. He must be old if he's in charge of all the vampires in the southern United States.

He catches me staring and chuckles. The laugh rings like sweetgum leaves on a spring breeze, but I know not to trust it. Maybe he's not what I thought either. Maybe he's not the evil bloodthirsty vampire prince who'd suck me dry for dinner if he could, maybe he's something much worse.

Or maybe he's not. Maybe he's more human than I thought. I almost laugh at that stupid thought. It's not possible. I'd be foolish to think it.

"So how much?" I press.

He laughs louder.

"What's so funny?"

"Normally 'how much' is the question I would be asking you."

So he bribes people often. This shouldn't come as a surprise, but my disappointment stings anyway. I don't know why I'd hoped he would be better than my expectations, that he'd somehow care about humans. He doesn't. He can't. They never do.

"Your other guests might like to sit and chat, but I want to get out of here as quickly as possible. So why don't we cut the crap and finalize the money?"

He steps closer. "What makes you think I'm going to give you money?"

I glance down and glare at the lapels of his designer suit, not quite able to hold his gaze. It's probably a vampire thing, that all encompassing "feel it in your bone marrow" type of look meant to ensnare humans, but his eyes are too mesmerizing. "It's clear to me that this casino has more than enough money," I challenge, "and still, your pit boss ignored my mother's obvious distress. Your employee broke the law. If I report it, not only will you have to pay a hefty fine, but I'm guessing that even you, Adrianos Teresi, North American *prince*, will have to answer to an even more powerful vampire than yourself."

He's across the room one second and standing a foot away the next. The scent of warm cedar, bergamot, and honey wash over me. The curls of his golden hair catch the light. Up close, his youthful appearance is more predominant, almost startling. Even though he looks to be in his mid-twenties, there's no possible way that he is. I don't know for sure, but I think someone this powerful had to earn his position through many years of servitude, which is how I know he must answer to someone. Everyone does.

"Are you threatening me?" he snaps, disdain eating his expression. Heat flushes across my cheeks. His pupils dilate and

I lose my breath; he can smell my blood. How easy would it be for him to kill me right now? To sink his fangs into my neck and suck the life from my veins?

Don't think about it…

"Maybe I am a threat to you," I challenge back. "And why do you really care for my mother's money? You got her blood. You don't need to take her paycheck, too."

Amusement sparks in his eyes. "And what if your mother faked her incapacitation? What if it was all a stunt to extort *us* for money?"

I gape, wanting to punch the smirk clean off his face.

"That's impossible. My mother loves this place. Besides, there were witnesses."

"Yes." He smiles wide. "There were." His tongue lightly runs across the tip of one fang as they slowly extend. My senses kick into overdrive, my pulse erupting. I need to get out of here.

He's dangerous. Beautiful—they usually are—but deadly as midnight.

"I'm not afraid of you," I lie. "If you kill me, you'll be tried and will face true death."

Okay, I actually doubt that would happen, vampires are good at getting away with things, but still, I have to appear strong in his presence or else I'm going to crumble.

He smiles and retracts the fangs. "How old are you?"

I'm caught off guard by the question. "I'm not even close to twenty-five, if that's what you're thinking."

He studies me as he leans back on his heels, still towering over me by at least a foot. I shrink.

"I'm eighteen," I finally say, irritation spreading through my body like a virus. I have absolutely nothing to hide here. He's the one who hurts people, feeds on human blood. He's the monster. "In case you suck at math," I'm quick to add, "I still have seven more years to make your job difficult if you keep hurting my mom."

Actually, it's closer to six. My birthday is coming up.

"Your mother is a grown woman who is free to come and go as she pleases." He says it like she's to blame here, not like she's a victim to their compulsion and her addiction. It curdles my stomach.

"Don't lie to me. I know your people use compulsion on her. You creeps love to prey on people like my mom."

"Compulsion is illegal." His voice is steel. "I assure you, we abide by the law here at The Alabaster."

Lies.

Sure, it's illegal, but it's also nearly impossible to track. No doubt it happens more often than people would like to believe. No one wants to think they were manipulated, especially not when they refuse to admit to their addictions, and especially not when they're entering into what they believe is a win-win situation.

Blood for gambling.

Blood for drugs.

Blood for sex.

The vampires have no shame.

"Like I said, I'm only eighteen. Let's make a deal, Adrian. Are we going to talk numbers? Maybe I should just go ahead and file that police report now." I raise an eyebrow.

He looks me over for a long second and then steps back, peering down his nose at me like I'm a bug he'd like nothing more than to squash. "I'll play your little game only because I am growing tired of you," he sighs dramatically. "I'll give you five thousand dollars."

I consider the option, ignoring the thrill of it. Be rational. Five grand is enough to get us through August and well into September. Hopefully, even longer. I could ask for more, negotiate, but I don't want to risk more money for what I'm about to do.

I don't want to be greedy like those gamblers down there. Knowing when to walk away is the only way to win.

"Fine by me." I reach out my hand and smile as sweet as my Grammy's pecan pie. Goodness, I miss that woman. She passed away two years ago and ever since it's like Mom's been in the casino nonstop. Grief does horrible things sometimes. We'd like to think so, but not everyone is strong.

Adrian seems pleased with himself, but he doesn't shake my hand.

All the better.

"I'll call down to the cashier," he says coolly. "They already know to look for you."

"Great." I head for the elevator, eager to press the call button. His lingering gaze sticks to me like a tattoo. I stop and turn back while I wait for the doors to open. "If they already knew to look for me, then why play this game?"

His smile is dangerous. "Maybe I like to play games. I do run a casino, after all."

I roll my eyes and turn away.

"You never told me your name," he says just as I step inside.

But I'm already gone.

As soon as I'm downstairs, I swing by the cashier, pick up the cash, and get Mom ready to go all in a matter of five minutes. I wrap her arm through mine, and as we make for the exit, I snatch my cell phone from my pocket. The number is programmed in, and the dispatcher answers on the second ring.

"I'd like to report a crime," I say, as we're about to make our escape. "Vampires took too much blood from my mom at The Alabaster Heart Casino and she passed out."

As I back up against the first set of doors, I catch ice-blue eyes from across the lobby. *Uh-oh.* Adrian crosses to me instantly, so fast it happens in the space of a single blink, and grips my wrist between his steel-trap hands. They're cold. His touch sends a shockwave through my entire body. Mom shrieks and I shift her behind me.

"What did you just do?" Adrian clips.

"Don't touch me." I shove him away, a feather against a rock. I have zero strength on him, but he lets me go anyway. He shakes his head, angry thunder rolling through him like an incoming storm. I cross the threshold and raise my hand in a wholly inappropriate gesture as my parting goodbye gift.

I can't help it. Like a fool, I look back for one last glimpse. It leaves me with dread in my chest. Adrian is watching me like I'm a whole new kind of game he wants to master, one where I end up dead. The sun is a welcome friend, but it's setting fast. We need to get home. One thing I said I would never do is cross a vampire.

But vampires can be deceived too. They're not the only ones who can play games.

Did we set any terms or conditions? Did we shake on anything? He never once required the money to be an exchange for silence, never once asked for anything from me. All he did was offer five thousand dollars. As far as I'm concerned, this hellish casino has exploited my Mom for years. Maybe now she and I will not only make it through another month, but hopefully Adrian will ban us from the casino altogether.

Wouldn't that be nice?

I made a new enemy today. I know it was reckless, but the money is a thick wad of redemption tucked neatly in my pocket. And the truth is, cheating vampires feels really freaking good.

THREE

The police requested we come into the station right away. I like this place. It's all busy and bustling and no-nonsense. I've been considering looking into law enforcement and being here makes that feel possible, like maybe there's more out there for me. I'm totally excited!

The whole college thing didn't work out. I can't afford it and don't have good enough high school grades or test scores to land scholarships. Plus, growing up with a mom like mine made me scared of debt. It's fine. Right now I'm a server. It's decent money and all, but it's nothing I would want to do for the long haul. Let's be honest here, I'm way too sassy and independent to be in the service industry long term.

As I look around the police station, I imagine myself here instead, dressed in a crisp uniform, packing heat in my holster, and with an important job to protect innocent people. It's a nice thought, offering a chance at meaning in my otherwise murky future.

"This isn't necessary," Mom crows to the officer. "It was an unfortunate accident. My fault, really."

I glower over at Mom. "Stop trying to play this off like it was nothing. The casino took advantage of you."

She waves her wrist around. "Oh, I'd hardly call it that."

"They could've killed you!"

Officer Perez leans closer, tapping his pen against his notebook, worry etched onto his thick brow. "Facts are, Mrs. Blackwood, it's against the human-vampire law to take that much blood. Now, *we* can't go making any arrests in this case because it's outside of our jurisdiction, but what I can do is report the incident to the Vampire Enforcement Coalition. They take these filings very seriously and have their own ways of punishing vampires." His mouth turns down in a grimace. "I'll tell you, I've seen some of it in action and it's pretty nasty. I definitely wouldn't want to be working for the VEC."

Okay, first off, how do I get a job for the VEC? Because I'd love nothing more than to punish the suckers. But second, is this guy for real? Are the police too scared to actually do anything about what happened?

The image of myself working as a police officer slips away in an instant. I don't want to go into law enforcement if this is how it's going to be. I can't imagine how frustrated I would feel knowing someone is guilty of a crime but unable to go after them. I know vampires are scary and all, but humans still need to stand up to them.

"So we're just supposed to believe the Vampire Enforcement Coalition actually cares? Who's running that organization, anyway?" I fold my arms over my chest and glare. I think we all know where this is going…

He shrugs, his face reddening. "A mix of humans and vampires."

I bark out a laugh. "And we're supposed to trust the vampires to punish themselves? Give me a break, man."

"They have a whole watchdog group set up and their own police force for this very reason." He raises his hand in reassurance, but I can tell even he knows it's complete crap. I mean really, the absurdity is like handing a toddler a rainbow lollipop and then telling the child *not* to lick it. Never going to happen.

I shake my head. "But the guy who runs the casino is the vampire prince of North America."

"Adrianos Teresi?" The cop frowns. "Yeah, he's one of the main vamps over there at the VEC and not someone you ever want to piss off. You should stay far away from him."

"Great, so now we know for sure he's not going to get punished. What's he going to do? Slap himself on the wrist?"

"I'm sorry, Ms. Blackwood, but that's all we can do." He straightens in his chair. "And Adrianos isn't the only vampire affiliated with the VEC. They have checks and balances. We have to trust that someone else will punish him."

"If checks and balances actually worked, do you think our country would be in the position it's in?" I scoff. I hate politics because it always fails the exact people it's supposed to help. I think that pretty much goes without saying in a country where vampires are *legally allowed* to take advantage of the people who need protection from them. "You have younger cops, don't you? Officers under twenty-five who don't have to worry about compulsion? Let me talk to one of those guys."

"Yes, well, it doesn't work that way . . ."

"Why not?"

"They have to refer back to the VEC as well. Everyone does."

I blink a few times, absolutely disgusted by this red tape bureaucratic garbage. "This is nuts, you do realize that, right?"

"Think of vampire law like a Native American reservation law. They have their own enforcement, too, and when someone goes onto their land," he gestures to my mother, "or into one of their casinos—they should know the risks."

Mom shrinks in on herself.

"So you're blaming her now?" I point to my mom, even though the man does have a point. A lamb can't expect to walk into the lion's den and come out unscathed. But still, victim shaming is victim shaming, and it doesn't sit right with me.

"No, that's not what I mean," he rushes on. "I'm just saying that there are inherent risks that people take when they go to places like The Alabaster."

"These are vampires we're talking about here," I chastise, "this is not something we should be playing around with, at The Alabaster or anywhere else. If we keep letting them get away with crimes, how much longer until they're the ones in control?"

"I'm sorry that I can't do more for you." He fidgets, and I close my eyes.

I'm so mad I could scream. I don't know if I've ever felt more helpless and disillusioned. Forget about the suckers getting more control of the humans, they already have it. If the laws aren't enforced then what's the point of even having them? To give us the illusion of safety, to make us think we know what we're doing, that everything is going to be okay.

It's not.

"Listen," he whispers under his breath. "We both know compulsion is illegal, but they do it anyway. It allows them to turn the cops crooked if we go near them. Same thing happens with politicians. Even if we could send the under twenty-fives in, we wouldn't want to risk it. We don't know when someone's prefrontal cortex actually forms, the scientists say twenty-five, but there's not an exact date to brain development."

"Fine," I grumble. Maybe he's right. Just because something is illegal doesn't stop the leeches from doing it. The idea that sometime around my twenty-fifth birthday my brain will become permeable to the same tampering makes my stomach slowly harden like drying cement.

I hate them. I hate them all.

"Come on, Mom." I take her hand and we stand. "Let's go home. This was a waste of time."

Mom is all too happy to leave, and despite Perez's assurances that this will be taken seriously by the VEC and that we should stay and answer the rest of his questions, I get us the heck out of there. Deep in my gut I know the VEC won't do anything about this. Everyone is afraid of Adrian, or I guess, technically it's Adrianos. Still, I feel justified in my actions against him. The vamps deserved a taste of their own manipulative medicine, and quite frankly, we deserved to get some of our money back.

Mom doesn't agree.

As soon as we get into the car, she lets me have it. "Evangeline, how could you? We can't make enemies with the vampires!" Her voice shakes. "This is not going to end well."

I laugh bitterly. "Humans and vampires are already enemies, Mom. What are you even saying right now?" I'm driving since she's still weak, and my fingers tighten over the cracked plastic of the steering wheel. My knuckles turn white.

A tear slips down her ashen cheek, and I have to stop myself from lashing out at her even more and remember that she's weak and she's lost a lot of blood today. "I'm so embarrassed. Did you see the way that officer looked at me?"

I hold back a growl. "You don't actually care about that cop. You're embarrassed because you lost face with your casino buddies."

And probably the vamps themselves, but I don't add that part.

We argue the rest of the drive home, and after we pull into the carport, she storms inside, locking herself in her bedroom to pout. I run the rent money over to Mrs. Maybee who lives on the other side of our little duplex, because once again I'm the responsible one in this house. I try to remind myself that it's not all mom's fault, she's an addict and the vampires are feeding off of that, but I'm still mad as hell.

The gambling has always been a little bit of a problem for Mom, but since Grammy died of cancer it's gotten to the point of no return. When Gram was sick I thought maybe Mom would change. She was so busy taking care of her mom, she stopped going to the casino. But then Gram died and Mom went back ten times more often. I honestly don't know how I'm going to fix this, or if I can. I'm terrified she's going to either end up homeless or dead. And where would that leave me? Even though I'm the more mature one in our relationship, I still can't imagine being an orphan.

I stomp into my room, shove the rest of the cash into a sock, and hide it in the air conditioning vent above my bed. Rummaging through my disaster of a closet, I pick out an outfit for tomorrow, pajama shorts and a tank for tonight, find my toothbrush and makeup bag, and toss everything into my raggedy jean backpack. I text Mom on the way out the door. **I'm sleeping at Ayla's house tonight. If someone rings the doorbell, don't answer it.**

Ayla is my best friend. She has been ever since middle school when all the other girls got boobs and boyfriends and we stayed awkward for another few years. Luckily, our boobs and boyfriends came later. Not that I have much of either at the moment compared to Ayla. The girl is voluptuous with a capital V.

I would never answer the door without using the camera. Mom types back. **We'll talk some more tomorrow.** And then a few seconds later. **Why do you always act like you're the parent and I'm the child?**

And then, **I'm tired of your judgement.**

And a quick, **You need to learn to trust me. I'm the grown up here, Evangeline Rose Blackwood.**

I scoff. She could've fooled me! Just because she can yell at me through text by using my full name doesn't make her the mature one here. But that's not what I type. Instead, I type, **I only do what I do because I love you.** And leave it at that.

I'm glad about the doorbell situation though. Vampires can't enter homes without being invited in by someone who actually lives there, but they could easily compel her into letting them in if she answered the door and looked into their eyes. This is common knowledge and the main reason why literally *everyone* has doorbell cameras installed these days. She knows better, but still, I can't shake the rage I saw on Adrian's face when I left the casino earlier. He probably wants me dead for the stunt I pulled, and he seems like the kind of man who is used to getting what he wants.

I shiver and try to erase his image from my mind.

There's a lot of speculation about compulsion in general. Can all vampires do it or only the older ones? Do they really do it often, like I think they do, or not at all like they claim? I wish I knew the answers.

Mom texts back yet again. **Fine, you can go. Have a good time with your friend. Stay inside at her place tonight and don't take off your necklace. I'll see you tomorrow.**

I don't bother with a reply. Protection from a crucifix necklace is only a superstition, everyone knows that. But I feel like it's a declaration to the vampires that I think they're an abomination, so I wear it all the time. Plus, mine's kinda cute and fits in with my whole down-with-the-patriarchy aesthetic, in an ironic kind of way.

The sun is beginning to set, casting everything in a hazy glow of creamsicle orange, so I speed walk down the street and toward my best friend's place. She lives on the other side of our neighborhood, the fancier side, where the houses have their own fenced yards, the garages are all enclosed, and most people don't rent.

Can I sleep over tonight? I text Ayla, already knowing she'll say yes. **Mom and I had a huge fight and I can't be in the same house as her right now.**

Well, shoot! What did you do, Evangeline Rose Blackwood? Ayla immediately texts back, using my full name like she knows my mom does all too often. It drives me crazy, but coming from Ayla it makes me smirk.

Not me. Her gambling again. Is all I say.

It's followed by a quick, **Of course you can stay here. See you soon! Hugs!**

I slide the phone into my back pocket and wipe a bead of sweat from my forehead. You'd think the setting sun would have cooled things off, but it's early August. The humidity is not fun in Louisiana and it's only going to get worse the next few weeks. The heat doesn't let off here until October.

Don't call me by my full name Miss Ayla Elizabeth Moreno, I text again, trying to lighten the conversation before I show up at her door.

Then don't be a menace to society. Her reply is almost instant.

I laugh aloud at the inside joke dating back to a high school assembly in which our crusty old principal lectured us on what was and wasn't appropriate for teen behavior. When I challenged him on the hem length requirement for girls, he called me a menace to society. True story.

My full name is Evangeline Rose Blackwood. Pretentious, right? I hate it. It's way too "Southern Pageant Girl" for my taste, which is exactly why my mother picked it. She's always wanted me to be like her, to pretty myself up for pageants until I was old enough to pretty myself up for a wealthy man. Unfortunately for her active imagination, by age eight I'd rejected her plans, including the name, and have gone by Eva ever since. Mom still calls me Evangeline, or worse, Angel, but she's the only one who's allowed to, on account of the whole "growing me in her uterus, spending twenty hours in labor, and raising me all by herself" thing.

Besides, following in her footsteps was never a guarantee for happiness. Look at how things turned out for her. Mom married into a wealthy family when she was only twenty years old and, from the outside looking in, it seemed like she'd be set for life.

No such luck.

My father was the son of a well-to-do old European family. He was also the black sheep who went off to America for college. They wanted him to return home, but he ended up getting into a medical school in New Orleans and fell in love with the city. It was during med school that he met my mom who was working as a receptionist for the school. He'd fallen even more madly in love with her than he had NOLA and that was all it took for him to commit to staying. After a year of dating, she'd gotten pregnant with me and they'd eloped without the big European wedding or even the blessing of his parents.

Strike one and two, according to his family. They cut him off completely.

When he died in a horrific car accident when I was a baby, his family apparently reached out to Mom and asked her to move overseas so they could help raise me. A Southern girl through and through, Mom had refused, and that was strike three because they put us out of their minds without another word. Just like my father, we were dead to them too.

Nobody from Dad's side of the family has ever contacted me. Not one.

I look like a mixture of my Caucasian mom and the one picture I have of my father. I don't know a lot about him because Mom can't say a word without getting weepy and shutting herself in her bedroom. But their wedding picture still hangs on our living room wall. Judging from his appearance alone, he's got to be Spanish or Italian or something Mediterranean like that. With his creamy olive tone and thick dark hair, it's no wonder she fell head over heels.

I can see myself in him more than I can my mother, and something about that makes me happy and sad all at once.

My inky black hair is stick straight no matter what I do to it, my slightly almond shaped eyes are brown as molasses, and my prominent cheekbones make me stand out among my friends. Sometimes people ask me if I'm Asian or Polynesian. I've even gotten Native American on a couple occasions. I don't mind looking like the personification of the American melting pot, it's not like I've ever been to Europe anyway.

But my complexion is pretty close to Mom's pinky cream, and I have her big pageanty smile too. I've now grown taller and thinner than her because I never inherited her womanly curves, but I'm okay with that. I'm a natural athlete, which is great if you ask me. I was hoping a track scholarship would come my way, but that obviously never happened.

I graduated in May and my plan is to figure out what I want to do with my life, which is kind of laughable at this point. It's been three months since graduation, and my "figure out what I want to do with my life" plan hasn't made an inch of headway. Actually, I'll argue that after that disastrous visit to the police station it's gone backward.

I tuck away the disappointment about that to unpack another day. Right now, the Moreno's cute Spanish style house is a welcome friend, and I bound up the driveway. When I knock on the big blue door and wave to the doorbell camera, I expect Ayla to answer it. But it's Felix who pulls it open. Ayla's older brother by eighteen months, Felix is my longtime crush. One year ahead of us in school, Felix goes to Tulane University in the city. He lived in the dorms his first year and plans to live in off campus housing next year with some of his buddies, but he's been staying at home this summer.

Let's just say, it's been the best thing about this summer. I missed Felix last year.

"Hey, Eva." His smile quirks, and his chocolatey latin eyes sparkle. "You're sleeping over tonight?"

Ugh, why does my brain immediately want to take that question and ask him one of my own? *Like—Yes, Felix, I am. Do you mind if I sleep in your bed?* But I don't have much experience in that department, and I'm pretty sure my best friend would kill me if I started dating her brother. Actually, she has warned me of that many times over the years even though she knows how I feel about him. Doesn't stop a girl from dreaming, though.

"Yes," is all I say about sleeping arrangements as I follow him inside. "How's the internship going?"

He's working at some fancy downtown bank as a paper pusher but doesn't talk about it a whole lot. I mean, what is there to say? It's probably super boring.

"Eh, it's the same old 9 to 5." He winks and immediately changes the subject, "So what's new, Eva? Any guys I need to beat up for you?"

The picture of him beating up some jerk for me is definitely something I can get behind.

"Unfortunately, no." I pretend to think hard. "But I'll let you know when someone crosses me."

"You do that."

My mind flashes to Adrian, and I picture the two battling,

Felix coming out victorious for my honor in the end, and then the two of us making out. Definitely an image I want to tattoo into my fantasy memory bank.

"Hey, you." Ayla appears and pulls me into her bedroom, closing the door softly. "Stop drooling over my brother, you hoe."

"Stop having such a hot brother," I retort. And Felix really is a hottie. He's got a bad boy persona with scruffy two-day-old facial hair and dark curly black hair. His eyebrows are stronger than most and his eyes have that deep-set commanding thing going on. He's tall and muscled and he even got a sleeve tattoo this last year. And to top it off, he's an athlete. But not a typical one; he plays lacrosse for the university. Honestly, how can Ayla blame me?

She crosses her eyes and sticks out her tongue. She's basically the girl version of Felix but shorter, with dyed blue hair and lighter eyes and *all the curves*. Ayla's the friend I've always counted on, and now she's leaving me behind to go off to college herself and pursue her dreams. My heart squeezes. "I'm really going to miss you."

"Me too." She frowns and gathers me in a hug, offering the first bit of comfort I've had in ages. Her signature vanilla spice scent wraps around me and I try to commit it to memory. I don't know what I'm going to do when she's gone.

FOUR

I wake up with a start, my eyes popping wide open. I blink into the shadowy ceiling and freeze. Ayla sleeps next to me, her body curled into a tight ball, her breath soft whisperings in the darkness. Exhaustion grips the back of my eyeballs, but there's no way I could go back to sleep right now. My heart races, the pulse drumming in my neck.

I heard something—a noise that woke me up.

A thump, maybe?

I don't move, don't breathe, listening intently until I hear it again. *Thump, thump, thump.* It's inside the house. Footsteps. Soft, quiet, sneaky, "trying not to wake anyone," kind of footsteps.

I think back to the encounter with Adrian and fear tightens around my neck like gripping murderous fingers. I imagine what it would be like to have fangs sinking into my tender skin, to feel the hot slice of them, to experience my limbs going limp and my body draining of life. Angry tears burn my eyes. Did Adrian come after me? He could have sent his minions to search me out, but that vampire seems like the type who'd want to do the job himself.

I can't believe I played him like that. How stupid can I be? Maybe Mom's right. In the light of day, my actions against Adrian felt empowering, but now in the middle of the night, I feel nothing but vulnerability and fear and the weight of a million what-ifs.

I force myself to sit up and slip from the warm bed, padding softly to the dark hallway. I follow the sound out toward the living room, my eyes slowly adjusting to the darkness. I need to place distance between myself and Ayla just in case the vampires found me here and somehow managed to enter her house uninvited. But also, as foolish and "girl in a horror movie" as it is, I want to locate the source of whatever that thump was that woke me up.

I freeze. A figure is standing near the kitchen counter, tall and unmoving, with the broad shoulders of a man. My throat goes dry.

He moves quickly, taking two steps toward the refrigerator. When he opens it and Felix comes into focus, I let out a breath of relief and sink back into the darkened hallway. I'm an idiot. One encounter with a vampire and I'm already imagining crazy scenarios in my head. I watch Felix for a minute. He puts a lunchbox in his backpack and tosses in a couple bottles of blue Gatorade. He must be getting ready for work. The clock flashes above the stove: 4:10 a.m. I didn't realize his internship started so early. I don't know of any banks that open before 9:00 a.m.

But he's not dressed in professional attire. He's in athletic wear, black basketball shorts and a black hoodie. He's probably hitting the gym before work. Or maybe they have lacrosse practice super early?

Just as I'm thinking that I'm verging on stalkerish behavior over here, he rearranges his bag and lifts something long and wooden from within. The tip glints silver in the refrigerator light and my jaw falls open. It's a silver-tipped wooden stake—the kind used to kill vampires.

Maybe he takes them with him when he goes out at night? A lot of people do these days, it wouldn't be that unusual. Except when he lifts his hoodie and fastens the stake into a holster securely above his waistband, something within me screams that this is more than everyday protection. There's a practiced movement to the way his hands grip the weapon that speaks to experience handling it and handling it well.

I want to ask him about the stake, to emerge from the shadows and confront him, or at least talk about this. What is Felix hiding? And also, how in the heck can I get in on it? Because if he's hunting vamps then I want to do it with him. But just as I'm about to take action and reveal myself, he finishes getting his bag ready and heads out to the garage door, disappearing from sight. Before I can think twice, I race back to Ayla's room, snag her car keys off her desk, and sprint out the back door. Since there isn't room for all the cars in the garage, the Moreno kids park in the driveway. By the time I'm approaching Ayla's prized navy blue Mini Cooper, Felix is already pulling his black SUV around the street corner.

I jump in, start the engine, and follow.

Adrenaline pumps through my veins, enough that every time I start to question my actions, I'm able to push them away and focus on not losing sight of Felix's tail lights. I'm careful to keep my distance, considering nothing about Ayla's ride is inconspicuous. I wish I had my own car at a time like this, but alas, I'm broke. I follow him all the way through the twisting suburban streets, onto the freeway for a few minutes, and then downtown into the banking district. The further we get from home, the more I lose my nerve. Maybe he's not out to hunt down suckers. Maybe there's a gym in this part of town that he belongs to. Executives and business professionals have to workout too.

He pulls the SUV into an underground parking garage. I park at the other end of the garage and watch as he gets out of his car and goes through an unmarked door with a fingerprint keypad to gain access. For five long minutes I stare at the metal door that's now closed behind him, feeling like a stage-five clinger. Why did I think I could follow him and learn anything? The guy is working or exercising or something. So what if he has a stake on him? That's a smart move, doesn't mean he's a hunter. I'm being dumb.

But I still can't forget the expert way in which he handled that stake.

I sigh and lean back into the seat, ready to head back to Ayla's house and squeeze in a few more hours of precious sleep, when the metal door swings open and Felix reappears. He's no longer alone. Two other guys are with him, each carrying a large black duffle bag. The new guys are also dressed in black athletic gear, and they all climb into Felix's black SUV.

It's a lot of black, like a totally suspicious amount. If I didn't know any better, I'd think this was a bank robbery, but I do know better. Felix may look like a bad boy, but he's a good person deep down to the core. He's not robbing anyone. So what's going on here?

They pull out of the garage and I follow him again, this time driving away from the city and back toward the suburbs, then farther to the outskirts of town where the suburbs become the rural areas which then becomes the swamp. As we leave the city behind, I have to drop back even farther so he doesn't recognize Ayla's car. I almost lose them a couple times because of it.

It's after 5 a.m. now. This time of year, the sun will be rising soon. The sky is turning that royal blue color when the sun is making its way out, but it's still pretty dark. I continue to keep back as I follow them—to a cemetery. And let me tell you, there's nothing like a swampy old cemetery at night to give you the heebie-jeebies.

"Okay, guys," I say to myself when I slow the car and park. "What are you up to?"

I'm farther down so I have to jog in. I'm suddenly feeling ridiculous because I'm wearing nothing but the pink lacy pajama shorts and white cotton tank top I brought to Ayla's. I thank the bra god's, or goddesses, that I still have one on, even though I'm so out of my element here. At least the bugs have gone to sleep and aren't having a meal of my legs, which if it was that extra special time around sunset, I'd be a goner. I'm a little cold and I'm *a lot* spooked, but I'm also curious and determined to figure out what's going on.

"We should go back to the car and wait. We weren't supposed to do this until sunrise," an unfamiliar male voice says. He's within the cemetery walls, his gravelly voice catching my attention like a fish on a line. I edge toward it. "We shouldn't break protocol. I don't know if this is a good idea."

"I think it's a great idea," a different voice replies, "maybe we'll get lucky."

"I doubt that. Where did they say it was?" The unfamiliar man speaks again.

"Here," Felix's voice adds. I'd recognize his deep smooth timbre anywhere.

I follow them through the maze of headstones, tombs, and mausoleums. The water levels are too high to bury bodies underground this close to the coast, so our cemeteries are like above-ground mazes. The tombs make it easier for me to follow these three men without being seen, but it's also freaky as hell, and I'm starting to shiver from fear instead of the cold. My sparkly white flippys are going to be ruined from the mud, but that's the least of my worries.

The sunlight will crest the edge of the horizon soon. They're going to catch me and then what?

"Well, if any are in here and wake up," the first unfamiliar voice speaks again, "they'd better hide quickly or the sun will get them soon."

I freeze. They're talking about vampires. They have to be.

"More like I'll get them," the second voice jokes.

I take another step forward and wince when my ankle catches on the edge of a tomb I didn't see in the darkness.

"Shh—" Felix snaps. "Did you hear that?"

They're fast. One second they're several rows of graves over and the next they're coming right for me. Whatever they're hunting, I've now become the target.

I stand there, frozen, really not wanting to be impaled by a silver tipped wooden stake, but also not sure where to even go, when Felix steps between two towering tombs, weapon raised and ready to strike. I scurry backward. "Don't!"

His body goes rigid. "Eva?"

I grimace, caught like a deer in the headlights, but it doesn't matter, because that's when something behind me screeches, something not quite human.

"Get back," Felix growls.

I turn, and standing not three feet away from me, with her fangs gleaming white and eyes bloodshot, is the pale face of a vampire. She lunges for me.

FIVE

I'm knocked to the ground, the back of my head slamming against a tomb in the process. Pain rings through my ears, but that's the least of my problems. I scream as the vampire hurls herself on top of me. Felix is quick to intervene, wrenching her away before she gets the chance to make contact. She jumps back just as he swings the stake toward her heart. It's close, but he misses. She shrieks an animalistic scream, her frizzy blonde hair a wild mess around her dirt-stained face. She's dressed in a long white gown and the closer I look at her, the more I realize what she is.

She's not just any vampire. She's new.

The most dangerous kind, because even though it's illegal in the vampire community to suck blood directly from a human without consent, newly-sired vampires are too thirsty to care about the laws. Their hunger is even rumored to be stronger than the blood bonds that forge them to their masters. The threat of true death is nothing compared to their mind numbing urgency to feed. This woman is no different. She crouches down among the grass with flexed fists, ready to pounce.

Male arms grab me from behind and pull me back against a broad chest. "Stay calm," the young man whispers. He presses something cold and hard into my palm. A stake. I grip it tight for dear life. It's all I have. It's everything.

Felix edges closer to the vamp. "You try to hurt us and I will kill you," he warns. "That's if the sun doesn't get you first."

She hisses, but he's right. The sun will be out soon, and if she's exposed, the light will burn her alive. But right now, dawn feels a million miles away, each second stretching into eternal darkness. Even though Felix's threats are menacing and we all have stakes at the ready, this woman is probably strong enough to kill the four of us. She'll suck us dry, one by one, until we're nothing but husks.

"You're not my master," she hisses. "Or did my master send you to me as my welcome gift?"

The male arms still wrapped around me shift to push me behind his large frame.

"Oh, yes," she continues. Sick clarity spreads across her moon pale face. "You all smell so good." Her eyes zero in on me. "Oh, and what's this? Virgin blood." She licks her lips.

Hot bile rises to my throat and blood warms my cheeks. New vampires are ruthlessly strong, and this one appears to have barely risen from the dead, literally clawing her way from her grave. The blood of virgins is rumored to have some kind of draw for vamps, but I don't know why.

I'm not going to stick around and find out.

Fight or flight mode kicks in, and I choose flight, taking off at an all-out sprint. I excelled at track while in school, so I'm fast, but even I know I'm no match for a newborn vampire. Even still, I have to try, especially while she's distracted by three aggressive vampire hunters. I don't know exactly where I'm going, just as long as it is in the opposite direction of her and toward the main road. I need to get to the car and get away from this cemetery as fast as possible.

"Wait!" Felix calls after me. He utters a few curse words when I don't respond, but I don't care. I can't be here. I shouldn't have come and I need to go right now.

My eyes have adjusted to the darkness but it's still not light enough to see every obstacle in the pre-dawn misty light. I trip over raised tree roots and graves a few times but scramble back up even faster, adrenaline careening me forward with each hurried step. Behind me, the vampire woman screeches into the night. She's closer—making chase.

Too late, I realize my mistake and the reason for Felix's curses. Earlier, I just so happened to stumble upon her, a lucky break for a new vampire, but now that I'm running, I've started a game of cat and mouse. It's like the advice I heard once about never running away from a mountain lion. You're supposed to make yourself big and scare it away. Running only makes the animal want to eat you even more.

And now this vampire is definitely hunting me down.

I have to choose to fight if I'm going to stand a chance, so I stop and whip around, the stake tight in my hand and poised to strike. I hold my breath in an attempt to hear better, but the graveyard grows eerily quiet, and my blood pumps through my eardrums, reminding me of how vulnerable I am. I ran too fast and too far, and now Felix and his friends are calling out from different directions. They're not close. Not like her scream was.

I look around for Felix anyway. I need him. There's nothing but darkness and shadows and the reality that I'm the idiot who snuck after him in the middle of the night, and because of it, I'm about to become a corpse.

I wait, my breath slowing like silent anguished prayers. I wait for her to come. I wait for the only two options left—to die or to kill.

She appears, jumping from the roof of a tall mausoleum, flying right for me so fast that I almost don't see her coming. She's like a ghostly apparition of death—eyes bloody orbs and fangs long thin daggers. I don't stop to question myself. I just swing the stake and aim for the heart.

It strikes, slicing through the white dress and sinking deep between cracking ribs. She wails, her thin body falling against mine, the tip of a fang nicking my arm. A flash of white-hot pain erupts through me. It feels like the shock of hitting my funny bone, but it's so much worse. The pain subsides as quickly as it came and the woman falls to her knees, reaching up toward the heavens.

"No!" she screams, and then she crumbles into dust.

Gone.

"Holy hell," I mutter. "I can't believe that just happened."

Talk about dumb luck.

Heart thundering, I brush off the dust and study my arm for bite marks where her fang got me. There's nothing but a tiny prick of blood that I rub away with one swipe. Was I bitten? I'm not really sure. I felt her fang pierce my skin, but I wouldn't call that a bite since she didn't get anything out of me. My blood was never taken. But because the vampire royalty has kept their secrets guarded, I have no idea what the consequences of this might be for me. At least I know that I can't be turned into a vampire. Not unless I feed on one who feeds on me, and then I'd have to be buried in a cemetery. Three nights later, I'd either wake up and claw my way out of the grave or the vampire venom would finish me off for good.

That's not going to happen. I'm not rising from the dead any time soon. I'm okay. It was just a scratch. It was nothing.

I let out a shuddering breath as Felix appears. His dark hair is disheveled and horror hangs on his face, followed by anger, and then something else I can't quite read. I prepare to defend myself but I don't have to. The man cuts through the maze of graves and pulls me into a tight hug. He's never hugged me before this moment.

"I thought you were dead," he mutters against my hair.

I release a frightened laugh. "Yeah, so did I."

His heart thuds against his chest, matching the rhythm of my own.

Too soon, he steps back and surveys me up and down, assessing the damage, but there is none. "What were you thinking following me out here?"

I scoff. "Um, excuse me, what were you thinking telling me you're working in banking this summer when you're obviously hunting vampires?"

His two friends trudge from the shadows, chuckling at my antics. "The woman has a point." The attractive African American one nods to me. He's the guy who gave me the stake and essentially saved my life. "But hey, looks like you're a vampire hunter, too."

I shake my head. "No, I'm not."

He points to the bloodied stake in my hand. "Could've fooled me."

I squeeze it tighter. I might never put this stake down.

The third guy frowns, not really watching us anymore but surveying the spooky cemetery. "Let's get out of here." His voice is soft. It's the same voice that didn't want to be in the cemetery at dark.

"The sun is rising soon," Felix says, "we don't need to rush." He points to the black duffle bags I'd forgotten they'd brought with them. "We need to place those stakes before we go."

"Oh . . ." Realization dawns on me. These guys weren't exactly out here to hunt vampires. They were here to place stakes around the graveyard, probably in hidden caches. I've heard this was something vampire hunters do since graveyards are the literal breeding grounds for vamps. It's not a bad idea. I'm pretty sure stakes anywhere and everywhere is an awesome idea, come to think of it.

A chill rolls over my exposed skin as everything comes rushing back to me, my mind unpacking what just happened. I don't want to be here anymore, either.

"Well, the sun's not up yet," the third guy continues in his levelheaded way. "We can place those stakes later because whoever sired that vampire is probably close by."

I thought I was afraid before, but now the consequences of my actions creep over my skin like tiny spiders as I realize what I've done. Killing a vampire isn't just killing a vampire. It's not one and done, and be done with it. Vamps don't work like that. They're connected. They feel each other through their blood bonds and are ruthlessly protective of their creepy little families. The woman I just obliterated hadn't become a vampire all on her own, someone had chosen her, had fed on her, offered their own blood, and then had buried her. This was all planned. Maybe she woke up early, maybe she woke up late, but either way, whoever made her would be coming back. And that someone might not be pleased to find me standing over her ashes with a bloody stake in my fist.

"We're leaving." I point the silver tip toward Felix. "And you're riding back in my car."

"You mean Ayla's car?" he quips.

"Felix!"

He shrugs. "Fine, but I don't have to answer your questions."

Oh, he knows me so well.

I raise an eyebrow at the boy I grew up with who is apparently someone else entirely. I'd be on the verge of laughing if I wasn't so freaked out. "Umm—you can answer all my questions, and you will answer all my questions."

He smirks. How can he smirk at a time like this? "Yeah, we'll see about that."

SIX

"Give me the keys," Felix says, sliding into the driver's seat. I'm a little too shaken up to drive after having just killed a vampire and all, so I have no problem passing over Ayla's keys. I retrieve a hoodie from her backseat and put it on, slipping the stake into the front pocket, and then get in the front seat.

"What do you want to know?" His voice is strained.

"How about everything?"

He nods once but his mouth turns down. "Well, I'm sworn to secrecy on most of it."

"I'm pretty sure I've already figured out you're a vampire hunter. What group are you with?" There's several that have been talked about over the years, each trying to prove they're better than the last.

His lips twist. "I can't say."

"So that's how it is, huh?"

"We're all under twenty-five if that's what you're wondering."

"Yeah, I sort of guessed that considering your buddies look about your age, but that wasn't what I asked."

"It's not a group you would have heard of."

I lean back against the heated leather seat and sigh. "Now I'm even more curious."

Maybe it's good that I haven't heard of them considering most of the hunter groups I have heard of only came to light after everyone in them had been killed. Vampires live openly in society and have rights now, which means you can't just hunt them down without repercussions, especially when the world leaders and everyday people can be easily compelled. Yeah, we have treaties in place, compulsion was made illegal, and we live our human lives with a semblance of normalcy, but at the end of the day, the vampires have the most power and everyone knows it.

When we turn right and the guys driving Felix's black SUV turn left, I have to ask where we are going.

"I'm taking you home," Felix deadpans. "Obviously."

That doesn't sit well with me. I wanted to know more, not to go home. Even though I was still shaken up, my mind was also whirling with opportunity.

"Take me to your leader," I say.

"E.T. phone home?" Felix rolls his eyes. He's trying to make me laugh and lighten the tension. He can be aloof at times, but he's not a broody person and knows how to crack a good joke;

however, right now, I don't want to hear it.

"No, I'm serious, Felix," I continue, passion sparking like a firework. "I want to be a vampire hunter, too." It makes the most sense for me to pursue this. I hate vampires. I want to help humans. Win-win.

The car grows quiet as he flexes white-knuckled fingers over the steering wheel. "That's not a good idea, Eva."

"It's a brilliant idea!"

"Why?"

"*Why?*"

"Yes, why on earth would you want to hunt something so dangerous? Most of us end up dead."

Okay, that was pretty rich coming from him. "Obviously, I'm willing to risk my life if it means getting rid of the vampires. I hate them. I hate them more than you could ever understand."

"Oh, I think I could understand."

I wonder what the vamps ever did to Felix. His family is so perfect and have managed to stay far away from the suckers. Not like me. "So why do you hunt them? You know I have to ask."

He goes still. "Nope. It's personal."

"You're really not going to tell me?"

He sighs, "Maybe someday, I don't know. Please, just drop it. Drop the whole thing. It's a bad idea. You have too much going for you to get caught up in this shit."

"Says the guy going to Tulane. You already know I graduated high school with no prospect of college. I thought maybe I'd go into law enforcement, but one trip to the police station . . . you know those guys are useless when it comes to vampires, right?"

He chuckles darkly. "I do know."

"Right. The cop gave our claim over to the Vampire Enforcement Coalition, which is literally run by vampires. What a load of crap."

"What claim?"

I wave him off and continue, "Nonsense to do with my mom, what else?"

His jaw tenses and his face turns into an unreadable mask.

"I need something meaningful to do with my life, Felix. You saw how fast I ran tonight, right? I did track forever, so I'm in shape. And I was good with the stake. I got that one on the first try, didn't I?"

"You did," he grumbles.

"So who do I need to talk to about recruitment?" I don't think I've ever spoken so openly with Felix, but my entire body is thrumming with electric excitement right now and I can't stop myself from going for this new opportunity.

"Eva, listen to me." His voice is tight. "It's too dangerous."

"Well, they'll train me. I'll learn some fighting skills or something."

"It's too dangerous," he repeats, this time emphasizing each word harshly. He turns to glower at me. "Do you have a death wish?"

"Hello pot, meet kettle," I growl. "I'm already in danger. I killed a brand spankin' new vampire sired by someone who's not going to be happy about what I did. What if they can trace it back to me?"

"They can't."

"Don't be so sure. Not to mention, are you ready to hear why I went to the police station to file a claim with the VEC?"

"Okay, why?"

I can tell he's growing annoyed with me, but I can't stop myself from pressing this. Now that I've killed one blood sucker, I need to kill another. They're evil, vile, horrible, and need to go. I don't care if it's illegal and dangerous and maybe even a lot stupid because I could be part of something important. For the first time in ages, I actually feel like I've found some direction in my life. "Yesterday the casino messed with my mom and took way too much blood," I confess.

"I'm sorry to hear that." And he means it. Felix knows all about my mother's vice. It seems like the adults have vices in one way or another, though I still haven't figured out what his wholesome parents are up to in their free time. I'm pretty sure they've eluded the vampires all together. It's not impossible, it's not easy, but if anyone can do it it's the Moreno family. Ayla and Felix's grandparents fled Cuba to immigrate here and have worked dang hard to get to where they are today. They've since retired, and Mr. and Mrs. Moreno now run the furniture and interior design shop. Ayla plans to go to school for design so she can take over for her mom one day. Felix is doing business administration for the same reason. They're good kids, living the American dream.

This guy is the one who has everything going for him, a perfect future all mapped out, and yet he's still a hunter. How can he sit here and tell me I can't do this? I have nothing, literally nothing, to lose.

"And," I press on, going for the kill shot. "I pissed off a vampire prince yesterday."

He whirls on me, slamming too hard on the brakes. The seat belt holds me back from a case of whiplash. "Felix!"

"You did what? Who?"

"Adrian Teresi." I'm being smug about it even though I shouldn't be.

Felix's body freezes. The sun has crested the horizon so I can see his features better, and while he's gone from weary to joking to angry during our conversation, now the man just looks afraid. I don't think it's an emotion I've ever seen him wear. It takes the wind right out of my sails, and my mind flashes back to the terror I felt when the newly sired vampire almost killed me tonight. That was child's play compared to what a vampire prince could do to me.

"Please tell me you don't know Adrianos Teresi." Felix's voice is tight.

"Well, I can explain… " I go into detail about everything that happened at the casino, and by the end of it, Felix is bright red.

"Do you know what you did?" he yells—yes, yells—through the car. "You put a target on your back! Adrian is the most powerful vampire in Louisiana and one of the most powerful in the country, maybe even the world, Eva, what were you thinking?"

"How bad can he really be?" My chest tightens.

"Are you seriously asking me that right now? We've been trying to take Adrian down for years, but the guy is untouchable. He's got his fingers in all the worst vices, Eva. All of them. If you think gambling is bad, you have no idea what he's a part of."

My entire body goes cold and I try not to picture what that means.

"So all the better to recruit me to your hunter group." I lean back in the seat, arms folded and mind made up. "Let me help you kill him." I smirk. "I actually think he might like me."

Felix shakes his head and doesn't speak to me the rest of the drive home. He pulls up to my little duplex and stops the car. "My stuff is with Ayla."

"I don't care. You need to get out."

"Felix—"

"I mean it. You can't do this, Eva. You just can't."

I glare but get out of the car. Who is he to tell me what I can and can't do? I slam the door and storm up my driveway. But soon realize I don't even have my key. Screw this. I whirl around, but he's already driven off, so I head toward Ayla's place on foot. I'm going to get my stuff, at least. He can't stop me from doing that. I need my key and I don't want to wake up Mom to explain why I don't have it.

When I get back to the Moreno's, my bestie is still asleep, none the wiser to what I just went through. I want to shake her awake and tell her every little detail of the horror involved in killing a vampire, but my better judgement stops me. She's leaving for college up north in three weeks. I'm going to miss her like crazy when she's gone, but I also love her enough to want the best for her. Right now, she thinks her world is safe, and it probably is, especially in the small town where she'll be attending college. I'm not going to be the person to take that away.

I quietly gather my things and send her a quick text on my way out the door. **I woke up early and decided to head home. Let's hang out later! Maybe shopping? I want to help you pick out a new bedspread for your dorm.** Her phone is on silent so I know it won't wake her. Offering to go shopping helps ease my guilt a little at keeping secrets. The girl loves shopping; I do not.

When I slip out the front door with my backpack loaded over one shoulder and my house key ring dangling from my index finger, I spot Felix climbing into his black SUV. So his friends came back for him. I run up to the window before I can stop myself.

His friend who had handed me the stake in the graveyard is still in the driver's seat. The quieter one sits in the back so Felix can ride passenger.

Felix motions for them to drive away, but his friend just smirks and rolls down the window. "Good morning, Beautiful," he says, his green eyes sparkling. He's got a southern accent, the kind people don't have when they grew up in the city. This is farmville-speak. I like it. It suits him. And damn, he's gorgeous. Tall, dark, and handsome—has Ayla met him yet? She's going to freak.

"Good morning to you, too." I pop my hip and fold my arms over my chest. I meet his mischievous gaze, then Felix's angry one, then nod to the guy in the back. "Tell your recruiter I want in."

Tall, Dark, and Handsome smiles like the Cheshire Cat. "Excellent. I'll do that."

"No, you won't," Felix spits.

The guy only laughs and rolls up his window, driving off and leaving me alone on the sidewalk. I have a feeling that guy and I are going to become friends. A vampire hunter with a sense of humor seems like the kind of person I'd want to be friends with. I grin to myself. This is going to be fun.

I pull the bloodied stake from the front pocket of Ayla's hoodie and look it over—the silver tip, the finely polished wood, the weight and length of it—all feel right in my hand. Replacing it back in the pocket, I walk home, a mixture of emotions rolling around in my gut. Am I a total idiot? Am I brave? Am I naive to think anything will even come of this? I don't have the answers to those questions, but there is one thing I do know. I killed my first vampire, finally doing something of value with my life, and I'm not going to stop now.

The unsettling feeling of being watched prickles at the back of my neck. I turn but the street is empty. Nobody is there. Of course not, I'm just being paranoid. But as I walk home, that feeling only intensifies. I start to speed walk. The sun is up. This is irrational but I can't shake the feeling…

A car engine revs and a black sedan rolls up next to me. It drives slowly, keeping pace. The windows are so tinted I can't see inside. Can vampires ride in cars if they're not directly exposed to the sun? It seems foolish for them to risk something like that but I don't know the answer. I imagine a human thug jumping from the car and throwing me inside. That's all I need to get thoroughly spooked.

I take off at a run, gripping the stake in my right hand to make sure whoever is in that car can see it. My feet pound against the pavement and my heartbeat thunders against my eardrums like a battle cry. The car speeds away with a screech of tires. When I get home, the scent of burning rubber lingers with me all day.

SEVEN

The tangy scent of barbecue greets me as I hurry into work that afternoon. And thank goodness it's strong enough to overpower the awful burning rubber smell that's been haunting me. I'm a server at one of the city's oldest and most popular restaurants downtown and I'm beyond grateful for this job. Pops would be a tourist trap if the locals didn't love it so much, but they do and for good reason. We're a greasy spoon kind of place known for authentic Southern food like spicy gumbo, traditional crawfish étouffée, world famous melt-in-your-mouth pecan pie, and so much more.

It's no surprise that the line to get a table is around the block as I weave my way through the crowd to get inside. Serving here comes with excellent tips, I just wish I could get more shifts. I'm one of the newer employees, with only a few months of day shifts under my belt, and tonight is the first time I'll really get to experience the dinner rush. Pops is the kind of restaurant where servers stay on the payroll for years, so I want to impress Eddie, the evening manager in charge of scheduling and my key to making more money.

I'm done counting on Mom to keep a roof over my head. She's in a downward spiral, and even though I'll do anything I can to save her, I refuse to become her collateral damage. New Orleans is probably the least safe place to be homeless in America. Everyone knows it's got the most vampires of any city on the continent, or that's what people say anyway.

I can picture my life the way I want it to be, working the busy evening shifts at Pops, hunting blood suckers through the night with Felix, and sleeping away the day. Who knows? Maybe I'll be able to get my own apartment. Except I have to look after Mom or else she *will* end up homeless or dead, so I should probably keep living in the duplex. Regardless, vampire hunting was a far-off possibility yesterday, but now that it's in my thoughts, now that I've actually done it, I can focus on little else. I have five or six good years left before the vampires will be able to get to my brain, I might as well end as many of them as I can while I still have the chance.

"You've got section four," Marla, the hostess, greets me. "I just sat table twelve."

"Great." I give her a friendly wink and bounce off to take care of my customers.

The shift is so busy that it flies by way faster than my daytime ones. We're a half hour from closing when I'm given what will hopefully be my last table for the night. The men are at least twenty years older than me and definitely intoxicated, if the stench of alcohol and their beady bloodshot eyes are anything to judge them by. I put on an unaffected smile and stroll over to take their orders.

"What can I get for you tonight, gentlemen?"

One of them blatantly checks me out, eyes lingering on my bare legs. Pops' servers wear black shorts and t-shirts, nothing too revealing, but this guy doesn't care and isn't being the least bit discreet. "Any secret menu items you can offer?" His voice is a low jeer and the other three guys chuckle at his sleazy antics. "I've got the money," he continues, "so maybe you can offer a discount?"

What a perv.

I step back and glare. "I can't offer you anything that's not on our menu, but maybe you'd like to speak with my manager?" I motion to Eddie.

Eddie is a massive African American man who looks like a bouncer and is probably packing heat under his oversized clothing. There's a reason he's on the late shift. It's no secret Pops has a lot of money coming in on the daily, and we're right in the middle of the French Quarter, aka New Orleans Party Central. People can get desperate when they're running low on funds.

One look at Eddie shuts these guys up but not without a few grimaces. They leave me alone after that, ordering and eating their meals without any more advances, and leaving without lingering around. As they go, I catch them complaining about a popular vampire-run nightclub nearby called The Crypt that they want to go to. The guy who propositioned me is grumbling about the high cover fee.

Since humans can't give blood every day without wasting away to nothing, the vampires keep meticulous records of how much blood we "donate." Donations equal entrance, so explain to me how it's a donation and not a payment? Anyway, when people aren't eligible for donation they have to pay actual money for their vices, and the prices aren't cheap. The vampires have taken over just about everything seedy—bars, strip clubs, casinos. Rumor has it even illegal drugs and sex work are included on the list.

I've always wondered about blood alcohol levels or drugs tainting the donations, but obviously the vamps don't care because they keep encouraging it. Maybe they even like tainted blood. Could it be more desirable to them? Can they drink alcohol? I have no idea. And I don't really care.

"You did good, kid." Eddie pats me on the back on the way out after I've finished for the night. "I'll make sure you get a couple more evening shifts next week."

I smile brightly and thank him before heading out to the

parking lot. Mom's old silver Corolla greets me. I love that car. I'd buy it from her in a heartbeat if she didn't need it for her day job. Scratch getting an apartment, I need to buy my own car so I don't have to keep borrowing hers. At least I didn't have to take the bus today like I do during my daytime shifts when Mom is at her bank teller job at a local credit union. It's a miracle she still has that job, to be honest. If they knew about her gambling addiction, nobody would trust that woman around giant wads of cash.

But Mom has a way about her, a way that can easily fool everyone. Just not me. She's the kind of person who makes you feel at ease while also wanting to impress her. I credit her two-faced nature to all those pageants and to growing up in the South where the phrase "bless your heart" comes second nature. Don't get me wrong, I love my mom deeply and I know so much of what's going on isn't her fault, but I'm also tired. So, so tired.

The back parking lot is usually busy, but by this time of night it's emptied out. The Corolla is one of the only cars left out here. A chill creeps up my spine. It's that paranoid feeling of being watched all over again, only this time it's dark. I ignore it and walk faster to the car, keys ready to go. Something skitters across the pavement behind me. I whip around, but nobody's there. Maybe it was an animal? A racoon or stray cat wouldn't be out of the question.

My mind races a million miles a minute, imagining that table of rough men I had. In my thoughts, they're not at the next bar, but actually spying on me from the shadows, closing in to attack.

Or worse, it could be a vampire…

I do have enemies now and what about that car that followed me? Someone could be out here.

But nothing happens.

I make it to the car, unlock it with the key fob at the last second, and climb inside with a sigh of relief. I'm going to have to ask Eddie to walk me to my car at night next time I snag one of these coveted shifts. That's if I'm not taking the bus home. Or a taxi. All depends on what Mom needs. Considering my pocket is full of tip money, I need to be smarter. That right there puts a target on my back and is definitely worth the nighttime spookiness factor.

I lean back in my seat and slip the seatbelt into position.

The passenger door flies open and a man slides in next to me. Before I can scramble away, he snatches my wrist in his iron tight grip.

"Don't scream," Adrian Teresi speaks low.

His blue eyes and pale skin practically glow in the darkness. My skidding heart turns animalistic, trying to claw its way out of my throat. I can't scream because I can't speak. I can't even move! Everything inside me is urging me to run, to get away, and that this man—*this thing*—is here to deliver my death.

Frozen panic doesn't last long as my voice comes rushing back. "Get away from me!"

"Tsk, tsk." Adrian squeezes tighter and glares. "You should have thought of that before you stole from me."

"I didn't steal anything. You gave that money to me."

"I gave it to you under the agreement that you wouldn't call the police, but you did, so the way I see it, you stole five thousand dollars from me." His eyes narrow. "You have caused an issue for me within the VEC and I do not take kindly to it."

I heave my wrist away again, and this time he drops it. Part of me wants to try and make a run for it, but I know I won't be fast enough. The other part of me wants to stay and play Adrian's little game just to see if I can win. Where's that stake when I need it?

My mind fumbles through where I stashed it last, and I remember. It's under the driver's seat, probably inches from my foot. If I can just grab it quick enough, I can kill Adrian and—

"Looking for this?" Adrian holds it up. His blue eyes flash murderous.

Now I've truly run out of things to say.

"I should stake you right here and now," he purrs, "see how you like it." But he doesn't. Instead, he squeezes his hand and splinters the weapon into pieces, hissing when the silver tip of it grazes his skin. It sends a little puff of smoke into the car. He throws the remnants in the backseat.

Geez . . . I'm going to have to talk to Felix about getting me a full-on silver stake because apparently the wood ones are economy class. Then again, I hear genuine silver is hard to come by these days. The suckers saw to that before they revealed themselves. They had ages to plan, after all.

"What do you want from me?" I say at last, staring Adrian back, eye to eye. He's an oxymoron if I've ever seen one. He looks young, mid-twenties at the most, but his eyes and his mannerisms speak of centuries of experience. Not for the first time, I wonder how old he really is. I mean, being a prince must make him ancient, right?

"I already told you what I want, Angel." He nods toward the steering wheel. "Drive. There's somewhere we need to go."

So he found out my mom's nickname for me. I shouldn't be surprised. "Evangeline," I correct.

"Drive!" he roars. "Or do you need me to do it for you?"

"Sorry, buddy, but does this look like a taxi to you?" I glare. "Get out of my car."

Faster than humanly possible, he snatches both my hands and slams them so forcefully against the wheel that pain thunders up my wrists.

Tears spring to my eyes. "What the hell? I'm breakable you know!"

"Drive," he demands again. "Or I will, and you might not survive that. You decide."

I might not survive how he drives? Is he serious with this? Anger burns hot in my chest, but I don't see another way out of this, so I finally do as the man—the creature—says and put the car into drive. I cling to the anger, letting it consume me, because it's better than the alternative: blinding fear!

I go where he directs me and I even think maybe we're going to the casino I hate so much. When we drive right past it, I suddenly don't hate the place as much as I thought I would. At least the casino is known territory, vampiric sure, but known. Whatever this new place is he's taking me to, it can't be good. Vampires own so much property now and if he wants me dead, there's countless places he can take me down without a single consequence.

That sends my heart pounding and my blood pumping. I wonder if he can smell it.

"You know, if I disappear the police will have to look into it," I start to ramble, "I mean, I did just make a report against you."

Compared to mine, his body is still as granite. I'm starting to shake. "And pointing this out will help your case, how?"

"They talk to the VEC and—"

"As I've said, I know all about your little report to the VEC," he cuts me off. "I *am* the VEC. And now I have shit to clean up in my own house."

My throat goes dry. Of course, he is the VEC. I already knew that. "But if you're the VEC then why are you so upset?"

"It's myself *and* others." He's not gloating. He's seething mad. And maybe a little annoyed. And possibly nervous. No, I'm totally picking up on my own fears and projecting them. No way is Adrianos-freaking-Teresi nervous. He's just pissed off.

"Turn here." He points to a shipping yard, and my stomach nearly drops to my butt. I stall the car at the stop sign, not wanting to go in there. From the looks of it, it's not good. Places like these are where murder documentaries end, and I really don't want to die tonight.

"I said turn." He grabs the steering wheel and forces it to the left.

In we go.

We drive past huge shipping containers and the occasional ruffian, but otherwise the place is pretty dead. He maneuvers me through the narrow lanes until we reach a tiny parking lot by the black water's edge. The reflection is so dark, all I can picture is spilled blood.

"Get out," Adrian commands. I deflate, because this is it. This is really the end. Some small part of me was hoping I'd have an out by this point, but that's impossible. Where would I go? How would I get away? It's so remote out here, nobody will even hear me scream.

I don't move. I can't.

He throws open his door. "Get out or I will rip your throat out and feast on your corpse right here in this shitty car."

That does the trick. I scurry from the car, and just as quickly, he's at my side. His hand is an iron lock on my arm as he pulls me toward an empty dock.

"What are we doing here?" I croak. "This is it, isn't it? You're going to kill me and throw me in the river." I'll be out to the swamp and eaten by alligators before anyone can find my body. Of course, I'll probably be drained of blood first. My mind races through the scenario, seeing it unravel in horrifying detail. My knees start to buckle and my body goes ice cold. I can practically taste the river water already. Or will his fangs ripping through my throat be the last experience of my life? I try to muster up some courage but it's useless.

"Can you please relax? I'm not going to kill you but if your fear pheromones don't let up soon I might not be able to help myself."

"Oh…" I don't know what to say to that. Neither of us speaks for a long minute. I will my heartbeat to slow and I take long quiet breaths that taste like nightfall.

"I have business to attend to," he says at last. "And you're going to watch."

So I guess I'm not going to die, at least. I blink and look around, finally noticing the rainbow of lights of the classic New Orleans ferry against the surface of the water. I squint to look closer, and recognition hits me like a punch to the stomach. This isn't just any old ferry. It's the floating casino, a giant floating party that takes off after sunset every weekend night and doesn't dock until the early morning hours. I hate it more than The Alabaster, even though I've never stepped foot on it, because it's where Mom ends up in the most trouble with no one to save her.

Last summer we had a scare where she didn't come home after going on one. She showed up two days later with a black eye and a drained bank account, refusing to tell me what happened. That day was the day I knew that things weren't ever going to get better.

"You want me to go on there?" I frown. "I'm not old enough."

He looks at me like I'm the world's biggest idiot, and maybe I am, but sorry, I have no intention of stepping foot on that boat.

Adrian has other ideas. The casino boat honks its low horn and slows to a creep as it nears the edge of our dock. The noxious sound of music and gamblers in the throws of debauchery drifts over the water. It edges closer and closer, until it's only a few feet from where we're standing.

"After you," Adrian demands.

Realizing I can't fight this, I take a large step and practically jump onto the boat. Adrian is right behind me. We're on—and the dock recedes quickly. The boat never even stopped.

I shouldn't have taken that five thousand dollar bribe. Or maybe I should've taken it but not called the police. But I did both and here we are. I'd really hoped I'd never have to board this boat, but I guess there's a first for everything. I glare at Adrian. "You don't have to do this you know."

"You're right, Angel, I don't." He returns the glare. "But I want to."

EIGHT

I'm handed off straight away to the woman whom I immediately recognize as Adrian's receptionist, Kelli. She's dressed in a revealing velvety blood-red gown and is downright stunning, but her whole vampire-vibe makes my skin crawl even more than Adrian's does. Nothing about her is warm or kind or welcoming. Nothing. She doesn't speak a word as she directs me into a little dressing room and hands me what can only be described as clubbing attire: a tiny black mini skirt, disco ball sparkly halter top, and towering silver high heels to match.

I don't bother arguing and quickly change out of my Pops uniform and into the ridiculous outfit. I run shaky hands through my long black hair and tell myself not to throw up and to be strong. At least the boat isn't rocking too badly, or I really would lose the little staff dinner I ate earlier tonight.

"Where should I put these?" I lift up my clothes. My phone

is tucked inside the bundle. Adrian still has my car keys. Kelli groans like I'm such a bother but hands me a tiny sparkly purse backpack and I shove everything inside.

"Can I pee? I haven't gone in hours."

Her eyebrows draw in on each other. Does she think I'm some kind of animal? Well, vampires probably don't pee, so maybe I'm pathetic in her eyes, but at least I don't drink blood. One of those things is considerably more disgusting as far as I'm concerned, *thank you very much Miss 80's Mean Girl.* I suddenly have the idea to buy her a copy of the children's book *Everybody Poops* and snort to myself.

"Quickly," she snaps and points me to a tiny washroom.

I lock myself inside and consider prying open the window, leaping into the river, swimming to shore, and making a run for it. Total lunacy. Knowing my luck, I'd probably drown. And if I didn't, Adrian would find me and then he really would rip out my throat and feast on my corpse. There's nowhere safe I could go. I'd have to leave New Orleans entirely, but a vampire prince probably has enough power to hunt me down if he really wanted to. There's no place to hide—the sun sets on every last corner of this planet. So instead of jumping, I take care of my business, wash my hands, and return to Kelli.

She looks like a Kelli and like she was turned in the eighties on account of her bad hair dye alone. It's over-the-top brassy bleached blonde but slicked back into a high ponytail so it doesn't look *too* bad. Vamps can't change much about their appearance after they're reborn, so Kelli's bad hair color is stuck with her for eternity and I'm petty enough to care. Her eyes rove over me as if I'm a sad little wannabe and she's the queen bee. Of course, she's no queen, but there you go. *"Hey, sweety, you're a receptionist, so get off your high horse,"* is what I want to say to her, but I would also like to live through the night.

"You don't wear makeup?" She smirks.

"Uh, neither do you."

"I haven't needed it since 1990." She tosses her shiny ponytail to the side. If she's trying to rub her supernatural beauty in my face she doesn't know me very well. "All human women should wear makeup though. Poor pathetic things."

There's that word, pathetic. I totally called it. I shrug. "Like I care?"

"You should."

"I don't."

She raises an eyebrow, moving on from my makeup-free face to assessing my obvious lack of curves, but this time says nothing.

Whatever. I couldn't care less what the leech thinks of me.

"Now what?" I ask, attitude sparking my question. She rolls her eyes as if she'd like nothing more than to crush me under her thin red stiletto. I'm sure she could.

"You got me in trouble with Adrian, you know." Her hazel

eyes narrow. "Apparently, I was supposed to watch you or something, like I didn't have other things to do than to babysit a teenager."

Oh, so that explains the animosity. Noted.

"I would say sorry, but I'm not, and I don't like to lie."

Her eyes flash and her pupils dilate. Oh crap, is she going to eat me now?

"Why am I here?" I ask, changing the subject.

I can tell she wants to say more, but she smiles as if she would rather show me. She offers a smirky, "This way," then escorts me to the casino floor.

For one thing, it's smaller than The Alabaster. Much. But that's to be expected considering this is a ferry and not a brick-and-mortar building with an additional hotel highrise attached to the back. It too, reeks of cigarette smoke and booze. And blood. Many of the windows are open to let in the breeze, so at least there's that. It's usually pretty muggy this time of night, and my hair sticks to my neck. The patrons are all dressed up, ignoring the humidity like it's nothing. Fancy dress is part of the requirement for getting on the boat—the regular casino couldn't care less. Either way, the patrons all have that sick sheen to their eyes that speaks of greed, and the pale pallor to their skin that screams of blood loss.

Unlike in The Alabaster, vampires are everywhere. Most have bloody cocktails in their hands, and some of them join in on the gambling. My stomach roils as I look around for Adrian.

I don't see him, but bony shoulders and long auburn hair sure do catch my eye. Sitting at one of the Texas Hold'em tables with her back to me is my mother.

Has to be.

There isn't a blood bag hooked up to her, but there may as well be because we don't have the money to be here and, at this point, I'd almost rather her give blood than money we don't have. Okay, not really, but I can't believe this!

"Ah, there you are." Adrian appears at my side. His familiar scent of warm cedar and bergamot washes over me, but underneath it is the iron of blood, and I want nothing more than to claw his eyes out. "You clean up nicely." His tone is mocking.

"What is she doing here?" I hiss, nodding toward Mom.

He chuckles darkly. "She's the business I was talking about. Your mother is here to teach you a lesson."

"And what lesson is that?" Though I'm afraid I already know.

"You cannot stop her gambling," his tone is no longer amused, "and you cannot stop me from doing anything I wish." He yanks my body around like a rag doll and his stone-like fingertips dig deep into my upper arms. I wince and tears spring to my eyes. I refuse to cry which only makes it harder to push them away.

"You're hurting me," I seethe.

That only makes him squeeze harder. "You are not going to

step foot in my casino ever again. Is that clear?"

I should agree to his demands, I know that, but I don't. I hold back a response and meet his steely gaze with one of my own. Just because the pain of his crushing fingers is overpowering and I'm about ready to bawl my eyes out over it, doesn't mean I can't be a defiant brat. He squeezes harder.

"Fine," I say at last.

He releases me and strides purposely toward my mother. His hands are clenched into fists but they might as well be sledge hammers. I know the strength in just those fingers, what could his whole fist do? Is he going to kill her?

"No!" I rush after him.

He doesn't listen.

"Are you Paulo?" He asks the man sitting next to my mother. The man turns and asks, "Yes, why?" Adrian then grabs the sweaty Mediterranean-looking guy, lifts him clear off his seat and snaps his neck.

The body collapses to the floor with a dull thud.

Humans scream and scurry from their seats, but a couple of the vamps are quick to meet them, compelling the humans to sit back down, insisting they didn't see anything. The vamps work quickly; it doesn't matter that there are less of them when they're the wolves and we're the sheep.

It all happens so fast, and my mother doesn't even notice me standing there, gaping like an idiot who should've seen this coming. Within the course of a minute, she's back to playing her game as if there isn't a dead man at her feet.

Something happens to me that rarely happens, if ever; I'm speechless.

Adrian can't do this. He can't kill a man. It's illegal. Vampires are out in society under certain agreements, and they can't just go around killing people. Except, apparently they *can*. Same as vampire hunters can kill and get away with it. Sometimes things that happen at night, stay in the dark.

Adrian motions to Kelli who sashays over seductively. If I didn't know better, I'd think that annoying smirk of hers was permanent.

"Yes, Master?" she asks coyly, batting her lashes.

"Enjoy your treat," he tells her with the flick of his wrist, "but get rid of the body."

"Throw him over the side?" She's giddy now and I'm honestly about to puke.

"As long as he's not going to wash up anywhere, I don't care what you do with him."

She picks up the body as if it weighs nothing, sinking her teeth into the dead man's neck like it's a juicy steak as she walks him out of the casino. His blood drops are the only thing that's left of the guy, but I'm sure those will be gone soon, too.

And none of the humans even give her a second glance. They're entranced by their casino games. It's not their fault, but

I still want to scream at them to wake up.

I feel like I'm sinking into the hardwood floor. My entire life is a ticking clock, counting down until my prefrontal cortex is developed and I join the sheep. My legs are weak noodles and I try not to lock my knees. Last thing I need to do is pass out in a place like this. I probably wouldn't wake up.

Adrian steps closer, and I inch back.

"Do you see now, Angel?"

I nod once. "Yes, I've seen all I need." Fear is thick in my tone, but I can't deny it, not for a second. Adrian terrifies me. He is *not* someone I want to cross.

"We have places like this, places where people disappear. Paulo back there chose to make enemies with a friend of mine so I took care of him. Did you notice that you're the youngest one on this boat tonight?"

I nod again. Of course it's for good reason that nobody here is young. The vampires can kill and compel and wash away their sins in the swamp. They can make it seem as if nothing had ever happened. Youth who can not be compelled. We'd be able to expose them.

"Despite our efforts to lower the gambling age, I assure you that this boat will always be reserved exclusively for my older clients. And if I ever have the misfortune to see you in one of my casinos again," his tone slices through me as he delivers the final blow, "I will kill you." And just to twist the knife, he adds,

"And I will take my time."

"You won't see me again after tonight." My voice cracks, sounding like it's a million miles away. But I mean it. I am so done.

"Good."

"Who's your friend, Adrianos?" a man questions. He slides up next to us so silently that I nearly jump out of my skin.

I turn to find another vampire, one just as beautiful as Adrian—or maybe I should say Adrianos? *Nah, too fancy for me, I'm sticking with Adrian.* Where Adrian's beauty is light—bright blue eyes and golden hair—this man is dark. His skin is quite olive for a vampire, casting him with an oddly alluring complexion. His jet black hair is slicked back and his eyes are the color of warm brown sugar. He looks older than Adrian, like he was in his mid thirties to early forties when he was changed. The tiny laugh lines around his eyes and mouth are still visible, a tiny snapshot to the human he once was. His stance and smile are welcoming, and he's quite handsome for an older guy, but my senses rise up in warning.

I want to step away. I don't, but only because it would give the wrong impression. He doesn't need to know that everything about him unsettles me to the core.

He can't be trusted—none of them can—but there's something about this one that feels different. I'm not sure how to put words or emotions to it, but it's definitely there, like a painful itch I can't scratch.

"Where's your new child, Hugo?" Adrian asks, changing the subject off of me.

Hugo's body turns rigid. "Dead." His tone turns bitter. "She didn't make it far from her rising. When I went to retrieve her, her grave was empty and I felt no bond."

"Do you think she rose early?" Adrian almost sounds sympathetic. Almost.

"Yes. I'm afraid she rose on the second night instead of the third."

"That's a shame. Maybe the sun got her?"

Hugo raises an eyebrow and slides his gaze over to me. "No, I'm convinced it was hunters."

NINE

My brain catches up to the speed of their conversation. My own prickly fear taints everything they're saying. Hunters killed his new child? Just thinking about a grown adult—someone who had an actual human life—considered a vampire's child makes my skin crawl. There's a good chance that whoever these two are talking about was the baby vampire I staked last night. I was defending myself, but that doesn't mean I have any regrets about my actions. I'd do it all over again if I could.

I have to force myself to keep calm. I don't need my heart rate rising and tipping them off to anything I might be thinking. As far as I know, the old stories about some vampires being able to read minds are just that—stories. I release a slow breath and attempt to clear my mind anyway.

"Hello, dear," Hugo says, his eyes now locked on mine. "Are you Adrian's newest fledgling?"

I nearly choke. "What does that mean?" I ask, trying to keep my voice from shaking, though I have an inkling "fledgling" means next in line for soulless immortality.

He smirks. "Well, if not his, then maybe you can be mine?"

"Brisa will never allow you to choose another child so quickly," Adrian quips, "you know that. Don't push her."

Hugo's face contorts into a grimace, as if he wants to say something but is forcing himself to keep the words locked inside. Finally, he utters a smooth reply. "You're right, Adrian. And it's such a shame, don't you think?"

Adrian doesn't respond, not with words or his face. He's a stone wall.

Hugo's bronze eyes run down the length of me. "We could use more vampires like you. Young. Beautiful." I step back, but he pulls me to him, pressing my body against his in an iron grip. "With a streak of defiance in need of breaking, I see. My favorite."

He wants to turn me? The very idea of it makes me sick, but the revulsion in my stomach is nothing compared to the fear stirring my thoughts. Maybe he assumes I'm one of those pathetic groupie humans hanging around vamps, trying to get turned. Maybe he thinks that I'd readily agree to his offer, that I'd jump at the chance. If he knew who I really was, that I was likely the one who killed his sired vampire, I have no doubt this vile creature would tear me to shreds.

I don't move. I can't. Even if I wanted to, Hugo has caged me in his arms.

"What's your name?" His breath is sweet and metallic. He smiles wide and runs his tongue over the tip of an extended fang, as if to entice me.

Adrian sighs heavily. "We're going now," he sounds extra annoyed, "and Evangeline is my fledgling, so if you wouldn't mind unhanding her, that would be much appreciated."

The two men stare each other down and it's as if I've become the newest toy tossed between schoolyard bullies.

Hearing Adrian call me Evangeline and not Angel doesn't make me feel any better, neither does him calling me the word "fledgling," but him pulling me back from Hugo somehow does. Hugo just laughs and hands me off like it's nothing to him, like I'm one of many possible fledglings and saunters away to go sniff around his other choices.

I'm still stuck on what Adrian just said about me being "his." The term fledgling itself makes me want to punch someone, preferably someone with fangs. But before I can question Adrian on it, he's ushering me from the casino and out onto the river boat deck. The night is quiet and dark, the air has lost some of it's humidity, or maybe the chill is coming from within me. Either way, the boat has docked. It's late. I'm bone-tired, but I'm also more awake than I've ever been in my entire life.

"You'll make sure my mom gets home okay?"

"Your mother is capable of getting herself home. Don't ask me for favors."

I don't speak as he leads me from the boat to a sleek black sports car sitting in the nearby lot. We're no longer near the shipping yard we were at earlier. It's all lit up here, but I don't see Mom's Corolla. Adrian opens the passenger side door to his sports car like a proper gentleman, as if this is a date and he didn't just threaten my mother's life and kill that Paulo guy in front of me.

I hesitate to get in. "Can I please go home then? Or, I mean, can you take me back to my car?" My voice is meek and pathetic, my thoughts are jumbled. He's won, and I want nothing to do with him, at least not until I've trained with the hunters and could possibly take him down like a proper badass.

"I'll drop you off on my way to the office," he says. "You're lucky I'm not angry anymore, Angel. I do tend to take my temper out on the road."

"So I should be thanking you for not having road rage?"

He chuckles. "I have plenty of rage with or without the road."

Sounds promising—not! I slide into the smooth leather seat and force a quick, "Well, thank you, I guess." Thanking him is the last thing I want to do.

He stares at me for a long second, our gazes colliding like fire and water. "You're welcome. But after this, remember, I never want to see you again." He slams the door in my face and all I can think is that I absolutely agree with that sentiment.

Still, I'm met with relief, because whatever that fledgling talk was all about, it must have been a bluff to get Hugo to leave me alone. And thank goodness, because he gave me the absolute creeps.

What else gives me the creeps? The fact that Adrian knows where I live. I don't have to give him directions. He heads the right way as if he's driven these roads a million times before. Maybe he has. Maybe he's lived in this city for ages. Not for the first time, I wonder about his age. Exhaustion weighs heavily, muddling my thoughts, but then it hits me again.

"Wait. Where's my car?" I thought that's where we were going.

"Your mother will be bringing it home later. Kelli will give her the keys."

"I thought you said you weren't going to do me any favors?"

"Don't flatter yourself."

Quite frankly, I find it odd that Adrian wanted to drive me home, odd and worrisome, not flattering. A warning signal tingles down my spine.

When we're pulling up to the driveway, he answers my question as to why he'd want to drive me home with a single, punishing blow. "I can come into your house anytime I like," he says. "And I can kill you." He points to my bedroom window. "I know that's where you sleep. On the other side of that thin pane of glass is your bedroom. And then the bathroom, and then your mother's bedroom is at the back of the hall. I know your little home well."

"You can't—"

"Your mother already invited me in, Angel." He turns on me, baring his fangs. "She gave me an open invitation. And I've been inside every room, I assure you. Don't give me a reason to come back."

I'm frozen. What a total violation of privacy! I want to scream, to run. I want to fight. *Something.*

"Because I will come back if it's warranted." His glacial eyes narrow. "And I'll like it."

I nod once and spring from the car, needing to put as much distance between him and me as possible. He got his point across, threats have been sufficiently made, and I need to protect Mom and myself. So I'll do what he says. I saw what he's capable of. But I also need to find a way to get Mom to stay away from his casinos. She's not going to make it much longer if she keeps living at this pace. Forget about money and being broke, they'll suck her dry.

Adrian drives away, and I groan. I don't even want to go inside. I'm still wearing the clubbing attire Kelli dressed me in and my stuff is shoved into the little bag in my hand. Instead of retrieving my house keys, I dig out my phone.

I leave my house dark and hoof it to Ayla's place, texting her on my way. She texts back immediately, welcoming me with a spattering of excited emojis like she always does. The girl has no idea what's going on in my crappy life, and I want more than anything to tell her, but I can't put this on my best friend like that, especially right before she leaves on her college adventure. I'm seriously going to miss her. How will I get on with my life while she's away? I don't have anyone else like her. I wish she were sticking around town for school like Felix did, but I also can't fault her for following her dreams. If anyone deserves to study at one of the best interior design programs in the country, it's that girl.

The streets are silent and empty. It's almost two in the morning and even though I know I'm an idiot for being out here alone, I kind of don't care. My eyes have adjusted to the darkness and I know the way to Ayla's well enough that I play a game where I decide to keep my phone's flashlight off, walk briskly in these ridiculous high heels, and hope to blend in with the black. At least, I tell myself it's a game and not that I'm freaked out that Adrian will come back for me. Or worse, Hugo.

I don't want to be at home if that happens.

An SUV pulls up behind me and my heart speeds, but then it passes and I let out a shaky breath. I need to chill the heck out. I'm not going to be able to become a vampire hunter if I'm so spooked all the time. The SUV screeches to a stop and flips around, coming right for me. I tense, I don't have a stake on me. The headlights are lighting me up and blinding me. So stupid! I should have gone home. I'm fast, but not fast enough to outrun one of them. What if that's Hugo and he followed Adrian? I'm a sitting duck out here, looking like a glittering disco ball.

The window rolls down and a man speaks low. "Eva, what the heck are you doing out alone at night? Are you trying to get yourself killed?"

Felix.

I kick myself for not realizing it was his SUV sooner. I also praise Jesus!

"I accidentally locked myself out of my house," I totally lie. "I'm heading over to sleep at your place."

The fun African American guy from last night leans over from the passenger seat. "She's going to sleep at your place, Felix." He snickers. "Lucky bastard."

"Shut up, man. She's my kid sister's best friend," Felix quips back. "She's practically a sister to me, too."

Ouch. My heart sinks a little, but I'm not surprised. Alas, once in the friend zone, always in the friend zone.

"Come on," he continues, "get in. I'll drive you the rest of the way."

I'm not about to say no. I jump into the backseat where, again, the quiet guy is sitting. His dusty brown hair and haunted green gaze give him sort of a sexy standoffish vibe. He nods at me once and then stares straight ahead, as if he's deep in thought again and couldn't care less about a girl in a tiny skirt and disco ball top sitting next to him. Heck, a guy like that is probably busy curing cancer in his head—he's that serious.

"So did you talk to whoever you needed to talk to about me joining your little group?" I lean between the two front seats and waggle my eyebrows at Felix.

"No way," Felix replies at the same time that his funny friend says, "I sure did, honey."

"What is wrong with you, Kenton?" Felix glares at his friend. "We talked about this!"

"You talked about it," Kenton replies casually and winks at me "I like this chick. You're one of us now."

"No, she's not."

"I've killed a vampire, haven't I?" I lean back in my seat and cross my arms over my chest. "Pretty sure that should grant me entrance to your little club."

"Our little club?" the quiet guy beside me speaks up. "You've no idea what you're asking to get involved in here, Eva."

"Exactly," Felix interjects.

"I didn't realize you even knew my name," I shoot back at the brooding quiet guy. "And you are? You haven't spoken two words to me and now you have an opinion?"

His face hardens to stone and he doesn't answer.

"That's Seth," Kenton supplies. "He's one of our lacrosse teammates and fellow hunters." He meets Seth's surly gaze through the rearview mirror. "Sorry, but Tate wants to meet her."

Ah, so all three of them play lacrosse. Note to self, lacrosse boys are hot.

"You told Tate?" Seth and Felix say together, both pissed off.

"Hey, he asked me why we left early for our assignment and it came up. You can't get anything past that guy."

"He wasn't mad?"

"At us? Sure. At finding a new hunter? No way. He's excited to meet Eva."

I don't know who this Tate person is, but by the way the other two guys are acting, I can assume it's their boss.

"Hi, Eva here." I raise my hand. "I'm sitting right here, remember?" I lean forward and almost kiss Kenton on the cheek for being awesome but think better of it. "When and where am I meeting this Tate person? Name it and I'll be there."

TEN

A couple days later, I'm dressed in my favorite athletic gear and riding with Felix to meet this Tate character. Felix is pretty pissed that this ball is rolling and there's nothing he can do to stop it. He figures that he might as well be there for the ride so he can make sure I don't get myself killed.

His words, not mine.

He made me lie to Ayla and tell her that I also got an internship at the bank and joined the same gym nearby. She bought it without question. In fact, she was excited for me, which made lying even worse. It's a good thing the woman is going to college soon or else there's no way I would be able to keep that up. I've always told her everything. But Felix is right to not want to get her involved, and if his parents found out about what he's been up to, it would put us all in danger.

"So what can you tell me about Tate?" I ask, fiddling with the air conditioning. I decide I'm really just nervous, so I sit on my hands instead.

"You'll find out for yourself," Felix replies and then goes back to acting like I'm not even in the car. So lame.

I've been wondering about this Tate person for days, but I guess Felix is right.

We wind through the downtown financial district and pull into the same parking garage from before. Felix parks and we head over to the unmarked door. Felix uses both a fingerprint scanner and a keypad code to open it. I'm not really sure what to expect will be on the other side. My brain has conjured up a mix of superhero movies' hidden lairs and squashed them all together. The bat cave would be pretty cool, except for the fact that bats gross me out. So what if they're kind of cute? They eat bugs and their poop is toxic.

We walk through a sterile, blank hallway and then down two flights of stairs. When we open the next set of locked doors, this time using a different keycode from what I can snoop off of Felix's quick fingers, we're greeted by what's essentially an upscale underground bunker/office/gym. It's a huge room— all polished concrete and shining chrome, with sleek gray and white surfaces. There's an open space with workout equipment along the edges and a sparring pad in the middle. Everything is airy and tall, and the second story looks down with glass rooms lining the perimeter. The windows are tinted, so I can't see what's behind them. Offices? Maybe more than that, maybe a kitchen, maybe even bedrooms. There are no windows to the outside. Whatever this place is, it's super nice, super secure, and beyond what I expected. I look around, studying the people here—there aren't many, and most of them are college-aged looking guys. They keep their distance but eye me with blatant curiosity.

I assumed the vampire hunting groups were ill-equipped on account of the fact that adults can't be trusted to get involved. This place—these guys—appear to be anything but.

It's with that thought in mind that an older man descends the metal staircase and my jaw practically drops to the floor.

"Hello, Eva." He sticks out his hand when he reaches our group. "I'm Leslie Tate. It's nice to finally meet you, Eva."

I don't know what to say but I shake his hand. How can he be here? Isn't having anyone older than twenty-five a huge problem for the safety and security of an outfit like this?

"I know what you're thinking." His gray eyes wrinkle around the edges when he smiles. "But I'm immune to vampire compulsion."

"Uh, say what now?" I blurt. "That's not possible."

Tate raises a bushy eyebrow. "I assure you, it is."

Hope loosens my body and I find myself smiling. "Can you show me how?"

"I wish I could," Tate goes on. "But it's an ability I was born with."

"Well that sucks," I grumble, and Felix elbows me in the ribs. "I mean, it's awesome for you, of course, but it sucks for me."

Tate nods and runs his hand through his salt and pepper hair. "Don't worry. I'd feel the same way if I were in your shoes. You're what? Eighteen?"

I can't help but frown. "Yeah, almost nineteen though."

I hate getting older. I should want to grow up, and I do, but every day older is just one day closer to losing my mind to the vamps. What if they turn me into an addict like they did my mom?

"We keep people around until they're twenty-four-and-a-half," he pauses for a second, "that's if they don't die first. I have to be honest about that fact. We lose almost half of our hunters before they age out of the program."

"I know what the vampires are capable of." I swallow hard. "Don't worry about me. I want to be here more than I want to be anywhere else."

Something about that seems to concern Tate. Sadness softens his features. "We will verify your age with your birth records. You can hunt with us until it's time to erase your memory of ever having been a hunter."

Umm . . . My eyes practically bulge out of my head. "Excuse me? Erase my memory?"

This is getting weirder and weirder. How on earth do they have that kind of tech? Did I just walk into the world of Men in

Black? I half expect Will Smith to appear with that silver "lose your memory" light pen thingy. I almost want to look around for aliens.

"There's so much more to our world than you know," Felix offers regretfully. Considering he didn't want me to get involved, that sourpuss tone makes sense. Now all I want to do is ask a million and one questions.

"So wait, are you saying other supernaturals exist?"

Tate's sigh is deep. "You'll learn all about that in time."

"Are you a werewolf?" I blurt. I can't help myself. I mean the man has bushy eyebrows and powers and if vampires are real then maybe werewolves are, too.

He chuckles. "No, I assure you I am not a werewolf. It isn't safe for you to know more than that."

"Why?" I look to Felix but he shrugs as if he doesn't know the answer either.

"Well, first of all, we have to see if you're loyal to us and not the vampires," Tate continues.

I scoff. "Loyal to the bloodsuckers? No way. I hate them."

"Unfortunately, it's happened before."

"It won't happen with me." I fold my arms over my chest. "My mom is a gambling addict because of those creeps."

Tate frowns. "I'm sorry to hear that, but we'll still have to confirm that you can be trusted."

"Alright, fine. What do I have to do to prove myself?" Because at this point, I'll do anything.

"A simple lie detector test will suffice."

A trickle of excitement passes through me. I've only ever seen those things in movies and television. I don't mind the thought of it. Not one bit.

An hour later and I end up telling Tate everything he wants to know. He takes a particular interest in my dealings with Adrianos Teresi even though there aren't that many. I never mention that Adrian has threatened my life should I ever step foot in his filthy casino again. I figure if Tate asks me to go to The Alabaster for an assignment, I'll bring up my problem with that then. Sort of an, "asking for forgiveness is better than asking for permission" mentality. I'm careful to be honest while still not saying anything that might jeopardize my ability to get in with this group. If they knew I'd made an enemy of the most powerful vampire around, they might send me packing, and I wouldn't blame them.

"Congratulations, you passed," Tate says as he removes the lie detector wires from where they'd been taped to my skin. We are up in one of the rooms—just us—but I already feel comfortable around Leslie Tate, like he's the father figure I never knew I needed. His energy is warm and magnetic. There's just something about him that's good. I don't know how else to describe it.

"Great." I smile, my mind already three steps ahead. "So what's this group called, anyway?" I've heard names over the years of other groups, like the Midnight Slayers, The Nightwatch Club, The Buffy's, which was a total throwback to the nineties hit television show, and countless others.

"We don't have a name," Tate says. "It's safer this way."

"I guess that makes sense." But honestly, I'll just end up giving it it's own name in my head. The Bank Vault Vampire Hunters has a nice ring to it.

"We're going to start with your training." Tate shoots me back into reality and levels me with a knowing stare. "Are you absolutely sure you want to do this? I can wipe this from your memory now. No hard feelings."

"Yes. I'm sure." Inwardly, I do a little happy dance. I'm excited to get back out there and fight the bad guys, but I understand training will take time and that I need it.

"You have to know what you're getting yourself into," he continues. "You could die. You could be tortured. You will lose the friends you make here because they'll die or they'll age out and forget about your interactions together. And of course, there's always the possibility that a vampire could catch you and turn you into one of them."

I swallow. "Can they turn people against their will?"

"They can and they will. Keep in mind, a situation like that would lead them right to us. This is why it's important you're never caught."

I worry my bottom lip between my teeth and think it over. "If I'm somehow caught and turned, is that it? There's no going back?" These are stupid questions that I already know the answers to but I can't help but ask.

"Well, the bloodthirst will be unlike anything you've experienced as a human. However, I do know of people who were changed against their will and were able to get into the sun before feeding." A haunted expression crosses his face. "But once a new vampire feeds, that's it. They'll never have their humanity back."

It's hard to imagine being burned alive by the sun, but then it's also hard to imagine drinking someone dry and having a vampire master lording over me. If it happens that I get turned one day, I hope I'll be strong enough to seek out the sun too. I think through all these possibilities for a long minute, through everything terrible that could happen to me, then swallow and offer another nod. "I'm in."

"Somehow, I knew you'd say that." He shakes his head. "I've seen your kind before. Let me guess, you feel like you have nothing to lose?"

"I mean, I wouldn't call my *life* nothing, but I don't have a lot of prospects for my future, if that's what you're asking." No college. No boyfriend. Not much of a family unit. Only one close friend in Ayla, but she's going off to live her life. I am probably the perfect candidate for a job like this.

His lips thin and he changes the subject. "Our actual hunters are our best, brightest, and quite honestly, our bravest. Even your friend Felix isn't a hunter, yet," Tate goes on. This revelation is news to me. "He's only been with us for four months. He's still a novice. We recruited him and two of his lacrosse teammates from Tulane. They're on the reconnaissance side of things right now and not considered hunters yet. Once they get more experience under their belts, they'll be able to do the offensive work and start making kills."

Ah, so that's how Felix knows Seth and Kenton. That also explains why those guys were in the graveyard placing stakes in caches a few mornings ago. But that didn't explain why they'd gone out while it was still dark. I suspect they weren't supposed to go in there until the sun came out, so I decide to keep my mouth shut. Something tells me those guys were hoping to find a newly sired vamp that morning. I don't blame them because I want to hunt too.

Tate escorts me back to the gym and introduces me to the hunters and the novice. I count sixteen in all, twelve men and four women. "Everyone, this is Eva. She's new. She's going to be joining the novice crew a few months late, so she'll be working overtime to catch up."

He points to Felix, Kenton, and Seth. "You look out for her like she's your own sister, you got it?" So my guys must be the novice crew, a.k.a., the newest recruits. I can work with that.

I give Felix a sidelong glance. His dark hair is all disheveled from running his hands through it, and his pillowy lips are set in an annoyed pout. I widen my eyes as if to say, "Yay, isn't this fun?"

He glares back.

Oh, yeah, I'm pretty sure treating me like a little sister isn't going to be a problem for him. He's certainly had enough practice.

ELEVEN

I'm running through the darkened forest, leaping over fallen logs and ducking under low hanging branches. My boots squash dead leaves like crumpled paper. Between that and my panting breaths, it's hard to hear the vampire chasing me. He could be anywhere by now. My heart thuds against my chest and my mouth goes bone dry. My hands squeeze tight around the wooden stake. The monster is coming for me.

I can't escape it.

I can't outrun it.

So I press my back against a tree, ignoring the rough bark that claws at the exposed skin above my tank top, and try to focus. The metallic scent of blood trickles through my senses and something wet drips down my arm. I've accidentally cut myself.

And now he'll know right where to find me.

I refuse to die today, refuse to let this demon get the better of me. I've been training for this very moment for nearly two weeks, and now that it's here, I'm determined to win. Still, nerves fire warning shots in my belly. What if I fail?

The tree behind me rips away, roots and all. I scream and scramble back as the vampire pounces on me like a sleek cat. His glowing eyes are wide and crazed with bloodlust. His skin is translucent under the moon-drenched night. I swing the stake, same as I've practiced a thousand times, but at the last moment he veers to the left and bears down on me, fangs sinking into my neck. He rips me open, blood arcs and pain erupts. I scream and then drown in my own blood until it's over and I am nothing.

"Damn it!" I growl and rip off the virtual reality headset. I'm covered in little round sensors taped to my skin and I want to rip those off, as well. The dim lights of the small room brighten and Tate slips through the doorway. The treadmill floor below me has stopped. I sit up and shake off the failure. "I really thought I had him that time."

Leslie Tate offers me that same knowing smile he's given me about a million times since I started training in the virtual reality simulations. Okay, not a million, but it sure feels like it. At first I found the smile endearing, but now I imagine it's pitying and all I want is to see it morph into pride. I don't know why, but I suck at this. The others make it look easy. Everyday we get one session with the simulation and everyday I fail to stake the vampire. Tate doesn't want our team to start practicing simulations together until we can all stake the vampire on our own. I'm the last to get there and I worry that the guys are starting to get impatient.

"What is wrong with me?" I ask. "Honestly, what am I doing wrong?"

"It's normal to struggle at first," Tate assures me.

"But from between the simulations, to the sparring down in the gym, and the grueling workouts, I'm still miles behind the rest of my team—way more than a couple months. I'm holding them back."

"Do you know why you're here, Eva? Your friends weren't supposed to go into the cemetery until sunrise. Yes, I know all about how they broke protocol, and they were reprimanded for that, but look what came from it? You."

I guess that's true, but why am I struggling so much? Felix sure hasn't been afraid to let me know I'm behind. On more than one occasion he's encouraged me to quit the program entirely. It's really starting to piss me off. Kenton is all for me being here and is more than willing to help me train, but he doesn't hold back when sparring with me and I've yet to best him. Seth hasn't said anything to me at all. He's the epitome of the silent brooding type, and it's like he doesn't want to acknowledge my existence. Maybe he's sexist? Maybe he just doesn't like me? I can't say I'm his biggest fan either.

"What if I got lucky when I killed that new vampire?" I run my shaky hands through my hair and stand up, peeling the sensors off of me as I go. "Beginners luck and nothing more."

"You're stuck in your head." Tate begins helping me remove the sensors off my back. "Instinct hasn't taken hold yet, but it will. In the meantime, you need to keep practicing and getting stronger. Next week, we'll start training with crossbows, and then we'll move on to silver bullets."

I cheer up. "That sounds fun." A thought occurs to me. "Why don't we start with the silver bullets? Seems easier than having to get close with a stake."

"It's not possible to kill a vampire with a small bullet, unfortunately. It will slow them down and sometimes scare them off, but it's not enough to actually end them."

We walk from the training room and down the metal free-standing staircase. Below me, Felix and Seth are fighting on the sparring mat. They're evenly matched, and from the sweat pouring down each of them, they've probably been at this for a while.

"Silver immobilizes vampires, it weakens them because they're allergic to it, which is why we tip a lot of our stakes with it, but doesn't kill them on its own," Tate continues our conversation. "Always remember, wood through the heart or direct exposure to sunlight are the best ways to kill a vampire."

"Oh yeah, I've seen some videos of them bursting to flame in the sun. Everyone has." A few years ago one went viral online. It was shared millions of times and sparked quite a bit of debate. Facts are, there are people out there who support vampire rights. And then there are even some vampires who are on social media. They're basically celebrities now but I refuse to follow any of them. I chew my lip, wondering how vamps must feel about the sun—the one thing that they'll never ever be able to stop from happening every day. "I'm sure they'd do anything to become immune to the sun, wouldn't they?"

"Oh, they would, and trust me when I say they're researching how to withstand sunlight *and* staking."

Research? I try to picture it and grimace.

The idea of vampires withstanding death would only lead to one thing: human harvesting. There's no other way I can see that going except for us to be treated like cattle while they lord over the world. They may be great at spinning the facade, but they're never going to live peacefully with us since they need our blood to survive. Right now they've got a good thing going with this whole blood bag in exchange for vices thing, but that will be pushed aside if they have nothing to fear. If they can't die, then humans are doomed to a life of servitude.

"Is there another way to kill them?"

Tate looks at me sidelong and I can't help but wonder what he is if he's not a werewolf. He said he wasn't. Whatever he is,

I hope he'll tell me soon. "Vampires can rip each other apart. They can also starve to death without blood, which is a slow agonizing death that can take decades."

Huh, well they would deserve it. Same as I've seen videos of them bursting into flames, I've seen videos of them killing innocent humans, not to mention, I'll never forget what Adrian did to that Paulo gambler guy right in front of me as if the man's life meant nothing.

"Do you know why they won't drink from humans directly?" It's the question the world has debated for ages but has never been able to find an answer.

"They do drink directly from humans sometimes. When they do, I can guarantee it ends in a kill or the making of a new vampire. Turning a new vampire is highly regulated by their royals. They're picky about who they allow into their covens."

"Yeah, but what's the big secret with the bites? What does the vampire venom do to humans that would make the royals be so strict about something like that?"

"I have theories, but I don't know for sure." Tate's gray eyes sparkle, like now I've really got him going on a subject he's passionate about. "But we'll save that for when I can confirm one way or another."

I'm beginning to feel like he's dodging my question.

"But—"

He holds up a hand to silence me. "Unfortunately, when

it comes to vampires, speculation can mean the difference between life and death. I've learned the hard way to keep my theories to myself until I can prove them."

"Well, that sucks."

"Not as much as vampires do," he cracks a total dad-joke and I roll my eyes.

It also sucks that I still don't know how or why he's immune to vampire compulsion. It also sucks that my team won't talk to me about this either. Anytime I ask about Tate, they tell me I need to take it up with the man himself. For now, I'm being patient, but hopefully I'll have answers soon.

We start at 6 a.m. and train for six hours every weekday morning, ending right on time for lunch. I've been able to get my schedule moved over to three weekly night shifts at Pops so I'm busier than ever. I make the same amount of money in three night shifts at Pops as I do in five day shifts, so I'm ecstatic about this new development. But since my Pops shifts go from 4:30 p.m. until we close at 10:30 p.m., and half the time I have to take the bus home, it's made for a crappy sleep schedule. Needless to say, by Saturday night of my second week of this, I'm beat and in desperate need of a massage and a good long nap. Neither of which is going to happen.

Luckily, I don't have a Pops shift tonight. It's Ayla's last night at home before she's heading off to college and the two of us are planning to stay in and have a movie marathon of all her favorite romantic comedies. Cheesy unrealistic movies aren't really my thing, but I'll endure them all for her sake, say goodbye, and then crash at home and sleep in until eleven. Sounds like bliss.

I catch a ride home with the guys after training. Tulane started back up a few days ago so Felix moved back into the city but he's still been helping me out with rides when he can since our neighborhood isn't far. All his classes are in the afternoons and evenings to allow for the "internship", plus there are the lacrosse practices. These guys are super busy and I don't take these rides lightly—I know they're sacrificing their time to help me out. Sitting in the backseat next to Seth, my muscles practically melt into the leather and my eyes flutter closed. I don't have an ounce of energy left. Everything is sore. Felix pulls up next to my duplex. "See ya, Eva."

Kenton taps me on the shoulder just as I push open the door. "Hey, we're having our annual kick off party at my fraternity house tonight. Wanna come?"

I turn back to the guys. A slow smile creeps across my face, and what do you know, I'm not so tired anymore.

Felix shifts uncomfortably in the driver's seat and rubs his hand over his face. Seth groans, which I don't even know how to take. Last I heard, Seth is too cool for those parties. It's not his fraternity, anyway. Kenton is the only one who pledged, but when it comes to the big parties, everyone's friends are invited. Kenton waggles his eyebrows and nods encouragingly. "You know you want to."

Actually, I do. I've never been to a college party before, but that doesn't mean I wouldn't be welcome. I mean, this is a fraternity we're talking about here. So what if I'm not enrolled and can't answer when someone inevitably asks what my major is? I'm single, I'm pretty, and I'm not shy. I'll probably fit right in.

"Hmm . . ." I pretend to think about it, like it's a hard decision.

I'll have to clear this new plan with Ayla, but that girl is always down for a good party. I have no doubt she'd ditch the movies and demand we get all dolled up. Felix has never invited us to his parties before. We're only a year younger, but even in high school he managed to keep the line drawn while still being friendly. And I know it's not his party, but I also bet he'll be there. The thought of seeing him outside of the Moreno house and in his friend element makes me giddy. How much longer will he be able to think of me as a friend if I keep showing up around him in places where people can become more than just friends? Time to find out.

I wink at Kenton. "I'm in."

TWELVE

The place is packed. Bodies move together to the low bass beat of the music. It thumps through the house so loudly that the walls shake. The people who aren't dancing mingle along the edges of the rooms and in the hallways. They stand around in small groups with red plastic cups in their hands, trying and mostly failing to hear each other over the music. There's so many people here that some have spilled out onto the front and back yards. It's exactly what I'd picture a fraternity house to be with the crimson brick and creeping ivy, columns and balconies along the front, and loads of party boys intermixed throughout the crowd. Honestly, I can't picture Felix or Seth fitting in here, but it's no wonder that a guy as outgoing as Kenton found a place with this fraternity. He's got stereotypical-partier written all over him, but that's not a bad thing, not for him—he's fun!

Ayla and I snake our way inside. She's done her blue hair

back in two curly loose braids and sprayed silver sparkles down the part. Her silver crop top, black shorts, and silver gladiator sandals complete the look and accentuate all her natural curves. She can pull off that sexy latin flare like nobody's business.

I'm wearing a little black halter top dress and red Chuck Taylors. Not quite as dressed up by Ayla's standards but definitely by mine. Little does she know, I've got a stake strapped to my upper thigh. A girl's got to be prepared for anything. Since my hair doesn't curl to save my life, I've ironed it extra flat and added my favorite shine spray. Ayla's applied my makeup, complete with winged eyeliner and matte red lipstick, and I have to admit I look as good as I feel—and I feel like a badass.

"Come on." I tug at her, pointing to where Kenton is tearing it up on the dance floor. "That's the guy who invited me."

Kenton spots us right away and waves us over. "You made it!" His short curly hair shines under the dimmed lights and his eyes narrow in on my friend. "Hey Miss Ayla, it's good to see you again."

She grins and then the two start dancing as if they're old friends. They must have met through Felix this summer too. I wonder if Ayla has any idea what Kenton really does in his spare time and what she'd think if she knew he was a vampire hunter. Knowing her, she'd probably find it hot. Ayla isn't a virgin like me. It's not like she's out there hooking up with everyone, but she does like to have her fun as long as she feels respected. She says it's what young people are supposed to do and I need to get with the program, but I can't help that nobody else lives up to Felix's high bar. And I don't know, but the idea of sleeping around has never appealed to me. Maybe it's because I have a hard time trusting people. Maybe it's because I'm protective of my body. But I think it's because I'm holding out for true love. Sappy, I know, but it's important to me.

Large hands clamp down on my eyes from behind and Felix's voice murmurs in my ear, "Guess who?"

I twist around and wrap him in a tight hug. His body is lean and rippled with muscle from all of our gym time. "Hey! It's good to see you outside of work or your house, Felix."

And it is.

He chuckles. "Same."

His energy is looser, but I'm not sure if it's the booze or just catching him in a different environment. Even though the vamps were able to change the legal drinking age to eighteen a few years back, I don't drink because I hate the feeling of losing control. I also didn't miss the lecture from Leslie on the dangers of alcohol while being a vampire hunter. It was one of the first ones I got. The nature of our work puts a target on our backs, and mixing alcohol with that, especially at night, is a lethal combination. It's not that hunters have to swear off drinking, but we know that inebriation could mean the difference between life and death.

I catch the clean mint and rain scent that is Felix's signature smell and notice there's not a hint of alcohol underneath. Smart man. He turns and scans the room full of people, same as I've been doing every few minutes. Felix isn't going to let his guard down. Not really. Neither is Kenton for that matter. He may be dancing with Ayla, but he's not one hundred percent focused on her like he's pretending to be. Not being able to let our guard down is our shared curse it seems. One day, Tate says this will all be washed from my memory, but that's years away, and until then, I can't unknow what I know.

The party gains momentum and an hour later my heart is light with happiness, the muscles in my face have relaxed, and my body is loose and heavy all at the same time. A result from dancing along with my friends song after song after song.

A hot guy moves in on me and we introduce ourselves by yelling over the loud music. Carter has cornflower hair and dimples and good 'ol boy baby blue eyes. We start dancing straight away. Dancing with him sends a little shiver of excitement up my spine when I notice Felix watching us. The music changes, slowing into a low thumping beat. Carter has no problem using it as an opportunity to get closer to me. He smells good, a little heavy on the cologne, but at least it's a yummy one. His hands wrap around my hips and tug me closer.

"Alright, that's enough," Felix butts in.

Carter shoots him an annoyed glare which only grows

into a full on grimace when Felix physically inserts himself between us.

"What's the problem, man?" Carter raises his hands, his eyes darting between us.

I pop my hip and smirk up at Felix. "Yeah, what's the problem?"

Over his shoulder I catch Ayla rolling her eyes and mocking throwing up. "Ew, I can't watch you guys flirt-fight. I'm going to pee."

I know she doesn't like that I have a thing for her brother, and it's not like I blame her, *but who can blame me*? Felix is by far the sexiest guy here. Girls have been throwing themselves at him all night. And this whole dominance thing he's doing to me right now just proves my point.

"Do you want Carter's hands all over you?" Felix glowers at me. Okay, so he knows this guy. Maybe they're close, but I like that what I want is Felix's first priority, not what Carter wants. Still, I can't help but like this newfound attention. He's never shown it to me before despite my efforts over the last five years.

I smile ruefully. "Maybe I do."

"See!" Carter moves back in.

"Or maybe I'm just having fun, Felix," I continue, not even bothering to glance sideways at the other guy. Felix is the only one I see. "Haven't you ever heard of a girl wanting to have fun? Or maybe you're too serious all the time to recognize social cues?"

Carter lets out a resigned growl. "Okay, I see what's going on here. Sorry, but not my scene." He turns away, disappearing into the crowd. Gone to find new meat, just like that.

Well shoot, I didn't realize I was being so obvious.

Felix steps back.

"As far as I'm concerned you owe me a dance partner." I raise an eyebrow at him. To my surprise, he slips his arm around my waist and pulls me against his body.

"Don't make me regret this," he says playfully, his earlier tone completely gone. He sounds like the kid I grew up with, but his liquid brown eyes tell a different story. They're older, more experienced, and linger on my lips. It's all I need to know. I've been given the green light—Felix is officially interested. We begin to move together to the beat of the music, our bodies aligned in a way I've only ever dreamed about, and before long it feels like we're the only people in the room.

"Where's Ayla going?" Kenton interrupts.

"Bathroom." My voice is breathy.

"No." Kenton points and we turn to see the back of Ayla's head disappear out the front door. "She's with some guy."

I pause. "That's not like her."

Sure, she likes to party with guys, but she's careful and smart. She wouldn't normally take off with someone random, especially without telling anyone. Felix catches the same train of thought and peels away from me to catch up to his sister.

I'm quick to follow. Kenton, too. Seth isn't here since he's "above" the fraternity parties, but if he were, I'm sure he'd be by our sides. In that moment, it finally feels like we're a team. It's amazing to know someone has my back. Together, we weave in and out of the college students, dodging flinging arms and elbows, many with cups of sloshing drinks in their hands.

When we get out to the front porch, we spot Ayla straight away. Too bad we also spot her with *them*. They're way too beautiful to be human, with skin too pale to be alive.

Vampires.

THIRTEEN

I reach for the stake strapped high on my thigh, but Felix stops me. "Not yet."

He strolls up to the group as if he either has no idea what these guys are or he doesn't care. "What's up, bloodsuckers?"

Well, that answers that question.

They turn on us with a sneer, and one extends his fangs. Ayla's eyes go wide as saucers and she begins inching toward us. Unfortunately, one of the vamps tugs her back. "Where do you think you're going, Babydoll?" His group snickers. The three of them look like regular college aged guys, except their skin is too oddly pale to be normal, their best features are somehow accentuated to make them more attractive, and their eyes have a slight glow. I want to slap Ayla for not picking up on it straight away, but not everyone does, especially if they're inexperienced with vamps.

Kenton laughs darkly. "You do know you sound like a sexist prick, right? You might be ancient as dirt, but the rest of us are living in the twenty-first century. Go get your breakfast from a willing donor at one of your filthy little blood banks."

"You don't know who you're talking to," the sucker hisses and tightens his hold on Ayla. She squeals and goes white as a sheet.

Kenton lifts his shirt to reveal a stake strapped to his waist. "Right back atcha, buddy."

The vampires' eyes glow brighter at the threat, and all hell breaks loose.

The one who has Ayla arches down to bite her. She screams, and Felix pushes her out of the way. He punches the vamp square in the nose one second and procures his own stake the next. The other vamps have readied their stances, fangs extending. They move unnaturally fast, to the point of almost being blurry. Around us, the front yard partiers scream and scramble away, but I pay them no attention. My mind goes completely focused on the moment which seems to slow everything down as it plays out as if in slow-motion.

We're three on three. The vampires are ten times stronger than we are, but we have weapons and an Ayla-sized load of willpower on our side. No way are we letting our girl get hurt.

"You!" Kenton points to the vampire who tried to bite Ayla. "You asked for this."

He swings his stake with the force of a twenty-year-old who

lifts weights on the daily. The vampire deflects his blow, but Kenton was only a distraction. Using the training techniques we've been working on, Felix swings around back to sink his stake into the vampire's heart from behind. The beast screeches and explodes into dust. His two companions hiss and jump at us, as if they didn't just get the memo that attacking us gives us grounds to exterminate them. This is the way the treaties work. We're not supposed to hunt unless we're attacked first, not that we give a crap about the treaties most of the time. If we don't get caught, then we don't get turned into the VEC. Vampires can burn in hell for all we care.

I fight off my attacker and plunge the stake into his heart. I miss. He growls and backs off, his body healing almost instantly. "I'll kill you for that."

"Not if we kill you first." I lunge for him again. By now his remaining companion has also been killed, this time by Kenton. It's three to one, we're hyped up on adrenaline, and this creep doesn't stand a chance.

He must know it because he hisses and bolts.

A saner person would let him go, but I must be a little crazy tonight because I chase after him without a second thought. Something within me can't let him get away. He's a threat to not only my kind as a whole, but also to me directly, and now that he's seen our faces, he won't forget us. Last week Tate taught me that most vampires are excellent trackers. They get a whiff of their prey and they can follow the scent to the ends of the earth. I can't risk this guy having a personal vendetta against me and my friends.

My feet pound the pavement and my hand grips the stake even tighter. All my senses narrow in on the blur of black sinking into the inky darkness of the tree-lined street. He's too fast. I'll never catch up. But that doesn't matter now. I know exactly where he's going; I don't know how that's possible, but I just do.

I continue running, my instincts telling me when to turn left or right. I weave deeper into the neighborhoods surrounding the college, but soon those turn from residential, to businesses that are closed up tight for the night. I run and run and run. I only have one focus now—hunt and kill.

I'm approaching The French Quarter when a black SUV pulls up beside me. "Get in," Felix calls out.

I don't want to. I can feel that my target is closer now. He's slowed down. He's not far. Maybe he doesn't realize I'm on to him, that I'm hunting him. Maybe he thinks he's lost me.

But he doesn't know me.

I ignore Felix and continue to run, going deeper into the The French Quarter until I'm on world-famous Bourbon Street. It's packed and music pulses from speakers. I snake through the raucous crowd until I come out on the other side and it's much quieter and empty again. I keep going, turning down street after street. Many are too small for Felix's SUV and I'm pretty sure I've lost them but I haven't lost the vampire. I can still sense him ahead of me. I end up back on one of the main roads and spot Felix's SUV again. He flashes his lights. I wave but ignore him, darting into another tiny alleyway. I hear my friends getting out of the car in the distance and can't help but feel slightly annoyed that they're making too much noise. I'm going to lose the element of surprise if they don't shut up.

The summertime humidity curls its way up and around my legs under my dress. It's a good thing I wore my Chuck Taylors tonight. I might never wear high heels again, come to think of it. I slow and walk on the balls of my feet, crouching low. I can sense the water in the air, the stillness of the night, the lack of a breeze, the stench of old garbage in the bins, and the acute awareness of everything happening around me.

Voices break the silence up ahead. It sounds like a man is reprimanding another man. "Foolish," he barks.

"But I was ordered to spy on her." The voice is defiant and I recognize it as the one who threatened me. I've found my target.

Maybe there are two vampires now. No biggie, I'll just kill them both. My confidence is growing. I can't help but feel like these kills are a sure thing.

I inch around the corner of the building, listening for the muffled voices. "Did you let her follow you here?"

No more time to think. I jump from my hiding spot and

zoom toward my enemy. He doesn't have time to react before I'm sinking the silver tipped wooden stake into his heart. I feel the moment when I hit the intended target this time. The flesh of his heart gives so easily.

He bursts into dust.

Then I swing around, prepared to kill again.

"I thought I told you never to come back here."

I blink up into the face of Adrian Teresi and my blood freezes. It's like all the confidence I just had has rocketed clean out of my body. He narrows his murderous eyes and steps closer. He's going to kill me. It's then that I realize we're in an alleyway behind The Alabaster.

"I didn't realize," I whisper.

Just then, my friends shuffle up behind me, Ayla included.

Adrian peers at them and then back at me, his mouth curling in utter disdain. "What's all this? Did your friends come to kill innocent vampires, too?"

I scramble back. "None of you are innocent."

"And yet you were the one who hunted tonight." He glares at my stake. "And by the looks of it, you've done this before."

I open and close my mouth, unable to find words. I know what Adrian's capable of. How's he going to feel about me being a vampire hunter? And what will it mean for me now that he knows? Will Tate kick us out of the program? Vampires aren't supposed to be able to identify us. I have so many questions, all of which I'm afraid to know the answers to.

"Those vampires showed up at our college party looking for blood. As far as we're concerned," Felix interjects, "they started it."

Kenton nods. "And we ended it." He grips his stake tighter.

What my friends don't know is it sounds like those vamps showed up at the party because they were spying on me. That guy I just staked said someone had ordered him to go. They probably followed me to the party and saw an opportunity to take advantage of partiers, or more likely, lured Ayla away so they could question her about me. Adrian sighs as if dealing with a bunch of young hunters is the last thing on his to-do list for the night. He's not afraid of us. He's inconvenienced.

"I won't kill you," he says at last, like he's doing us a favor. "But only because those idiots weren't my protégés and, quite frankly, had no business in our coven to begin with." He chuckles darkly. "You may have just done me a favor, come to think of it, but that doesn't mean you can show your faces around here again." He flicks a hand toward us. "Now shoo."

And then his body levitates up and up until he vanishes into the darkness.

Ayla yelps. "Did he just?"

"Yes," Felix growls. "I've never seen one of them fly, but I've heard the stories."

"Only the oldest and most powerful, and therefore the

creepiest, can do that." Kenton whistles low. "C'mon people, let's get out of here before more fangers show up." He wraps an arm around Ayla's shoulders and tugs her in close. "I think you and I should have a little chat before you head up to college tomorrow about not going off with random strangers."

Ayla doesn't reply as the two shuffle ahead of me and Felix.

"You know what they say, right?" Kenton continues in a lighter tone.

"What?" Ayla's voice cracks.

He winks. "Some guys are only after one thing."

And in the case of vampires, it's nothing good.

FOURTEEN

"How's the new roommate situation going?" I ask Ayla. She's on speaker phone while I sit on my bedroom floor and apply matte overcoat to my freshly black fingernails.

"Getting better. She's cleaning up after herself now that we had that little talk. Hopefully she doesn't hate me, but we're sharing a room, have some decency."

I look around at my cluttered bedroom and snort. Ayla's a clean freak, but her new roommate is the opposite. It's a good learning experience for both of them, if you ask me. Not that anyone has . . .

"How's the training going?" she replies. "Any more run-ins with vampires?"

"Not yet."

It's been a few weeks since my bestie left for school and things have mostly gone back to normal. Well, as normal as they can be with my favorite person gone. Now that the cat's out of the bag, it's been so nice to talk to her about this crazy vampire stuff. Lucky for me, she wasn't mad that I lied about the internship. On the contrary, the woman took it all in stride, saying she'd have done the same thing to protect me and was grateful we were able to save her that night. She'd gone outside to bum a cigarette with that guy, something she does every now and then at parties, but promised she'd never be so careless again.

I believe her. In fact, she's been at school for two weeks and hasn't gone to a single party, let alone left her dorm room after dark. She's going to have to live her life eventually, but right now she's still too traumatized by what happened. I'm glad she's safe, but I also hope that she can learn to trust again. I doubly hope that she can sense vampires better now that she's had direct contact with some. They're not always easy to spot since they look like glorified versions of their human selves.

The phone beeps and an unknown call comes through. I almost send it to voicemail but instinct tells me to answer it. "Hey, I gotta take this call, talk later?"

"Later, babe. Stay safe."

My heart drops a little. The Ayla I know would've ended the call with something akin to "don't do something I wouldn't do" or "make me proud" or even "see ya later, alligator"—not "stay safe." I sigh, switch the call over, and answer with a quick, "Hello."

"Hello, is this Evangeline Blackwood?" The woman's voice is glossy and professional.

"This is she."

"I'm calling about your mother. You're her emergency contact, correct?"

"What's wrong?"

"She's okay, but you need to come pick her up. She refuses to leave and she's already donated well above the allocated amount of blood for her weight."

My body goes cold. "Where are you calling from?"

Not that I have to ask.

"I'm a nurse at The Alabaster Heart Hotel and Casino." Her voice changes from cool professionalism to an urgent whisper. "You need to come quickly. This won't end well for your mom and she's refusing to leave. Vampires aren't great at saying no to blood donations."

Vampires aren't great at saying no to anything they want, who cares who they hurt in the process.

"I'll be right there."

I hang up and jump up with a curse. My nails aren't dry and I don't have the car and I can't even believe this is happening right now. I consider calling Felix to come help, but he's pulled away since the frat party, placing me squarely back in the friend zone, and I don't really want to let him in on my family problems. Mom has the Corolla and taking the bus will take ages at this time of night, so I suck it up and order a taxi. Riding into the city will cost double during prime time, but none of that matters right now. I have to get to Mom.

I blow on my nails and hope for the best, gathering my things and running out the door, making sure to lock it behind me.

I know what I'm risking by walking in here. The risk was always there before, but this time it's tenfold, and I may as well be signing my own death certificate. I keep my head down, my curtain of black hair covering my face, and power walk toward the nurses station. It's set up right next to the cashier. No surprise there for an establishment that runs on blood and money.

"I'm here to get Virginia Blackwood."

The nurse offers me a grim expression and points. "She refuses to quit. I can't take the bag out without her consent. The vampires have a policy."

Mom is practically slumped over the edge of the Texas Hold'em table and that stupid bag hangs next to her, nearly bursting with her blood. The nearby vampire pit boss eyes her blood bag like it's his dinner. Someone's placed a chocolate chip cookie and a glass of orange juice next to her chips, but the goodies are untouched.

"You're kidding me," I growl at the nurse. "You can't take it out of her? There are laws about this."

"Humans only get to donate every so often, so the vampires don't like us to cut them off once they are hooked up to a bag."

"But the laws—" I press on.

She laughs bitterly and nods toward the pit boss. "He's the law tonight." It's a different guy than the one from last month, but even if it were the same vamp, I don't think it would matter.

Feeling helpless and pissed off, I charge toward my mother. "It's time to go."

She startles and turns on me with a grim expression. "What are you doing here? I'm fine. I know what I'm doing. Did that nosy nurse call you?"

She motions to the pit boss. "You'd better get a handle over your employees. Your nurse called my daughter, who by the way, isn't old enough to be in here."

Mom's never been like this with me. I can't even count on all my fingers and toes the number of times I've come to pick her up here. She always resists, but she's never so volatile.

"Why are you being like this?" I growl at her.

She widens her eyes and motions to her sad stack of chips. "The more blood I donate the more chips the house will give me to play with. Don't worry, I haven't had to touch the ATM yet. It's the weekend," she laughs cruelly, "why aren't you out with your friends? You know, having fun, like I am?" She sighs toward one of the patrons sitting next to her. "You'd think an eighteen-year-old would know how to have a better time than her old mom, wouldn't you?"

The greasy man grins down at her, his eyes traveling to her exposed cleavage and back up to her ruby hair. "Not everyone is as easy going as you are, Virginia." The way he says "easy" makes my stomach twist.

"Gah! Don't be a perv," I hiss at him. He only laughs. "Mom, we need to go. I'm serious. I can't be here and I won't leave you like this."

She turns her back on me and continues playing as if I'm not even there, as if I'm a bother to her and not her own daughter. I can't stick around. Adrian might've been alerted to my presence and on his way to kill me. I also can't make her go, she's a grown woman. "Will you at least let the nurse take that thing out?"

"Fine!" She throws her hands up and the blood bag shakes. "Send that busybody over and then go home, Evangeline."

I turn away with a huff, find the nurse to send her back over to my ridiculous mother, and make for the door. I don't ever want to step foot in here again. Mom is a lost cause because she won't admit the problem, she doesn't want help, and she's going to end up killing herself. Tears well up in my eyes, and my cheeks grow hot. What am I supposed to do? Just let her go? Ditch my own mother? She's the only family I have, but it feels like there's no other choice, and she's never been this mean before.

Arms of steel grab me from behind and lift my feet clear off the floor. I scream just as a black bag is thrust over my head. I claw at my attacker, but something hits me on the back of the head and everything fades to black.

FIFTEEN

I wake up sputtering to icy water splashing my face. I blink and try to clear my head, but my thoughts are too heavy to catch and my eyes flutter closed again.

"Wake up," the voice is cruel. I know that voice . . .

More water.

I careen back and find my arms and legs tied to a chair. "What the hell?" I force my eyes to stay open this time and take in my surroundings despite the pulsing headache at the back of my skull.

I'm in a small room. I think it's in a basement because it's shadowy and cold and barren. The walls and floor are all concrete. A single light casts most of the small room in shadows. Thick and scratchy ropes bind my wrists. Standing above me is none other than Adrian Teresi. A sour look is plastered to his face as he stares down his nose.

"You kidnapped me?" It's not a question though. It's the cold, hard truth. Is he going to torture me before killing me? I shouldn't have tested my luck by coming to the casino because it's painfully obvious that it's run out, and nobody is coming to save me.

His fangs extend.

They're about half an inch longer than the rest of his teeth. He leans in and breaths in my scent. "Evangeline Blackwood, I can't decide if you're an angel or a devil." His lips brush against the delicate skin of my neck. I lean away, but that only exposes more of me.

"*You're* the devil."

He clicks his tongue. "Careful. Your blood smells hot and fresh. It's practically begging to be mine."

I jerk my head back. "Please . . ." I don't want to beg, but I find myself doing it anyway. "Please let me go or kill me now, but don't play with me."

"Where's the fun in that, huh? You must want to be played with considering you keep coming back to where you don't belong. The Alabaster Heart is a casino, after all. Does the little lamb want to play a game with the lion?"

He twists around until his face is inches from mine. Everything about him is dangerous and beautiful. Gooseflesh prickles all over my body.

"I can hear your heart beating." He possesses my gaze with

his. I can't seem to look away. "It's the sound of an invitation. I could rip it from your chest right now."

This time, I don't beg. There's no point. But I won't go down without a fight. I thrust my head forward and crack my forehead into his nose.

He jumps back, growling. "You shouldn't have done that."

Maybe I shouldn't have, and maybe my head hurts even more now, but I'm still glad I did. I smile and glare. I have nothing to say to this sucker.

Procuring a white handkerchief from inside his suit jacket, he mops up his blood. His nose heals right before my eyes. Except for a couple drops on his white shirt, it's as if nothing happened. I heard it crunch, I felt it give, my own forehead hurts.

But he's healed.

"A less controlled vampire would've already killed you for that," he says calmly. "But you're fortunate that I have had centuries to learn patience."

Centuries? Just how old is this freak?

He picks up a stake, the same one I had strapped under my pant leg, and snaps it in half. "Who are you working for?"

"I don't know what you're talking about." It's a lie and we both know it.

"Let's cut right to the chase, shall we? I have your mother. I will kill her if you don't answer my questions, and then I will kill you."

I blink at him, fear cleansing me like boiling water. He's right. He holds all the cards and I've got nothing. What did I expect? This is a casino, he said it, and what do I know about casinos? The house always wins.

"What makes you think I work for someone?" I deflect with a question of my own, even though I know it's useless.

"You tracked that vampire the other night, and you obviously had hunter friends with you. You carry a stake on you at all times. You wear that crucifix everyday, which by the way, is a silly superstition." His jaw tenses and he grabs the necklace, yanking it from my neck and breaking it with an easy flick of his wrist. I yelp as he tosses it to the floor. "You, my angel, are a hunter."

I shrug and try not to hate him for breaking my necklace. Grammy gave it to me before she died but I won't give him the satisfaction of knowing what it means to me. "So? What does it matter now that you've got me. You can't compel me to do anything."

"I could keep you locked down here for years until your prefrontal cortex develops and then compel you. How old are you, again? Eighteen? Oh, but you're almost nineteen. Only two more weeks until your birthday. You humans love to celebrate your countdown towards death."

"What's your point?"

He smiles. "Six years isn't so long a wait for a vampire. It's but a drop in the ocean to me."

My mouth goes dry. He looked up my date of birth and now he's willing to keep me until I'm twenty-five. I imagine myself being a kidnapped girl, living years in this dark, dank room—a vampire as my only link to the outside world.

"But why should I bother with all that when I have your mother?" he continues. "Is her life not compelling enough for you, Angel?"

It is, but he doesn't have to know that. "Stop calling me that."

"Devil, then."

I take a deep breath. "My mother will end up dead either way. I came here to save her, as I've done countless times, but tonight she refused to come home. Did you see how much blood she donated? There's no saving her now, thanks to you."

"*She's* a gambling addict," he scoffs. "How is that my fault?"

"Compulsion!" My outburst echoes through the room.

"We don't need to compel the addicted." His laugh is bitter. "They come to us all on their own. You humans are weak."

"I'm not weak."

His smile quirks. "Trust me, you are. You're mortal. You're breakable. And just like everyone who has come before you, I will get exactly what I want from you when I want it and how I want it. I could even make you beg for it if I desired."

"And what do you want, Adrian?" I twist my neck. "This? You want my blood? Take it then. Get it over with."

"If I wanted your blood you'd already be dead. You already know what I want, hunter. Who do you work for?"

Like I'd tell him. But I need to drag this out while I think of something. "And what's in it for me?" I feign interest.

"Oh, we're back to negotiating, are we?"

"I guess we are."

"Well then, name your price and we'll see what I can do." His liquid ice eyes travel up and down my body, slowly, langually, and I shiver.

The thought strikes me and I can't stop myself. "Compel my mother never to gamble again."

He pauses. "You're smarter than you look."

"So I don't look smart?"

"You look like a twenty-first century teenager so one can only assume your education and experience are lacking."

"Typical narcissistic male." I roll my eyes.

This time his laugh is genuine and it unsettles me. "If I do this, I'll need more than just to know who you're working for."

I snort. "I'm not going to walk you in there and let you kill my friends if that's what you're after."

"I don't want to kill those hunters," he replies evenly, catching me off guard. "And I already know where you work. Your facility is under the city bank. No, Angel, I have other reasons for wanting to keep my enemies close."

I know I shouldn't believe him even though I want to. But he knows about our location, so maybe he's not lying.

"How can I trust you?"

His eyes flash triumphant. "A blood vow."

"A what now?" I haven't heard of this, but if it has to do with blood and a vampire then it can't be anything good.

"We exchange a small amount of blood and a promise," he says, "if either of us breaks that promise, then we die a very painful death."

"Eww, I don't want your blood! That's so unsanitary." I mean, seriously, that could have terrible complications for me. "Haven't you ever heard of HIV? I don't know where you've been."

"I can assure you my blood is pure, much more than that of a human. The vampiric virus kills off anything that tries to threaten my body."

"Still gross."

"And I can tell your blood is untouched."

If he means that I'm a virgin who's never done a drug in her life, then he has me there. But seriously, that's been *my* hard work and a series of a lot of unpopular choices, and I'm supposed to blow it all now on this guy? *Yeah, right.*

"I won't touch the hunters if you will agree to keep me informed on your handler's goings-on. I want to know when he leaves, where he goes. I want to know what he's teaching. Anything out of the ordinary about him. Anything at all."

"My handler?" My mind flashes to the man who's been nothing but kind to me.

"Yes. Leslie Tate."

I freeze, and he chuckles. "Oh, Angel. Who do you think I am? I run this city. Of course, I already know all about Tate, and if he were brave enough to face me, I wouldn't have to go through you."

I don't know what to say.

"And in return," he continues, "I will agree to save your mother from her addiction."

I think of my mother and the way she treated me tonight. I think of the bag, heavy with blood, of the money, being gambled like it means nothing. I want to save her, I do, but what if I can't? What if Adrian is her only hope? He can fly. He's powerful. He's old and connected and runs the city. If anyone can save her, it would be him. And as much as I don't want to betray Tate or my friends, Adrian is resourceful. He'll find out what he wants about Tate one way or another. At least this way my mom will survive until Christmas. Could anyone really blame me for that? She's the only family I have.

"You can't go after the hunters or Leslie if I do this." The second the words pop out of my mouth, guilt eats at my stomach. I'm not this person. I can't agree to do this. As much as I want to, it's not who I am.

"Fine, I will only fight a hunter if it's to protect myself." I can tell Adrian is getting excited. This isn't going to end well. "How does that sound? It's a good deal that I'm offering. You should take it."

"But—" I can feel the shame pull on my facial features. Adrian freezes. He sees it, too. He knows I'm going to refuse.

"The alternative is I kill you and your mother," he growls, his face going dark. He's not playing games anymore. "You make this vow or you die."

"Those are my only options?"

"Yes. I have no qualms about killing you both. You're lucky I'm even making this deal with you to begin with. Don't think I can't force you to do whatever I want, because I can." He smiles and his eyes shine brighter than ever. "But I'm a gentleman so I'm going to ask you. One. More. Time."

He's not a gentleman. He's a monster.

I release a slow breath, the implications of this conversation pressing down on me with the weight of life or death. He's right. What other choice do I have? Maybe it makes me a horrible person, but I want to live, and I want my mother to have a life free of addiction. I don't see another way out of this one, so I'll just have to hope that I can outsmart Adrian later and help Leslie Tate along the way.

"Fine," I snap. "I'll do it."

SIXTEEN

With a flash of movement too fast for my human eyes to follow, the ropes binding me fall to the floor in a stream of ribbons. I jump up and Adrian gives me space to stand and shake out my limbs. I want to run away, to fight, to do *something*, but I can't. So I stand there, frozen to the spot, glaring at the beautiful monster that I'm certain is going to be my ultimate undoing.

"You agree that you'll spy on Leslie Tate for me, and in return I'll relieve your mother of her gambling addiction?"

I nod. I've always been a confident person—I've always loved myself—but tonight, Adrian has taken some of that away from me, and I'll never forgive him.

His eyes narrow. "And you will speak of this agreement to no one?"

"Fine, but neither will you."

"Agreed." His smile is sinister as he drags one of his fangs across his full bottom lip, splitting it. Blood trickles down his chin.

"What are you doing?"

He answers by stalking in so close that I stumble back. He pushes me up against the hard wall, caging me in with his muscled arms. His spicy cedar smell dances through the air, reminding me of a Christmas tree—if a Christmas tree was sexy and terrifying. The long thin stream of blood continues to trickle down his neck; I grimace. His bottom lip is an entirely different color than his top, red as cherries with the pooling blood. Hunger flashes, lighting up his sky blue eyes like a thunderstorm. Did he change his mind? Is he going to kill me? I should be afraid, but strangely I'm not.

My knees weaken, and I grab hold of his arms to anchor me up. They're like steel beams welded to the wall. His strength is utterly unhuman, reminding me of just how vulnerable I am to be standing here.

"What are you doing?" I ask again, my voice trembling.

"Testing myself." His reply is low and guttural. Is he going to kiss me? *No*, a human man would be testing a kiss, but Adrian is anything but human. The bastard is testing his resolve *not* to drink me dry. I'm a toy to be played with and used, nothing more. He's like a little boy trying to see how long he can hold his breath under water. Eventually, he's going to need air. Eventually, I'm going to get myself killed.

"Test yourself on someone else," I growl. "I thought we were doing the blood vow?"

Something I can't quite describe flashes over his features. It's like annoyance and resolve and laughter all wrapped together. "We are." He snatches his right arm free of my grip and swipes at my face. He's so impossibly fast that his stubby little fingernail slices through my bottom lip, blood spilling to mirror his.

Surprised, I cry out, but he captures the pain with his foul mouth. His lips cover mine, our blood mixing. Metal assaults my taste buds, and I hate him even more than I thought was possible. This feels so wrong, and when he coaxes my mouth open to deepen the kiss, his tongue sliding across mine, it feels downright immoral. What kind of girl kisses a vampire and likes it?

Because I do like it.

My body buzzes and my heart pounds and my fingers crawl their way up and around his cold neck to ruin his perfect Adonis hair. He pushes our bodies against the wall, his hand still above me cracking the plaster. I've never been kissed like this before.

I feel like a wildfire and Adrian is my fuel. I need more.

As if knowing exactly what's going through my mind right now, he chuckles cruelly and peels us apart. He wipes his thumb along his bloodied lip and licks it clean. His has already healed. "Hmm, I thought so."

"You thought what?" I hate that my voice cracks. I hate that I want him to come back and kiss me again and that I'm hoping he'll say something about how good I taste.

"That you'd crumble and I wouldn't." The statement is like a cold shower.

Nevermind, I *don't* want him.

I glare, hating how right he is about me. Here the man stands, completely unaffected by what we just did. He's had lifetimes to engage physically with far more beautiful and experienced women. What am I? I'm nothing but a stupid teenaged girl, a game he played to win. Well, he may be the victor for now, but I'm not giving up. This is far from over.

"And what did you think of our exchange, little angel?"

I shrug. "That I've had better."

He laughs. "So have I." He is so clearly not the liar right now; it would be laughable if it wasn't so embarrassing.

"So that's it? The blood vow is set?" I fold my arms over my chest and tap my foot.

"Yes."

"But I didn't feel anything."

He smirks. "That's obviously not true." His eyes drink me in, and I redden. I also realize just how disciplined and powerful he must be if he could exchange blood with me without actually biting me. I didn't know that kind of restraint was possible for a sucker. Technically what we just did wasn't against vampiric law. There certainly wasn't venom involved.

"How do I know if any of this vow stuff is real?" I challenge. I still can't shake the fact that I didn't feel anything magical happen. Not that it's magic, well, maybe it is, I'm not really sure.

"Well, Angel, it's quite simple. If you don't hold up your end of the bargain, then you'll die. What's so hard about death for your human mind to comprehend? Don't you worry about your mortality on a daily basis?"

I scoff. "Whatever, let's go compel my mother right now and get this show on the road." I raise an eyebrow and try to mask my excitement. I've always wanted this for her—for us—especially since things have taken a turn for the worse, but I never dared to imagine it was possible. Now that it's about to happen, I want it more than ever.

"Patience is a virtue." He strolls away, and I follow, but first I pick up my broken necklace and stuff it into my pocket. "Haven't you ever heard that?"

"Talk of virtues is pretty rich coming from a murderous vampire, don't you think?"

"I can't help what I am, same as you can't help it. It's pointless to fight nature."

"Right. Like vampires are *natural*. I know for a fact you were born human just like the rest of us. You said it yourself. You're a virus."

He says nothing.

"So vampires can't help but kill?" I continue to poke the bear. "Great, maybe we can get that in writing and take it to the idiot humans who signed treaties with you guys in the first place."

He doesn't bother to respond. We continue walking through a labyrinth of hallways until we reach a stairwell. He opens the door. "After you."

He doesn't have to tell me twice. I want to save my mom and get out of here. The thin cut on my lip throbs and I feel completely bruised from his kiss. His mouth is like a brand on me now, one that nobody else will see but that I will never forget. I'm not proud of myself.

As soon as we're back on the casino floor, he points to the nearest bathroom. "Clean yourself up. You're going to attract unwanted attention with all that blood."

I hurry inside and wash my face and neck—even though I refuse to look myself in the eyes—and then scrub everything clean with a paper towel from the dispenser.

Smoothing my hair on the way out, I find Adrian waiting for me. He hasn't bothered to clean our blood off his smirking face. I don't think it's a vampire thing, I think it's a rub-this-in-Eva's-face thing. "You're truly sick, you know that?"

"I do know that." His eyes are sinister but playful, a terrible combination.

I have to look away. I gaze out at the casino floor with it's golden art deco style, totally bugged that it's more crowded than I've ever seen it before. These people are idiots for being here and I want to shake them all and scream in their faces, not that it would matter one iota. "Okay, let's go find my mother. Knowing her, I'm sure she's still here somewhere."

"You mistake me, little angel. I'm not going to do anything for your mother tonight."

I stop short and gape at him. "But you have to."

"No, the vow we agreed on is that you'll spy for me and then I'll relieve your mother of her addiction." He clicks his tongue, smiling ruefully. "We never set a time limit on when that relief would come, but we did set an order."

Realization burns bright as the midday sun. "That's not fair!"

He backs away. "Neither is taking my money and still reporting me to the Vampire Enforcement Coalition, but you did that, and now I'm doing this. Two can play the game of twisting words, Angel. Now get out of my casino and don't return until you have valuable information to report."

He disappears into the raucous crowd, leaving me to wonder why on earth I ever thought I could trust a vampire.

SEVENTEEN

I regret everything. What was I doing? Why did I give into him like that? I'm a terrible person. A better hunter—a stronger hunter—wouldn't have agreed. They'd have died before engaging in a blood vow with a sucker, especially Adrian-freaking-Teresi. I may not know Tate well, but I do know that he's been nothing but gracious to me, and here I am betraying his trust. And what if it ultimately comes down on my friends, too? What if I'm the weak link that causes the downfall of the whole organization?

I can't follow through with this. I just can't.

My mind whirls with regretful thoughts as I fail to find Mom in the busy casino. I look everywhere before finding the nurse who tells me she already left. I hope she's safe and okay. She probably ran out of money and went home. At least she's not in a hospital or dead somewhere. Defeated, I wait on the front steps of the casino for a cab to arrive. I know it's counterproductive, but I really hope Mom won some money tonight so she can pay me back for all this cab fare. September's rent is paid and I'm saving the last of the hidden sock money toward our next payment and my own money for a car.

I stare at my phone for too long and then sit on the steps. Exhaustion is heavy, and all I want is to be in my bed and for this night to undo itself.

But what if . . .

What if I do it, though? What if I find something valuable to tell Adrian about Tate and he saves my mother from addiction? I'd never have to come back to this casino again.

But I can't.

I won't.

So then, what? I'm going to die? I don't want to die.

Adrian is the one who said there wasn't a time limit on our blood vow, so maybe I can hide from him, and hold off telling him anything valuable. I mean, eventually I'll be old enough that Leslie will do whatever he does to erase my memory and that will be the end of it. The blood vow can't possibly work if I don't remember it, right?

Ugh, I don't know.

And now that I'm really thinking about it, something isn't adding up. How, exactly, is Tate going to magically erase my memory? And why is it that he's the only adult I've ever met who's immune to vampire compulsion? Felix said there was more to the supernatural community the first day I met Tate. Tate said I'd learn more soon. But he hasn't mentioned it again in the last month of training. There's got to be something else going on with that man. He claims his immunity isn't something he can share, but maybe he's lying, or maybe he just hasn't tested it enough.

I can't help but wonder if he's some kind of warlock. Are those a thing? There's enough voodoo witch-doctors in New Orleans for me to believe it's possible. But I don't know, Tate seems too level-headed for that. Or maybe he really is a werewolf, but with powers? Maybe he's something else. Elf? Are elves a thing? I know enough bookworm girls out there who would hope so, who'd give up their firstborn for a chance to be kidnapped by a High Fae and taken to some magical realm.

I snort and the sound rings out into the darkness. I'm starting to get away with my imagination, here. None of that is real. In my experience, the sparkly stuff doesn't exist. It's the things that go bump in the night that you have to worry about.

Well, when I get home—another fifty bucks poorer thanks to Mom—I don't want my mind to be a complete mess about this. I may not know the right thing to do, or if I even have a choice in the matter, but I'm going to climb into my warm bed with the decision that I'll deal with this problem when it comes back to bite me in the butt. Until then, I'm going to pretend this night never even happened.

Fat chance.

I tap my shoe against the concrete step and double check my phone that the car I ordered will be here soon, when a smooth voice behind me says a low, "Hello."

I jump up and turn to the man descending the casino's steps toward me. My hand presses against my chest. "You scared me."

"I have that effect on people."

My throat tightens when he approaches close enough for me to recognize him. "Hugo."

"Hello, Evangeline. I'd hoped I'd run into you again."

He sniffs the air and grins. "Are you hurt?"

Without thinking, I raise my hand to my injured lip. That only causes him to chuckle again. Everything within me is telling me to get far away from this one. He's not here to be my friend.

"There's something very familiar about you," he goes on. "Do you feel it, too?"

"We've met before," I try to keep my voice from shaking, but it's useless. "On the ferry, remember?"

"Oh, I remember." His eyes narrow into little slits. "But there's something more to this . . . connection."

"If this is some kind of pickup line, sorry but I don't date vampires." My tone is dry. This is my attempt to change the subject. Sarcasm usually is. The last thing I need is for this guy to realize the reason we might have a connection is because I killed his baby vampire lady a few weeks back. I'm sure now that it was her. Tate had said that vamps rarely make kin, so it stands to reason that the one I staked was Hugo's.

He doesn't take the bait. "This isn't about romance and you know it."

I swallow hard just as my phone dings and a car pulls up. "That's my ride. Gotta run!"

I dash down the remaining steps and into the car. Hugo doesn't follow me, though I can't let go of the horrible suspicion that I haven't seen the last of him.

When I get home, Mom isn't in bed. I check the garage and the car isn't in the bay. It's well past 2 a.m. which means she's either still at the casino and the nurse lied, or she went home with somebody else. I don't want to think about that one because she's never left me alone at night before. But there's a lot that's changed with the woman. Maybe I shouldn't be surprised.

I send her a quick check-in text and fall asleep waiting for her to reply. She never does.

I sleep through my alarm the next morning and not by a little, by a lot. When I eventually peel myself out of the bed and realize I'd turned it off this morning in my sleepy stupor, the time on the screen catches me by surprise. I'm three hours late for training. I've never been late before. I'm also used to catching rides with Felix, but he never bothered this morning, it seems. There's no missed call or anything.

Cursing my mom and Adrian, and Felix for that matter, I speed through the quickest shower of my life. I need to get the cigarette smell from the casino out of my hair. I don't want anyone guessing where I was last night. I finish up and hastily french braid my long wet hair back, slide into workout clothes, and run to the kitchen to grab a banana and fill up my water bottle.

Mom's car keys sit on the counter. I guess she made it home after all. She should be at work by now.

"Mom." I pop my head in her darkened room. "Are you okay?"

She mumbles something about calling in sick to work and rolls over, her little red head burrowing under a mountain of pillows. I don't have time to lecture her about the stunt she pulled last night, and it wouldn't matter anyway. Taking her car, I zip downtown to training and hope that I don't get into too much trouble for showing up late.

Well, I try to zip over, but I get caught in terrible slow-moving traffic and by the time I'm actually pulling into the underground parking garage, I'm four hours late. Half the day is gone. I wish I'd applied some makeup because I can already tell I'm blushing from embarrassment and probably look like I lost as much sleep as I did. They're going to think I'm hungover, and with my lip still healing, they may even think I ended up in a bar fight or something.

I do the fingerprint scan first and then number code my way into the facility, racing over to the gym area where I expect to find my teammates sparring. But it's empty. Taking the stairs up to the classroom areas, I find a group of hunters gathered outside of Leslie's office.

"What's going on?" I ask.

One of the girls turns on me with a frown. "He's gone."

"What do you mean, gone?"

She shrugs. "He wasn't here this morning so we started working out on our own. Finally someone got worried enough to break into his office. He wasn't there. He's not anywhere in the building. This has never happened before. Did you know he lives here? He has an apartment and everything. He's very careful about when he leaves and where he goes.."

I did not know that. "Thanks," I mutter to the girl and push my way through the crowd until I find Felix, Seth, and Kenton whispering in the corner.

"What's going on? Tate's missing?"

They go quiet and turn to me. "There she is," Seth says. "Hello, Eva. Nice of you to join us." He peers down at his watch. "A little late, don't you think?"

I wave in his face. "Uh, yeah, hi! I'm your teammate, remember? You're supposed to be on my side, not giving me crap for being late."

He rolls his eyes. "Giving you crap for being late proves I'm on your side. You can do better. Who else is going to tell it to you like it is?"

Fair point.

I turn to Felix, punching him in the arm. "Why didn't you wake me up this morning? You were my ride."

"I rang the doorbell twice."

Well, shoot. "You could've called."

"I'm not your personal alarm clock," he bites out. "And I drove across town for you not to answer your door."

Fair point.

I ball my hands into fists. "Why are you acting so rude to me? It's been this way for two freaking weeks."

"Really, Eva?" Felix shakes his head. "Think about it. What happened two weeks ago?"

"I don't know." That's a lie. Two weeks ago we danced and got close and I thought for sure we'd end up a thing, but then he backed off. It still stings to think about it. Rejection sucks.

He laughs bitterly. "Come on, Eva. Say it."

I'm not going to say it. What? That he rejected me? That's cruel. I've never known Felix to be cruel but maybe he is.

"Break it up, Mom and Dad." Kenton steps between us. "We have bigger fish to fry than your stupid argument."

I fold my arms and turn on Kenton. "So then what's the

problem with Tate?"

"The guy wasn't here when we arrived this morning." He points to the desk. "And look at what he left."

Centered on Tate's desk is a single piece of paper. Instead of a neat scrawl, the black words inked against the white appear to be written with a hurried hand.

I'm safe. I don't know when I'll return. Be careful. Stick together but trust no one. Things aren't as they seem.

My face goes white hot. Surely this doesn't have something to do with me, does it? He can't know about my deal with Adrian. That would be impossible. But what if he did? It makes sense, actually. He somehow knows about the blood vow and took off. A shard of guilt cuts through my gut like broken glass. Maybe I caused this. Maybe it's my fault. And what happens when the others figure out I'm the one to blame?

EIGHTEEN

I study the other hunters, measuring their faces for any possible suspicion that could be pointed in my direction. So far, there's nothing beyond what I'm also feeling—they are freaking the freak out. Because, seriously, what are we supposed to do now? Tate runs this operation. He's our leader. He tells us where to go, what to do, and teaches us how to do it. He's like the captain and the life-jacket *and the boat* and suddenly we're floating in the ocean on a flimsy raft.

"Listen up, everybody." One of the older hunters jumps up onto the desk where everyone can see him, or at least hear him considering it's crowded in here and there are still several people in the hallway. "I'm Cameron Scout, and I'm pretty sure I'm the oldest one here. I'm supposed to age out of the program in a few months."

Cameron is a muscled and stocky guy with spray-tanned

freckled skin and flaming red hair. He reminds me of a grown up Chucky doll who went to hang out on the Jersey Shore for the summer. He's a little scary, a little hot, and a *lot* creepy, and I wouldn't want to be on his bad side. Or his good side. Or any side, actually.

"Being the oldest here has to count for something, right? But hey, I'm not saying my seniority puts me in charge." He smiles, and my hackles rise.

"That's exactly what it sounds like," Felix mutters.

"But I'm a team leader and I've been around the longest, so I know how things are supposed to work around here," he continues. "So let's just keep things going business as usual until our fearless leader returns, okay?"

A bunch of the hunters nod, and considering my team and I are newbies, it's not like we have a dog in this fight. We'd be looked at like little yappy chihuahuas who think they're ten times bigger than they really are. My guys and I end up nodding along with the others even though this Cameron person is a tool.

"Team leaders, raise your hands, please," Cameron commands.

Next to me, Seth raises his hand. I'm surprised. I assumed our leader was Felix. I never thought to ask, and nobody said anything, but Felix is usually the one to drive us around and make demands and all that jazz. Felix doesn't bat an eye at Seth's raised hand. Once again, I'm reminded that I was late to this party and missed a few important things.

Also, if Seth is my leader, I might be in trouble. Seth doesn't like me. He's not a jerk, he doesn't say anything bad about me, but that's the point, *he doesn't say anything.* He doesn't even act like I'm here most of the time. Today was one of the only times he's even acknowledged my existence and it was to tell me how late I was.

"Okay guys," Cameron motions to the leaders, "hold back so we can have a conversation. The rest of you can go workout until we figure out our next step."

We shuffle out the door and Kenton curses. "We're so screwed. You guys know that, right? Does anyone even know how to work the simulations that's not Tate?"

"And don't forget we were supposed to be learning crossbows this week," I add and the guys groan in unison. Looks like I wasn't the only one looking forward to crossbows.

"Hopefully Tate will be back soon," Felix grumbles.

"But if he's not, we're going to turn into all those other hunting organizations that end up going south and everyone gets killed," Kenton goes on. I've never heard him be so negative and something about that makes this feel even worse. "Tate is what made us different and kept us safe. He's the only damn reason I agreed to do this job in the first place." He motions to the large state-of-the-art gym as we amble inside with the rest of the group. "I mean, the man single-handedly secured all of this without the vampires knowing. With him gone, it's only a matter of time before it falls apart."

There's at least one vampire who knows about our facility.

"Well, then we're just going to have to train harder than ever to make sure we don't get killed, now won't we?" I raise my eyebrows at Kenton. I hate seeing him like this but I don't blame him. We're all here for a cause, not a death wish.

"The woman has a point." Felix sighs, raking a hand through his curly dark hair. His bicep flexes and I have to look away. I'm mad at him. No more drooling.

"Fine, you two go first." Kenton points to the mat. "I haven't seen you spar yet."

"That's because we haven't sparred." Felix's tone is warning.

"Yeah," I add. "Felix is too holier-than-thou to spar with me."

"It's not like that." He glares down at me, but behind that glare I catch hurt. I have to stop myself from rolling my eyes, because if anyone should be hurt about the iciness that's been going on between us, it should be me.

"Then what's it like?" I fold my arms and pop my hip.

"I don't want to hurt you." He says it like it's obvious.

"Maybe you avoiding me is what's actually hurting me. Did you ever stop to think about that?"

Felix just stares at me. He knows I'm right. Did he really not catch on before?

Kenton chuckles and intervenes. "You know that if she doesn't get good sparring partners then you're only weakening her for the suckers, right?"

"Yeah. What he said! Or maybe you're scared I'm going to kick your ass?"

Felix shifts his glare to Kenton. "Fine." He picks up two of the rubber stakes we use to practice with and tosses one to me before stepping back onto the black mat. "But I'm not going to go easy on you."

"You wouldn't dare," I tease.

And then he lunges for me.

I'm quick to dodge him, jumping out of the way and landing in a fighter's stance. As we circle around each other, I'm reminded of two wolves challenging each other for the spot of alpha. Adrenaline spikes my blood. Everything around us blurs as I become hyper-focused on Felix. I'm quick, quicker than I've ever been before, dodging his moves milliseconds before they should strike. Deciding that I don't just want to be on the defensive here, I make my own move, dropping low and kicking out my foot, hooking it around the back of his ankle and pulling. It catches him, and he falls. I pounce forward, stake prepared to strike, but he blocks me with his forearm and flips me onto my back. Before I can react, the tip of his rubber stake presses to my ribcage, just over my heart.

I lost.

His body is weighing mine down and every inch feels like an answer to all my teenaged birthday candle wishes. This is what

I've been waiting for. I blink up into his chocolatey eyes, daring him to take this further. He shouldn't kiss me here, not where everyone can see, but I want him to want to kiss me anyway. I want him to think about my lips and nothing else. My hope leaps when his gaze flicks to my mouth and then holds.

He feels it, too.

"What happened to your lip?" He sits back up, rolling off me.

Oh, that . . .

"Why were you looking at my lip so closely?" I deflect, and he glares. It's not like I can tell him the truth of my healing lip, but I don't want to lie to him either.

"Eva," he challenges.

Well, maybe I can tell him part of the truth. "Someone got a little excited when he kissed me last night." I wink. "Don't worry, I liked it."

Also, not exactly lying because I did like that part.

My words cause the reaction I was hoping for. Pure unfiltered jealousy creases his brow and fires up his eyes. It ignites something primal in me. Before I can react, he jumps to his feet and stalks away. I guess this is his way of not wanting to show me his true feelings, but it's too late, I already know what I saw. Meanwhile, Kenton is busy laughing his head off from the sidelines.

I get up and brush myself off, ready to go another round, when Seth shows up.

"Evangeline, can I speak to you about something?"

His request catches me by surprise, but I decide to give the guy the benefit of the doubt. Also, I don't want to look as guilty as I feel today.

"Sure. Here?" I nod toward the mat. "Wanna talk while we spar?"

"No, let's go somewhere more private."

I follow him back up the stairs and into one of the smaller classrooms. We turn to face each other. I almost expect him to tell me to back off Felix, and I'm prepared to lay out all the reasons why it's none of his business who I date. Of course, I know that's a load of crap considering he's the leader of our little novice team.

"There's something I've been meaning to ask you." He levels me with that all-seeing gaze of his, and I try to appear causal.

"What's up?"

He studies me and it feels like he's looking into my soul or something. Geez, this guy is so freaking intense for only being twenty years old. "That night at the party when you tracked that vampire from Kenton's fraternity house all the way into the city . . ."

"Yes?" I let out a little breath.

"How did you do that?"

This isn't what I expected. In fact, I hadn't given much thought to that night since it happened. I've been so busy. "I don't know," I shrug, "I just did it."

"You have no idea how you were able to do that?" He's skeptical. "I wish I was there to see it for myself. Kenton and Felix told me about what happened. Felix has been going on and on about it. "

I shrug again and realize that's what Felix was talking about earlier. He's been upset because I ditched him to track that vamp. "I don't really know how I did it. The sucker pissed me off, I knew he was a threat, and when he ran, I followed him. It was like I just sensed where he was. Hunter's instinct, I guess."

He frowns. "Instinct?"

"Well, I don't know what else to call it." But now that he brings it up, it is kind of odd. I thought it was normal but now I realize it's anything but normal. People can't just track vampires like that. So, why me?

"Do you have any idea where Tate could be? Do you think you could track him, too?"

I try to keep my face clear of any guilt I feel when I think about Tate and shake my head. "I don't know if it was a one time thing with that particular vampire, but I don't have any idea where Tate is or any kind of instinct as to where to look. I'm just as worried about his disappearance as you are."

And for more reasons than I'll admit.

"Okay." He nods once. "Well, if you think of anything, or if anything else comes up, will you let me know?"

"Sure thing, boss." I don't say it sarcastically, but maybe he takes it that way because he frowns.

"I didn't choose to be the group leader, you know. Tate assigned me."

"Tate's a smart man." I pat him on the shoulder. "I'm sure you're a great leader."

He hums to himself and frowns. "Actually, I don't think I have been the best leader. I'm sorry I haven't been more welcoming to you. I'll do better."

"I definitely wasn't expecting you to say that, but I'll take it." I try to hug him but he escapes me by ducking under my arms and makes a break for the door.

"Baby steps, Eva," he deadpans, and I snort.

We go back downstairs with the others and train like we normally do, all the while wondering about Leslie Tate's disappearance and what that might mean for our futures.

A couple days later and things have almost returned to normal, except for the fact that Tate's still MIA. I'm back to getting rides to and from hunter practice with Felix and the guys whenever Felix has availability. Sometimes they have lacrosse practice that intervenes with our gym time, and I hate those days, because I hate to train by myself. I'm so used to doing things independently, that this feels different and special. I like that I'm not all alone in this thing. Being on a team has become a lifeline.

Felix has dropped his attitude and I suspect Seth has something to do with that. Today I'm sitting in the front and sneaking glances at the boy whom I've had a not-so-secret crush on for ages. He's still as gorgeous as ever. He's still this mysterious code I'm dying to crack. He's still fun and alluring. But… but I'm starting to get tired of waiting for him to make a move. I deserve someone who wants me as much I want them.

I know, shocker, right? This is what Ayla's been preaching to me forever, and it's what I've believed too, but I still couldn't shut my feelings off. Maybe it's time I find the switch and stop worrying about him like that. I have enough going on without having to add a complicated romantic relationship to the mix.

The thought makes me a little sad, but a little relieved at the same time.

Mostly sad.

When we pull up to the duplex, my entire body goes cold.

"The door is open," I croak.

Felix and the guys are out of the car in all of two seconds flat. I follow behind as we quietly creep up to the duplex. Sure enough, our front door has been kicked clear off the hinges. It lays in our tiny living room, parts of the painted red wood splintered across the beige carpet.

NINETEEN

Seth points to Kenton and he takes off to run the perimeter of the house. Then he and Felix escort me inside.

Our stuff is everywhere—literally everywhere—and tossed about like trash. A couple of our kitchen cabinets have been kicked in. Our round hallway mirror is smashed in the middle, splintering out like spiderwebs. I catch my stunned face in the reflection, a fractured image of a girl I can hardly recognize.

Something's happened to Mom. I'm sure of it.

We edge along the hallway into her room, but she isn't there. It only takes a few more minutes to case the rest of the tiny two bedroom duplex and realize she's not here at all. Am I too late? Is she dead somewhere?

"Mom?" I call out, helpless.

Silence.

At least there doesn't seem to be anyone else here, namely

whoever destroyed my house.

"I'm going to call her," I croak and then dial her number. To my surprise, she answers right away.

"Evangeline, baby," her voice is breathy, like she's been running. "I was just about to call you."

"Mom, what happened? Have you been home? The house is a disaster. Were we robbed?" My mind starts racing, imagining her hurt. "Do we need to call the police?"

"No!" she barks out. "Do not call the police."

"Mom, what's going on?"

"Listen, baby, I did something stupid." She goes silent. "I'm okay though. I wasn't there when they came to the house, but—"

"Mom! What did you do?"

"I borrowed some money from the wrong people, that's all. I'll pay them back. I'm working on it, but in the meantime I'm hiding out with a buddy, and you should hide out, too, okay? Go stay with Ayla."

I'm shaking. Shaking with fear. Shaking with rage. I want to yell at her that Ayla isn't even in the state anymore, but then I have to remember that this addiction isn't all entirely Mom's fault, even though it certainly feels like it right now. I still don't believe Adrian when he said they don't compel people because they don't need to. Maybe I'm looking for the best in people instead of looking for the truth.

"Are you okay?" Felix places a gentle hand on my shoulder.

I don't know what to say. He carefully removes the phone from my hand and finishes up the conversation with my mom before hanging up.

"You're coming to stay at my parent's house," he says, "you can take Ayla's room. It's fine. My parents will be happy to have you. They've been super weird about being empty nesters anyway."

My face has got to be candy apple red by now. I don't know if I've ever been more embarrassed, which certainly doesn't make the anger or fear feel any better. While Felix tells Kenton and Seth what's going on, I go to my room to pack up what I can from the mess of my things. I don't have much to begin with, but a lot of my stuff has been destroyed by whoever is after my mom. Tears burn my eyes and stream down my face but I force myself to work through them anyway.

Once I'm all done, I go to the air conditioner vent where I've got my sock of money hidden away, but when I reach inside, there's nothing there.

Of course, it's gone. What did I expect? The whole house is a mess, they probably took anything of value and whatever money they could find. It's not like a vent is the most original hiding spot. I want to scream, to riot, to find whoever stole that money and demand it back. But I know it's hopeless. There was only a grand left in the sock but I was counting on that money. I should've put it in the bank. I should've been smarter.

"What happened here?" I recognize Mrs. Maybee's shrill

voice and cane thumping against the floor from the duplex entrance. My heart sinks. And as usual, I'm the one who has to fix this with the landlady. Just great.

I wipe away my tears and go out to the living room. "I'm so sorry, Mrs. Maybee," I say. "I'll clean this up."

"Where's your mom?" Her face is scrunched up like a prune.

"Umm—I don't exactly know but she's safe."

"Were you robbed?" She thumps her cane against the floor to emphasize each word. Her face is no longer a prune and has turned ghost white.

I should lie, I know I should, but I freeze up and don't say anything.

"Get out," she finally snaps. "Just get your things and get out. Consider this your eviction notice!"

I don't know if she can legally do that because it's not like we're late on rent anymore and we still have plenty of time left on our lease, but I'm not going to stick around for her to call the cops and try to deal with this legally. If Mom is worried about the police then there must be a reason. Whoever she owes can't be happy with her. This isn't my mess, it's hers, but once again, here I am trying to clean it up.

"Now!" Mrs. Maybee growls.

Mortified, I glare at the woman but pick up my duffle bag and scurry from my house, the guys at my side.

"And don't bother coming back," she yells after me. "I'm fixing the door, changing the lock, and using your security deposit to repair these damages."

"You could fight her on it," Seth says, "there are laws to protect you in these situations."

"I'm sure there are laws to protect her, too," I reply, dejected, thinking about all the damages. "But it's a moot point considering my mom has taken off and my name isn't on the lease."

"It's going to be fine." Felix wraps an arm around my shoulder and leads me back to his SUV. He's trying to be nice, but even he can't make everything better. I've lived in that duplex for four years, and before that, in an apartment building a few streets over. This neighborhood is my home, my stomping grounds, and now what? Now I crash at Ayla's? Felix isn't even living there anymore now that school's started. And last I'd heard from Ayla, her parents are trying to make sense of their new life as empty nesters by remodeling a bunch of stuff. They're talking about turning her room into the guest room and have started transforming Felix's into a home gym. Ayla's been sending her mom mock-ups and helping them design everything. Who am I to come in and ruin their grand plans? I'm going to have to figure something else out. And in the meantime, Mom is heaven knows where, with heaven knows who, and loan sharks are after her.

My life is a mess, but I'm not going to cry about it anymore. I hate crying. I'm going to fix it. It was the last of Adrian's money that I had stashed in that vent, over a thousand dollars now gone.

Luckily everything I've been saving for a car is still in my bank account. I'll just have to use that money to find an apartment rental instead and keep taking the bus and bumming for rides.

When we get to the Moreno house, Felix runs inside to discuss the situation with his parents. Not surprisingly, his mom Yanet comes out to usher me into their home like I'm their long lost child and there's nothing they'd rather do than take care of me.

"Eva, honey," she says, pulling me into a warm squishy mom-hug. "I've always thought of you as a second daughter anyway. Don't even worry for one second." She's the middle-aged version of her kids. The whole family looks like gorgeous Cuban cookie cutters of each other. I sink into her for a second and then we're walking into the house.

"You don't know where your mom is?" She glances around, as if looking for something or someone. Who am I kidding? Of course, she's worried. My mom is an idiot and people are after her. They could be watching us right now. Yanet has to be wondering if her house is a new target.

"I'm sorry," my voice cracks, "she won't tell me where she is but she sounds okay."

"Well, that's a good sign." I can tell she doesn't believe her own words. "Come inside."

Yanet begins cooking dinner for our crew, and while they all hunker down on the couch to watch football, I go lay on Ayla's bed and begin searching online for rooms to rent but don't find anything. I was hoping maybe someone would need a roommate near the college, but it's looking like it's too late and everything is filled.

I could stay here. I could use the Moreno's generosity until my mom shows up with a solution. But what if we bring trouble to their doorstep? Whoever is after my mom could decide to use me as collateral to get her out of hiding. I can't risk their safety. I would never forgive myself if something happened to anyone in this household. I shouldn't even be here at all.

My bag is still packed.

I open the window, toss the bag with everything I own onto the lawn, and crawl out, leaving the comforting smell of Yanet's signature arroz con pollo dinner and the cozy feeling of family behind.

TWENTY

"Back so soon?" Kelli raises a perfectly groomed eyebrow from where she sits at her receptionist desk. She sniffs the air and cringes. "Humans really should shower everyday, you know."

"Is your boss in?" I drop the duffle bag at my feet and rub my aching shoulder. "I need to talk to him. It's important." And yeah, I wanted to shower after practice, but things took an unfortunate turn, none of which is Kelli's business. I totally want to punch the nasty smirk off her perfect face but I'm not going to fall for the bait.

She rolls her eyes and sighs dramatically, like it's such an imposition to do her job. "Is he expecting you?"

"I know you don't like me, Kelli," I snap. "But I've had a hell of a day and I'm not going to put up with your attitude. Just get me Adrian."

She stands and her fangs extend. "Do you know who you're

talking to, little girl?"

Maybe I should feel fear, but I don't. I have a stake strapped to my stomach under my baggy t-shirt and I could end her if I wanted. Of course, that would be the end of me too considering where I am right now. And anyway, I'm tired, I don't want to fight her. I just want to get Adrian's help. That's it.

But dang, I'm in a pissy mood. I can't help myself.

"I said please. Are you his receptionist or not?"

"Executive assistant," she growls. "There's a difference."

"Oh, so you pick up his dry cleaning *as well* as answer his phone? My bad."

A dark voice chuckles.

"Two things," Adrian's voice cuts through the tension and I turn to see him standing not a foot behind me. I didn't even sense his approach. He holds up a finger and whispers low in my ear. "First, you're foolish to bring a stake in here. If a vampire catches you with one of those, you're dead." He leans back.

Note to self: the vamps must not have the amazing hearing I assumed they did. Or maybe that's only for when they're hunting? Or maybe he wanted to whisper in my ear for dramatic effect and Kelli heard every word. Whatever it is, I don't ask.

"And second," he says aloud, "you two need to get along."

Kelli scoffs.

"Because you both work for me now."

I elbow him in the stomach and then immediately regret

it because I hit my funny bone and it burns like a mother. "Ouch!" Kelli laughs as I lean over and try not to cry. His chest is hard as rock, no exaggeration. Vampires are too strong for their own good. Also, how does he always know when I have a stake? The man is too good at spotting them. Maybe that's why he's managed to stay alive for so long.

"That's between us." I glare up at him.

"Kelli can be trusted." Adrian shrugs. "She's my protégé. She is bound to me."

Again, creepy.

"So you're saying I can trust you, then?" I roll my eyes. "Yeah, I'm not dumb."

"Do you have information for me already? Because if you don't, then I'd beg to differ." He stares down at me, his blue eyes swirling with excitement.

"Unfortunately, I do." I pick up my bag. "But we need to chat in private."

He eyes my duffle bag, curls his lip, and nods to the elevator bay that leads to his office.

"Let me guess," he says once we step inside. "You need a place to stay."

I pat my trusty old blue duffel bag with it's frayed edges. It's seen better days, but I still love it because I associate it to years of fun track tournaments. "Unfortunately, I'm currently homeless. It seems my mom borrowed some money from gangsters and now I have to hide out."

He glowers at me. "Angel, did someone drop you on your head as a child?"

"Excuse me?"

"You really think hiding out among vampires is a good idea?"

"I don't." I swallow hard. "I know I could get a cheap hotel room in a seedy part of town and probably be safer there than in a vampire casino. And sure, maybe I should do that, but I needed to talk to you anyway and I figured you could help me for a night or two until I find a place to rent. You've got to have empty rooms available. This place is huge."

The elevator stops and the doors open to his gorgeous office. The last time I was here, I was terrified and angry, and now I'm just . . . tired. Adrian ushers me into a plush leather chair. Outside the river sparkles under the blue sky. He leans against his desk, studying me like he thinks I'm either courageous or stupid or both.

"So do you have information on Leslie Tate?"

I grimace. "I do."

"And?"

"Mr. Tate has left the building."

"I assume he does that from time to time. During the daylight hours to avoid people like me, of course." He glances out at the highly tinted windows and frowns. "Did you follow him somewhere, perhaps? Maybe somewhere interesting . . ."

I follow his line of sight outside. It's the afternoon, so it's the time of day when he's stuck indoors. When was the last time that this man was able to feel the sun on his face? No, I can't think about those things. He's not a man. He's a monster.

"Leslie Tate is gone," I continue and Adrian's eyes narrow into slits. "He left a hurried note on his desk saying that he had to leave us, and that he's safe, but he doesn't know when he'll return. Oh, and he also told us to trust no one and that nothing is as it appears." I release a slow breath. "So that was fun."

He growls, slamming his fist into his desk with a bang. I flinch and gape at the cracked oak finish.

"And you're probably wondering what this means for our blood oath?" He rakes a hand through his Greek god-like hair and levels his gaze on mine. There's something so otherworldly about the fluidity of his movements; it reminds me who I'm dealing with, reminds me to be careful. He's not human. And I'm nothing more than food.

"There is that." I sit up straighter.

"The vow hasn't changed. You will keep digging up what you can, and when I get what I need, I'll release your mother from her addiction."

I'll admit, I do like this situation better now that Tate is MIA, and I want to help my mother, but right now I have to think about getting a roof over my head and food into my belly. I hate Adrian, but the guy has more resources than anyone I know.

When the time comes for him to compel Mom, maybe I can get him to get rid of her gangsters, too. In order to do that, I need to get on his good side.

I need him to like me. Vampires can like humans, can't they? I mean, some must like them enough to turn them. That's not going to happen to me but maybe I can get him to think of me with something other than utter contempt.

"Come." He strides back to the elevator and we return to the lobby. He tries to hand off my raggedy bag to a bellman, but I refuse.

"If you must carry that thing then fine, but let's go, I have a meeting in an hour."

I smile, channeling all that pageantry in my blood. "So you're going to help me?" I bat my eyelashes, feeling like a complete idiot. But hey, men like to save women and feel like we can't survive without them. This is a universal and timeless fact about the opposite sex.

He glances sidelong at me. "If your hunter friends know you're staying here, they're going to be mighty suspicious."

I frown. "Crap, you have a point."

"You can hide out here for a few nights until you find a place, but do not go out onto the casino floor, do not talk to any vampires—especially not my brother—and don't let your people know about this arrangement."

Considering I snuck out of the Moreno's house to come

here, this secret is going to be difficult to keep from Felix, but I bite my tongue. Adrian doesn't need to know about Felix. Something he said hits me as we stride toward another bank of elevators.

"Your brother?" I try to imagine another man who looks like Adrian and my insides almost spontaneously combust. Is Adrian awful? Yes. Is he also the most attractive creature I've seen in real life? Also, yes. Take Greek-god features and add vampiric beauty and make him look mid-twenties forever? Genetic lottery.

"You've met Hugo."

Eww, Hugo . . .

"Hugo and I are sired by the same master which makes him my brother."

"Trust me." I shiver. "Hugo is creepy on a cracker. I'll stay as far away from him as possible."

"Creepy on a cracker? Can't say I've heard that one before, Angel." His eyes travel up and down my body. "But it's not really him I'm worried about."

"What's that supposed to mean?"

"It means if he knows I'm interested in you, it's only going to make him more interested in you as well. You might try to stay away from him, but if he wants to find you, he will. His tracking skills are the best I've ever seen."

He's expecting the reaction that I'm feeling, which is fear of

Hugo, but what I give him instead surprises him. I waggle my eyebrows. "You're interested in me, eh?"

He laughs. The sound makes me smile. It's stupid.

We climb into the hotel elevator and zoom to the top floor. There is a small hallway and two hotel doors opposite each other.

"This way." Adrian uses a real key instead of a hotel card to open the door on the left. He stares at me for a long minute. "Can I trust you with a key?"

I don't know what to say so I nod. He shakes his head and mutters something about being foolish.

My jaw actually drops open when we enter into what has to be the presidential penthouse suite. The room seems to take up an entire floor, similar to his massive office. But it doesn't have the same businessman feel of the office. It's not intimidating or mid-century or sharp angles. This place is warm. The floors are dark hardwoods with turkish rugs. The couches are plush and welcoming. The cream colored walls have beautiful paintings hung on them, many of which have to be famous. I don't know much about art, but even I can recognize a Van Gogh when I see one. There's a small kitchenette that looks untouched, a couple of closed doors, a mammoth-sized flatscreen television, a fireplace, and of course, a view of the city behind thick bulletproof darkly tinted glass.

"If you're staying in my hotel then you'll need to stay close to me." He saunters to the kitchenette, removes a blood bag from the refrigerator, and plops it into the microwave as if it's the most normal thing in the world, as if he's making a freaking Hot Pocket. I can only stare as I watch him prepare his meal. The microwave dings and I imagine him biting into the bag like I've seen Felix drink directly from the milk jug. I can picture the rivulets of crimson that might stream down his face and neck. Instead, he slices the top corner of the plastic and pours the blood into a black water bottle, sealing the lid. It appears so natural. He walks back toward the door to leave.

"You can take whichever bedroom you prefer. Vampires don't use them for sleep, anyway. But you should stay in here when you're at The Alabaster if you're not with me. Don't go anywhere else. And let me or Kelli escort you to and from the hotel. You can call her using the phones in the bedrooms." He retrieves a key and hands it to me. "You can have this, just in case you need to get in and Kelli or I aren't available. Don't try to make a copy. I plan to replace the locks once you leave anyway."

The weight of the gold key feels heavier than it should, like it's attached to a million expectations. I shove it into my pocket. "Is it really so dangerous for me to be here? I've come to this casino many times to get my mom."

"It's always been dangerous, Angel. Your virgin blood makes you more desirable to my kind and they will seek you out. I may run a casino, but I'm not always a betting man. I need you alive to get use out of you."

He pushes open the door and steps into the hallway.

Realization dawns on me. "Wait, is this *your* penthouse?"

"Welcome home." He chuckles.

The door slams.

TWENTY-ONE

My phone buzzes in my back pocket but I ignore it. Again. It's probably Felix. He's been texting me nonstop for the last twenty-four hours, trying to figure out where I'm staying so he can check on me. He's all worried, but I can't exactly tell him the whole truth. I texted back last night that I was safe at a hotel and that I'd see him on Monday at our "internship." Apparently, that's not a good enough explanation for sneaking out of Ayla's bedroom window because he keeps sending follow ups that I don't know how to answer. Meanwhile, the person I want to hear from—my mother—is totally MIA.

I wipe a bead of sweat from my forehead and refocus on what I'm here at work to do: work! I load table fourteen's order onto my arms and stroll out to deliver the food. I head over to my next table that was just sat by the hostess only to find Felix, Seth, and Kenton there waiting for me. Felix stares at me hard, his eyes roving over me like he's looking for flesh wounds. Seth is unreadable. And Kenton already has his face stuck in the menu.

"Hey . . . guys. I didn't expect to see you here tonight. Can I start you off with some drinks?"

"We're here because you apparently forgot how to answer your phone." Felix's eyes narrow. "What's going on with you, Eva?"

"Would you recommend the ribs or the brisket?" Kenton interrupts.

"Shut up, Kenton," Felix growls.

Kenton looks up with wide eyes. "What's your problem, man? I'm hungry." He flexes his right arm and kisses his bicep. "It takes a lot of food to fuel this body."

I laugh, Felix and Seth roll their eyes, and the tension dissipates. "Definitely the brisket. Ours is amazing. But save room for the pecan pie because it's the best thing on our entire menu."

"That good, huh?" He waggles his eyebrows. "I'm not normally into sweets. You know I like it savory."

"Dude, don't be gross." Seth punches him in the arm but they laugh.

"Trust me, Kenton. You want this pie."

"Hello?" Felix waves his hand in my face. "Can you please tell us what's up with you? Why'd you ditch us yesterday?"

"I'm at work, Felix." I motion to the busy restaurant. "Can't this wait?"

Suspicion flashes behind his chocolate eyes, and I sigh. "Okay, fine. If you must know, I didn't want to stay at your parent's place because what if the people after my mom show up there looking for me? You saw what they did to my house. I love your mom and dad and can't risk anything happening to them."

He folds his tan arms and I have to keep myself from staring. What is it about his manly arms that has me so attracted? He's looking good today, but I've sworn myself off of the Felix-train. "Fair enough, but you could have told me that. We'd have helped you."

"Hotels are fine until I find a place," I rush, catching the eye of my manager Eddie heading our way. "What was I supposed to do, crash at your party house?"

I haven't been inside his house but I have been with them when he dropped Seth off once since they're roommates. The place looks like a typical off-campus party-house man-cave dump. I'd rather take my chances staying with Adrian, scary as it is.

"You could've stayed in my room at the frat house," Kenton says, his tone completely serious. "Plenty of girls do." He waggles his eyebrows to break character.

Seth gives him a sidelong glance and Felix looks about ready to rip his head off.

"Hello, gentlemen." Eddie approaches the table with that happy-go-lucky smile on his face, but I know this is his way of checking up on me. "Is everything okay over here?"

"Yeah, we're just having a debate about the menu." Kenton

grins ruefully. "Ribs or brisket? What say you?"

"I'm normally a ribs man myself, but nobody makes brisket like Pops." I smile at Eddie, mentally thanking him for saving me from this conversation.

Kenton hands me the menu. "Great. I'll take the brisket with a side of coleslaw and hush puppies. Oh, and a sweet tea and let's finish it off with that pie." He winks.

The other guys order and I get back to work while Eddie hangs around for a few minutes to chat. Eddie sometimes has to do this for the servers. It's his way of keeping us on task while also keeping the customers happy with his lively conversation and saving us from flirty or just overly chatty customers.

Later, when the guys pay their check, they give me a big tip and ask if I'll be needing a ride on Monday. I insist that I'm fine. I tell them not to worry, that I got it handled, and I'll let them know when I need something. I'm an adult. I can take care of myself. But it's not until they leave that I finally relax and get focused on my job. Being faced with that suspicion in Felix's gaze, not to mention Seth's unreadable intelligence, I know I need this money now more than ever. Adrian was right last night, I can't stay at The Alabaster for long, and I can't let the hunters figure out I'm there.

I take the bus back to the casino even though I hate the bus. I get a little carsick each time because it's way too hot and smelly and bouncy, but taking a taxi to and from work isn't going to do me any favors when it comes to saving money and I'm not walking alone through these neighborhoods at night. At least there's a reliable bus system. I have to be grateful for that. When I finally get off and walk into the lobby of the hotel, I veer away from the elevator bay and toward the casino floor. Adrian doesn't want me out here, but I'm just going to take a quick peek to see if Mom's gambling. She's hiding out, so I'm guessing that includes staying away from The Alabaster Heart, but I also know my mother. She won't be able to stay away for long, and I want to talk to her, to find out the full situation she's gotten herself into. Maybe it's not as bad as she says. Maybe I can help.

I've still got on my little black shorts and t-shirt from work, and the AC bites at the exposed skin. I keep my head down, the curtain of black hair a pathetic disguise, and fold my arms in on myself. I do a quick once around the area where the tables are set up but don't see her here. On one hand, I'm relieved she's not here. On the other, I hope that doesn't mean she's on the riverboat. It is Saturday night, after all. And on the other, other hand, I'm just hoping she's staying away from casinos and staying safe in general.

But I really wish she'd return my calls. I'm on the verge of giving up.

I also don't see Adrian down here and the only vampire is the pit boss, who's busy working. It's fine. It's not like someone is going to jump over the tables and bite me just because I'm a virgin which somehow makes my blood yummier. I recognize one of the regulars at the Texas Hold'em table and saunter over to his side, positioning my back to the dealer and keeping my head down. It's a full table, a full casino really, and the music is annoyingly loud. Hopefully, I won't get carded and sent away.

"Hey," I say casually to the guy, "you know my mother, right? Virginia Blackwood? She's the petite redhead who's at this table a lot."

He peers over at me from under bushy black and silver eyebrows. His eyes are red rimmed and his breath reeks of alcohol, which tells me he has more than one vice. The guy doesn't stand a chance. He'll probably be dead before the year's end. "Sure, I know her."

"Have you seen her recently?"

He ignores me for a minute to place a bet. I put a friendly smile on my face, waiting patiently, even though I'm far from patient right now.

"Saw her a few days ago. What was it?" He thinks back. "That was Wednesday."

"Yeah." I nod. "Me too. But I can't find her and haven't seen her since then. She said she's staying with one of her casino buddies. Do you know who that might be?"

He doubles down on his bet and stares at the cards as the dealer finishes the hand. "Yes!" He pumps his fist and pulls his winnings toward his stack of chips.

"Good job. You're really good at this." I'm trying to stroke his ego here, even though I know that he's probably going to blow through those winnings before the night is out.

He smiles for the first time and really looks at me, some of that alcoholic haze melting away. "Virgina has a lot of friends around here, not just me. I don't know what to tell ya, kid."

"Thing is, I'm worried she might be in trouble and I really want to find her."

He stiffens. "In trouble? If she's in trouble then keep me out of it."

Some friend.

"Let's say you needed to borrow money from someone around here. Who would that be?"

Please don't say vampires. Please don't say vampires. Please don't say vampires.

He laughs. "Vampires."

I frown. "That's what I was afraid of. I didn't realize casinos were keen to give out loans."

"Not the casino." he whispers and looks around, making sure nobody is listening in on us. "But there are others who have their little fangs mixed up with the mob, if you know what I mean."

I feel like sinking into the floor and disappearing. How am I supposed to handle vampires *and* the mob, especially if they're working together? I don't even know anything about mobsters beyond what they show in movies and television, but I do know that they are a law unto themselves and they're not the kind of people my mom should've borrowed money from.

"If you're smart, kid," he goes on, placing his next bet. "You'll stay far away from your mom and her troubles. Let her deal with them. You don't want to end up as collateral damage."

"Thanks." I grimace and walk away, my heart strumming against my ribcage because I know he's right. For as many times as I tell myself I'm going to give up on her, that I try to convince myself to do it, I also know it'll never happen. I can't. She's the only family I have left, she's my *mom*. Besides, I'm already in too deep to turn my back on her now.

I make a beeline for the elevator and sigh with relief when it arrives and nobody is inside. I hit the button for the top floor and close my eyes all the way up. When I get back to the room, I'm going to take a hot bubble bath and then go right to bed. Sounds heavenly. The elevator dings and I step off into the hallway.

I stop short and freeze. I'm not alone.

TWENTY-TWO

There are two penthouse suites up here. They take up the entire top floor, swanky enough for a prince. I already know the one on the left belongs to Adrian.

And the other...

A man in a black tuxedo has a woman in a silky ballgown pressed up against the door on the right. He's kissing her hungrily, she's groaning, and they definitely need to get a room. I try to sneak past, but my footsteps snap them out of their bubble.

"Ah, if it isn't Adrianos's little pet." Hugo turns to me and smirks, wiping a smear of lipstick from his mouth. He leans down to whisper something to the human woman. She murmurs a response and opens the door behind her to disappear into the dark suite. "I heard you were staying with my brother but I'll admit, I found it hard to believe."

"And why's that?"

He chuckles but doesn't reply.

"So I guess I don't have to wonder who has the other penthouse suite in this place, huh?" I shrug and point after his woman. "I think you'd better get in there and take care of her." My smile is fake as I pull out my key to unlock the door on the left.

"Before I do," Hugo appears in front of me, blocking my way and nearly making me jump, "I have something I wanted to talk to you about."

"Geez, do you have to do that vampire Speedy Gonzales shit?"

His black eyes narrow. "You haven't seen anything yet, my dear."

I don't know what to say to that, so I just raise an unimpressed eyebrow and try to appear aloof. Inside, my heart is pounding wildly and I'm certain he can hear it.

"You're staying with Adrian," he continues. "Nobody stays with him."

"So? It's not like the guy is here all that often, and you people don't sleep anyway. He's doing me a favor, that's all."

"You two are not involved?" He says "involved" like it's a filthy word.

"We're . . ." Oh, crap. What do I respond with here? That I'm working for the sucker? Do I lie and act like I'm in love with Adrian? Do I pretend to be his fledgling wannabe vampire groupie? I'm at a loss. "I don't know what we are."

He clicks his tongue. "Romance isn't my brother's thing. Sex?

Often. Business? Always. So what is it?"

"Business." One word. One simple word. Business. And yet it has so many implications when it comes to what I've wrapped myself up in these last few days.

"I appreciate you telling me the truth." He smiles and steps impossibly close. "I can still smell your virgin blood. Had you lied to me, I would have punished you."

"I work for Adrian. Not you." I wrinkle my nose. His eyes flash with anger one second and then with amusement the next. "And how can you people smell virgins? That's so weird, do you know that?"

"It dates back to when priests used to send virgins into graveyards to find vampires to stake. Virgins are attracted to us and we to you. Think of it like the biblical Adam and Eve story, only we're the serpent. We can't help but want to tempt you, young Eve. You can't help but want to be tempted. I can't explain it beyond that."

But maybe that explains why I was able to track that vamp from the frat party.

Yuck.

"I find you quite intriguing." He runs a piece of my hair between his long fingers. I don't move. I'm suddenly very aware of how vulnerable I am in this moment. With Adrian, I'm the angel making deals with the devil. With Hugo, I'm not Eve, I'm the simple field mouse standing at the mouth of the serpent.

"Now tell me, Evangeline, what would you do to have your own car? To have your own home? What would you do to be able to pay off the Italian mobsters who are after your mother?"

My body goes cold. "You know about that?"

"You made me curious, so I had you followed." My eyes bug, but he shrugs like the disgusting invasion of privacy means absolutely nothing to him. "I know why you're in that little uniform. I know you work for a bank during the day and at a restaurant at night. I know your mother is a colossal disappointment, failing you time and again. And I know your best friend in the whole wide world is away at college." He tilts his head in sympathy. "You're lonely."

"I'm not lonely," I whisper. Even as I say it, a pang stabs in my chest. He doesn't know me and yet he's somehow managed to uncover my deepest wound—the fear I'm not enough for people to love me.

"What did I say about lying, hmm?" He drops the piece of hair. "Evangeline Rose Blackwood, my my my, what a name. I do like it. It would be a great vampire name."

"I go by Eva." I glare.

"Well, Eva, I probably know more about you than Adrian does. What makes you think he's going to protect you, to help you? Leave him. Come be mine, and I'll give you anything you desire. I will *never* leave you."

His eyes shine with passion. His body radiates power. He plays a convincing character but I can't trust him. Deep in my gut, I know it. This has nothing to do with me. I don't *really* interest him. This is a pissing contest with Adrian and nothing more.

"You obviously don't know everything about me."

"Oh, what did I miss?"

"I'm loyal." I push past him and slip the key into the lock, letting myself inside. He doesn't follow.

"Think about it." He walks away as I close the door.

My knees go weak and I crumple to the floor, every inch of me shaking. Who am I kidding? I'm not loyal. If I was loyal, I wouldn't even be here. I wouldn't have ever agreed to the blood vow, no matter how precarious my situation was at the time. I'd have died before agreeing to be Adrian's spy. But then my mind flits back to what Hugo said about Mom owing money to the Italian mafia, and just the thought of her reminds me that when it comes to my family, I am loyal to a fault. How many times have I dragged her out of this place? How many times have I helped her? Defended her? Tried to save her? And I never seem to learn that she doesn't want to be fixed.

And where is she now, huh? Where is she while her daughter is hanging out around deadly vampires and making deals with them on her behalf? I retrieve my phone, knowing I'll find nothing from her, but hoping there will be something. Anything. A lifeline for me to hold onto for dear life and believe that she still loves me and that I matter to her more than the addiction.

There's nothing.

She hasn't called. She hasn't texted. I drop my phone into my lap, my face into my palms, and burst into tears. I don't know how much time passes. Minutes? Hours? Eventually, I lay on the floor. All the emotions I've knotted up inside of me are unraveling one by one. Anger. Sadness. Fear. Guilt. Frustration. Betrayal.

And yes, loneliness. Deep, deep loneliness. Hugo was right about that one.

I gladly fall asleep in it, letting unconsciousness replace the pain.

Sometime later, cold hands wake me up, lift me into cold arms, and carry me to a cold bed.

When my eyes flutter open the next morning, I long to feel the sunlight on my face. I peel myself from the bed and pad over to the window to throw open the curtains. It hardly makes a difference. These bulletproof tinted windows are too dark and only remind me of exactly where I am. I don't have anything going on today, but I don't want to stick around the casino either. The vampires roam around the city at night and are often gone, but since they have to stay out of the sunlight during the day and they never sleep, that means this hotel is probably full of them. Hugo included. I don't want to run into him again.

I shower and get dressed, trying not to think about last night, my conversation with Hugo, and especially not about my breakdown and Adrian finding me in a ball of sleepy tears on the floor. He'd carried me to my bedroom and tucked me under the covers. Why on earth would he do something like that? It's mortifying and confusing and not something I want to ever think about again.

I need to get out of this place. If I could go anywhere, I'd go to the beach. I'd swim in the surf and lay out on the sand and let the sun warm every inch of my body. But New Orleans isn't very close to good beaches for someone without a car. So instead, I brush my hair up into a wet ponytail and dress in a simple t-shirt, shorts, and sandals. I'm going to walk along the touristy boardwalk today. It's only a street away. It will be fun. This whole area of New Orleans is historic and draws in tourists from all over the world. There are so many fun places where I can window shop and people watch. It sure beats the alternative.

When I walk out into the family room, Adrian is sitting on the sofa with a newspaper in his hand and what would be a cup of coffee if he were human. I'm sure it's blood. If it weren't for his impossible Adonis Grecian beauty, his too-perfect movements, and the aura of danger that oozes off of him, he could pass for a normal man. I suddenly wonder what he looked like before he turned. I want to know his story but I don't ask.

"Good morning," I chirp.

He peers up from his paper. "Is it?"

My memory flashes to how he found me last night. "Look, I'm fine, okay? I've never been better."

He returns to his paper. "You're a liar, but fortunately for you, I don't care." As I go toward the door, he clears his throat. "I had some human food stocked in the kitchen for you."

Hmm, you don't care, huh?

As if on queue, my stomach growls. "Well, I'm not too proud to turn down a meal. And oh, look at you, you even got a toaster." It's sitting on the counter. I go to the cupboard to see what he got. I peel apart a bagel and plop it in the toaster. "I don't know, Adrian, some might say you're warming up to me."

He rolls his eyes. "I can't get warm, remember?"

"No need to remind me."

He saunters over and opens the fridge, retrieving a tub of cream cheese from between the stacked blood bags. I turn away and try to scrub the image from my mind. "We only have one coven in New Orleans. Most of the vampires live here in the casino. People are talking."

"And?" I plop the hot bagel sides onto a plate as he hands me a butter knife.

"And I don't like anyone knowing my business but me. How much longer are you going to be staying here?"

My heart sinks. "I don't know. I haven't made a plan yet."

"Do you need Kelli to help you find a place? She's rather good at her job."

"No offense, but I don't want Kelli or any vampires knowing where I live."

He levels me with a heavy gaze. "And yet here you are."

"Give me a couple days. I want to find a room to lease with one of the off campus college kids. I figure that'll be cheaper than getting my own place, and I should be around people my own age." I take a bite of the bagel. "No offense."

He laughs. It's real, not bitter or dark, but golden around the edges. It loosens something in my chest. I don't like it. "Fair enough. I'm the oldest vampire in all of North America after all." I choke, and he whacks me on the back. "Try not to look so surprised."

"I'm not. You've definitely got old man vibes about you." I look him up and down. "Total dinosaur." That's the complete opposite of the truth. He doesn't look a day over twenty-five and he's got sex appeal for days.

His eyes do the same—rove up and down my body. They linger on my legs. "Where are you going today?"

I shrug. "Walking the boardwalk. Taking some me-time. You know, self-care is self-love and all that? It's my day off."

"Good. Finish up and get changed. There's a dress in your wardrobe. You're coming with me."

"Uhh—what? Why? Where?"

"Downstairs to meet the rest of the coven. It's time we put the rumors about us to bed don't you think?" He walks toward the other bedroom, the one that I didn't claim. "Unless you'd like to put me to bed?" He says it like it's a dare. Is he flirting?

I glare. "Virgin blood, remember? I'm not losing it with a sucker. I'm already at rock bottom, no need to dig a hole."

He chuckles again. "Well, you might want to think about losing it soon, Angel. You're too attractive to us for your own good." He winks. "I'll even provide the shovel."

"Eww! In your dreams." He's totally flirting and I don't know what to do with that. I've never seen this side of him and I want to kick myself for enjoying it.

"One cannot dream if one cannot sleep. Never forget what I really am."

"You mean you're what nightmares are made of?" I bat my eyelashes.

"Exactly."

TWENTY-THREE

An hour later, I've curled my hair and brushed it into long Hollywood-style waves. It probably won't stay this way for more than two seconds, but it looks amazing, if I do say so myself. My face is made up with perfectly dark smoky eyes and bright red lipstick. I try not to think about the color too much or the last time my lips were this red. I slip into the little black dress hanging in the closet with the matching strappy high heels. The designer labels make me want to scream. Here I am, homeless, barely scraping by, and Adrian dresses me up in an outfit that probably costs more than a month's worth of tips.

"You can't bring that." He says the second I step into the family room.

"Bring what?"

"Don't play dumb." He flashes forward in that speedy vampire way, reaches under the hem of my dress, and rips the stake and holster clean off my thigh, throwing it to the hardwood. "I've told you. If one of my kind finds you with that, you're dead."

"So I'm supposed to walk into your creepy little coven lair with nothing to protect myself?"

"Not nothing. You have me."

He shoves a necklace into my hand. "Put this on. But you're not keeping it."

It's certainly not the dainty little crucifix I normally wear, which I'd decided to forgo today. Plus, I already had to buy a new chain thanks to this guy. Adrian's necklace is heavy and dripping with huge sparkly white diamonds. It can't be real. Can it? I snort. Who am I kidding? Of course, it's real. The vampires have billions of dollars because they've been around forever, and Adrian is their little North American fanger prince, after all.

I stop short. "If you're a prince, does that make Hugo a prince, too?"

Adrian offers a clipped, "yes" and goes stone-faced. He clearly doesn't want to talk about this more, so I clasp the necklace around my neck and follow him out the door. We ride the elevator down to the level below the casino floor. I don't want to think about the fact that we're now underground. This is a restricted area and Adrian uses his fingerprint to get the elevator to open. We're greeted with dark lighting, a spicy incense scent mixed with the undercurrent of copper, dramatic classical music drifting from a live orchestra, and beautiful people dressed up in suits and gowns. Some are humans, but most are vampires. There's probably two hundred vampires in this ballroom alone. I didn't know so many lived in New Orleans and a cool shiver rolls up my spine.

"Stay close to me," Adrian says, tucking me against him like we're on a date. Maybe we are? I don't like it, but I'll pretend I do for both our sakes.

We circle the room as he introduces me as his fledgling. It's not true—it will never be true. Fledgling is the term they use for humans who are trying to get turned, and it makes me want to scream to be called something so degrading. I try to hide my frustration and go along with it because it's not like I want these vamps to know I'm actually an aspiring vampire hunter and Adrian's little spy, but it's hard.

"Ah, there she is." Hugo appears next to us. A wine glass filled with inky blood rests in his hand and I have to look away. "Came for the fledgling announcement, I see? My my, you two are closer than I thought. Remind me, how did you meet?" Adrian glares and Hugo laughs. "That's right, how could I forget? She turned you into the police and you formed some kind of enemies-to-lovers bond over it." He pats me on the back. "You sure know the way to a vamp's heart."

"Careful," Adrian warns.

"Oh, come now, brother. I find it quite amusing! All that VEC nonsense is water under the bridge now that you've got your girl, isn't it?"

Adrian relaxes and cracks a smile. "What can I say? Eva's beautiful and smart. A winning combination for my next child."

I had no idea that Hugo had figured out that particular piece of our history. He knows all about the complaint I filed. At least Adrian is trying to play it off like it's all part of my charm. He smiles down at me like he finds me adorable. "Anyone who would dare to challenge me like that is someone who gets my attention."

"And she's just your type." Kelli approaches with her hand on her hip. "That's why you turned me, isn't that right, Master? Because I'm beautiful and smart."

He smiles at her adoringly. "That's right, daughter. I don't like to be encumbered with protégés, so I'm incredibly choosy." Kelli smirks and kisses him full on the mouth like a lover would, like they've kissed a million times, before sashaying away in her tight silver dress. I definitely catch a hateful scathing look from her on her way out. She's playing me up to please Adrian, but underneath the smiles is a savage beauty who wants me dead. *I didn't ask for this!* This whole family coven stuff they've got going on here is beyond weird. He calls her daughter but they kiss open-mouthed, and I don't even want to think of what else they do together.

"Come," he says, "you're sitting with me and Kelli up front."

Hugo stops us. "I find it so strange that you don't grow your family as large as the queen allows. Here I am petitioning for more children, and you only have one protégé left, and a young one at that."

"Differences of opinion." Adrian shrugs.

"Perhaps I can use a new angle to convince Brisa to reconsider my proposition. If you don't want to multiply your family, let me pick up your slack." His eyes bore into mine.

Adrian stiffens. "Did you not hear me? I'm announcing Eva this very day."

"But think of all the years you choose not to take a child," Hugo argues.

"Don't be a fool. You've asked Brisa many times, and her answer is always no. Perhaps, brother, you are overlooking one important factor."

"And what's that?" His tone turns sour and he finally tears his gaze from me.

"Our mother loves me more than you." Adrian doesn't say it playfully. He means it, and then he pats Hugo on the back to rub it in. My mouth drops open in shock. These two aren't engaging in sibling rivalry like I'd thought. They're straight up enemies.

They hate each other.

"Oh don't look so offended. I'm only kidding," Adrian laments, his tone, however, says otherwise.

Hugo looks about ready to rip Adrian's head off. "Are you

doing this because of what happened at that damned VEC meeting last month? It's not my fault you can't control what goes on in your own casino."

"Enough," Adrian stops him. "I don't have time to bicker with you yet again. Eva and I are expected somewhere else." When Adrian turns away to take us to our seats, Hugo directs that seething look my way. If he can't have me, maybe he won't want Adrian to have me either. Maybe he'd rather I be dead. This is not good.

"How often does your coven meet like this?" I whisper to Adrian, desperate to change the subject. We walk between aisles of chairs, his arm still around me.

Adrian doesn't take the bait. "Like I would tell you that. Now come on. I'm going to announce you as my fledgling to the queen."

"What?" My eyes bug out and I nearly stumble on my heels. "To your *queen*? I didn't agree to this," I hiss. And I didn't know the Queen was even here. I thought she lived in Europe somewhere!

"Quiet," he snaps back. "Do you want to survive this casino or not?"

"I was only supposed to stay for a few nights."

"And you will be leaving soon, but in the meantime, I need you to do this for me." He whispers against my ear, his soft lips featherlight, making my body tense, "Please."

"Geez, Adrian, you make me so uncomfortable."

And in so many ways I don't want to admit.

"Feeling's mutual."

We sit down at the front of the room, facing all the other chairs with the vampires and humans who are beginning to occupy them. He needs me here? Why? The prince brought me, someone he knows is a hunter, into his coven's sanctum. There's something more happening today than he's letting on, and he's definitely using me for some political game with Hugo and now his queen.

He stands and strolls over to a podium with a microphone. A camera is set up on a tripod to face it and another is set up to face the crowd. I feel like I'm at a conference or a school assembly. Dread settles low in my stomach. He begins to speak and the room falls silent. "Welcome to our family meeting. Tonight we announce our newest fledglings. Over time, as they prove themselves to us, and to Queen Brisa De La Cour, of course, they will have the honor of joining our ranks."

The crowd claps and my heart skitters. It feels like hands are gripping my throat. I shouldn't be here. *Squeeze.* This isn't right. *Tighter squeeze.*

The room darkens and a projector lights up a huge screen on the wall behind us. A young woman flickers to life, transforming the white backdrop to something else entirely. She's got a worldly European look to her, complete with a narrow face, pale smooth skin, long caramel hair, and large amber eyes. She looks cool—she also looks like a mean girl. While it's day here, she sits outside where she is in the darkness. An ancient looking city is lit up in the distance. I wonder where she is. I don't recognize it immediately but I feel like I should know, like I've seen pictures before. Going by her last name, I'd guess somewhere in France. Even though I'm still freaked out, I let out a breath of relief that the woman isn't actually in the building.

"Hello, my posterity. I miss you!" Her voice is wind chime sweet with a slight French accent. It sounds to have been watered down over her many years as a vampire. She's probably traveled the whole world many times by now.

"Your Majesty," Adrian purrs. "It's so wonderful to see your face again."

"Adrianos, my son, you are looking quite handsome tonight. It's good to see you in such a cheerful mood." She thinks this version of Adrian is cheerful? I try not to roll my eyes. He seems pretty sour to me. "Do you have the fledglings ready to announce? I've got another call with Saint Petersburg in an hour. You know how those Russians can get, not an ounce of patience in the lot of them."

"They are ready." He sweeps his hand toward the crowd. "Fledglings and their sponsors, please line up and introduce yourselves to Queen Brisa."

I sit frozen, watching as one by one the humans approach the camera at the podium and introduce themselves. At least we have to introduce ourselves to her via televideo. I don't know how I'd react to meeting a vampire queen in person. I wonder if she's the only queen. I assume so but I don't know much about their royalty since they keep as much as they can to themselves.

"What's this Hugo? Another one?" Brisa hisses when Hugo approaches with the woman I saw him kissing last night. "But you just turned that other girl, what happened to her?"

Hugo's face goes stony cold. "She woke early and hunters killed her."

My face warms. I want to sink into the floor and disappear.

"And so that makes you above the rules? No, no, this simply will not do. You know better than this, my son." Her voice turns razor sharp. "We do not allow too many fledglings. You are aware of the reasons."

"But we should want to grow our numbers."

"Hugo—"

"We should take over and harvest the humans in farms."

"That is not necessary or smart." Her eyes are daggers. "They will rise up against us."

"I'm not the only one who feels this way," Hugo bites back. The crowd gasps. Brisa goes silent and her cheeks flare red.

Adrian flies forward in a flash of movement, picking Hugo up by the neck and lifting him off the floor. "You forget your place, brother."

"I'm sorry," Hugo sputters, showing weakness for the first time since I've met him.

"If you are sorry," Brisa says bitterly, "you will kill your proposed fledging and offer her blood as an apology to me. As I am not here, I'm sure Adrianos will stand in as my proxy."

Adrian shoots the camera a dark look and drops his brother. Gone is the flirty man—he's all thirsty vampire now. Hugo's woman, dressed to the nines and staring with horror at the scene, holds up her hands and backs away. "Hold on, this isn't what you said would—" Hugo cuts her off, jumping on her and ripping her throat from her body in a matter of seconds. Blood sprays in a sickly arc. He throws the body at Adrian.

I hold back a scream, biting my fist as I whimper. I reach for the stake strapped at my thigh only to remember it's not there.

Nobody else screams. Not one.

Maybe that's the sickest part of it all. Not even the humans seem fazed by this horrific murder. It's as if they expected it to happen. Adrian scoops up the body and sinks his fangs into what's left of the woman's neck. Nobody reacts to that, either.

"You may go now, Hugo. Who's next?" Brisa calls out through the screen. "Hurry, please. I don't have all night."

Hugo storms from the room as twelve more vampires approach with one fledgling each and Brisa approves them all. When the last of them steps forward, my stomach flips.

Standing with Kelli is none other than Cameron Scout. I

wouldn't be able to miss that flaming red hair anywhere. He holds himself tall and proud, and when he catches my eye, he winks.

"What's your name, dear?" Brisa coos.

"Kelli. I'm Adrian's only living protégé."

Brisa laughs. "I know that, darling. I was talking to your beefy arm candy."

"I'm Cameron Scout, Your Highness."

"You're a perfectly built specimen." Brisa grins. "Well done, Kelli. This is a good choice for your first child. You've waited the required thirty years for this, I know."

"Thank you." Kelli beams. "He's very eager to be here and actually, there's something special you need to know about Cameron." I freeze.

No. No, don't do it.

"He's a hunter."

The room goes eerily still seconds before the other vampires start hissing. Kelli speaks above it all, unfazed. "I wanted to bring you someone extra useful to prove my devotion to our family, Your Majesty. Cameron is willing to turn over his team of hunters when we make him one of us."

The lying, disgusting, little Chucky doll twerp! I want to go over there and rip off his head myself!

Brisa's cool demeanor breaks into a wicked smile. "Well aren't you resourceful. But he better not be trying to deceive us, Kelli, or it's true death for you."

"He's the real deal," she assures Brisa. "We will prove it to you when he delivers his comrades to us."

"We'll see." She's skeptical, but she's pleased. I stare at the people standing before me and wonder—did Adrian tell Kelli to find Cameron? Did she do it herself? Or maybe Cameron came to her? I need to know what's going on. I just hope that my being here didn't somehow create this. First the blood vow and spying on Tate, and now this? As her maker, Adrian is bound to want to help Kelli now that she's got the threat of true death looming over her.

We're all screwed.

My hands are shaking and I have to hold them together against my stomach in a tight ball.

"And what about you, Adrianos? Did you take my advice?" Brisa asks, turning back to Adrian.

He's been watching everything unfold with his fangs still in Hugo's woman, drinking from her like he can't stop. Her skin is unnaturally snowy white and my stomach lurches to see it. At his master's question, Adrian drops the body into the pool of her own blood and wipes his face, turning back to the camera. His blond curls hang low over his hooded eyes. He looks like the devil.

"Of course, Mother," he says. "How could I not?" There's an edge to his voice and I'm reminded that vampires are bound to their makers. Adrian has to do whatever she asks. And so does Hugo for that matter. That's why Hugo was so quick to kill his lover, and Adrian was quick to make a meal of her body.

Well, that and they're vampires. They deal in death. Adrian had to have liked drinking from that body. It's his nature.

It now makes sense why Hugo can't just do as he wishes and make as many vampire babies as his evil heart desires. Someone else is pulling the strings. Queen Brisa. Thank goodness she's in charge and not Hugo or I'd be living in some dystopian blood harvesting farm right now.

"Evangeline." Adrian motions to me. I stand even though my entire body is suddenly made of sand. "Come forward, fledgling; come and say hello to your new queen."

TWENTY-FOUR

I feel as if I'm on a rowboat in the middle of a hurricane. I can barely keep my balance as I go to stand in front of the camera. Like dangerous waves, my heart slams against my chest. Like pouring rain, fear pelts my nervous system. My every thought is met with the horrible feeling of drowning, because if Brisa doesn't approve of me, she'll order me dead and that will be the end of it. I remind myself to kill Adrian if I make it out of here and force a pageant-girl smile to my lips.

I stare directly into the lens, knowing that on the other side, the queen of all the vampires is staring back and deciding my fate. After what feels like an eternity, her voice rings through the speakers. I never take my eyes off the lens. I can't bear to see her expression.

"You've outdone yourself, my son. She's unusually beautiful."

"Yes, she is."

My stomach goes hard. I don't like them talking about me like I'm some kind of prized race horse. Unusually beautiful? What, because my ethnicity is hard to pinpoint? I hate these people.

"Well, good, I'm glad you've finally decided to bring another child to our family." Brisa levels me with a daring expression. "I hope she proves herself worthy."

"She will."

"And what do you think of all this, dear? Is this what you want?"

It's a trick question. Of course I can't tell her the truth. "I'm honored to be here," I say, my voice silky with the lies. "I won't let you down."

"Good girl." The queen sighs and my eyes hold the screen. She looks truly pleased. "Evangeline. Pretty name. I'll be sure to check back on your progress. It's not often that Adrianos takes on a fledgling. Do as he says and you'll be his protégé. Don't, and well," she chuckles, "you saw."

I smile and nod, all the while wanting to strangle Adrian for bringing me here. That's after I kill Cameron Scout first.

And here I thought the bagels were him being nice. Vampires don't *do* nice.

The queen signs off and the room buzzes with conversation, everyone eager to discuss all that just happened. Nobody seems to care about the body on the floor. They're desensitized from death. Humans are food and nothing more, and even the humans here act like they're thinking that way. But what did I expect?

I stroll right up to Cameron. "Hey, buddy, you and I need to talk."

"That we do." He grins happily. "I was surprised to see you here, but now I'm glad to have someone else I can trust during this process. I'll be at the Neon House tonight at nine. Come, and we can make plans on how to help each other."

He winks again and then he slips into the crowd with Kelli on his arm. Bile turns my stomach. I'm going to be sick.

"Let's go," Adrian demands. He takes hold of me and steers me toward the elevator. It's the private one that goes to the penthouses, so we don't have to worry about a line. Once we're inside and the doors close, I vomit into the corner. I can't keep it in for another second.

"I'll get someone to clean that up."

I wipe my mouth, then turn and glare.

"I'm sorry I blindsided you, but I knew you'd never come otherwise," Adrian says. "I needed to take a fledgling, my Queen asked and I can't deny her. It's impossible. Don't worry, I won't turn you. This was all for show. Brisa will forget all about it. She's extremely busy and doesn't care if we choose to turn our fledglings as long as we keep the number of vampires where she wants them."

This is all a bunch of political crap that means nothing to me.

"I hate you."

"Good," he purrs. "You should hold onto that hate. It might keep you alive. No matter what happens, don't stop hating me, and remember this, Angel: I will always put my needs before yours."

The Neon House is a popular eighteen and older nightclub smack dab between The French Quarter and Tulane University. The music is too loud, the neon lights too bright, and the foggy smoke cough-worthy thick. I weave my way through throngs of dancers and search for Cameron. Sure enough, I find him near the bar with a group of douchebag-looking friends. I don't recognize any of them from the hunters' gym. They probably have no idea who the real Cameron Scout is. For all they know, he's going to be the one to kill them one day when he's a vampire. He well and truly is a snake.

"Hey," I say, sliding up next to him and smiling as brightly as I can manage to fake. "What's up?"

"You came!" His voice is too loud and a little slurred. He's been drinking. For a vampire hunter, he's sure not doing his job. And to think he took control of our teams when Tate left as if he were the best man for the job. Anger burns me up and I hate that I have to pretend that it doesn't. He hugs me like we're old friends. "Let's dance."

"I came to talk." I fold my arms over my chest and resist the urge to tug at the short hem of my white minidress. I fit right in with this scene, but I don't love the outfit. I can't help but wonder how different my life would be if I'd gotten that track scholarship. I'd have gone away to school and none of this would've happened. I'd be a normal girl, like Ayla, like everyone else here.

"We can dance and talk at the same time. It's called multitasking." Cameron grins like he's just realized he's a rocket scientist. I roll my eyes but follow him out to the floor.

"Mutual assured destruction," he says, putting his hands on my hips and tugging me against him to dance.

"What?" I yell over the pounding music and back up a bit. I have no intentions of making this "a thing" with him.

"That's what this is, you and I. You can't turn me in and I can't turn you in. We're in this together. If you go down, I go down, and vice versa. Might as well form an alliance."

I grimace. This Chucky doll is the last person I'd want to form an alliance with, and that's saying a lot considering my many recent lapses in judgement. "So why'd you do it, Cameron?" I pretend to be genuinely interested and not wildly pissed off.

"I could ask you the same question."

I can't show all my cards here. I don't know what to do, so I go with a semblance of the truth. Easier to keep my story straight that way. "I need to help my mom. She's in trouble with the Italian mob. Adrian can save her for me. The hunters can't."

"Woah, that's intense."

"Yes," I level, "it is. And what about you? What's your excuse for turning on the hunters?" It comes off a little too jaded but Cameron is far too pleased with himself to notice.

"I realized that the vampires are the winning team." The green glow of the neon lights gives his red hair a sickly filter as he stares down at me. "I'm a realist and I want to win. It's simple."

It's evil is what it is, but I can't let him know what I really think, so I nod. "I get that but how can you be certain?"

"There's more to this war than you realize. It's not just vampires and humans, you know. Leslie Tate is using us."

I stop short. "What do you mean?"

"Do you trust me?"

I snort. "Not as far as I can throw you."

"That's fair." He smiles. "But I like you. And I think we should talk about what happened to me so you understand me enough to maybe start trusting me."

"Okay, what happened to you?"

"I joined the hunters because I thought vampires were the evil I needed to fight but I was wrong. Something else is a lot worse than the vamps."

"Something else?" I sound skeptical even though deep down, I believe him. There aren't other supernaturals that we know of, just vampires, but wouldn't it stand to reason that if vampires are real, then other things are real, too? I've always thought so.

"Just hear me out, okay? Let's go over there." I nod and we move to a quieter corner of the room and stand side by side, looking out at the club. We're up on a platform so we can see everything going on down below. These people are having the time of their lives and here I am with creepy Cameron. My life sucks.

"My kid brother got sick with cancer," he says, and suddenly I feel like a brat for coining his new nickname. "Tyler was fourteen and I was seventeen at the time. It was terrible. The doctors did everything they could but Tyler was terminal." His voice cracks and he stares at his shoes for a minute. Part of me feels bad for the guy but the bigger part is still angry about what he did today. "So anyway, my father got desperate so he found a vampire and made a deal. The vampire would turn my brother immortal and in exchange my parents would be willing blood donors."

I grimace. "That sounds pretty brutal." It also sounds like something the vampire royalty wouldn't condone. Brisa doesn't seem like the charitable type.

"I didn't know anything about it until after Tyler's funeral when my father broke down and admitted to me what happened. He said that the vampire came to see Tyler on his deathbed. He watched him cry out and die, but refused to help. He just stood there watching it all unfold like he enjoyed it or something. And then when it was over, he left."

My heart hurts for the family. Nobody should have to experience something that horrific. "I'm sorry. That's terrible."

"Yeah, it was messed up. So you can imagine that when I went to college and got the opportunity to hunt vampires, I jumped at it. It was my way to heal through the pain of losing Tyler. But my parents? They never got over Tyler's death. They ended up getting divorced a couple years ago."

Okay, I still hate Cameron, but he's doing a good job of making me feel bad about that. This story just keeps getting worse.

"Here's the thing," he continues. "My mom never knew about the vampire. So she starts dating this guy, right? Something was off about him but I couldn't figure out what it was. Well, one day my dad comes around and starts freaking out, accusing the guy of being a vampire, saying this is the same guy that was supposed to help Tyler."

"Was it?"

His face hardens. "Same guy? Yes. Vampire? No. Remember, I'm a hunter by this point so I know how to spot a vampire a mile away and this thing definitely wasn't a vampire."

"So what was he then?"

"I still don't know for sure, maybe a demon, a fae, some kind of warlock, I don't know. But I do know this; that guy was truly sick. He fed off Tyler's illness and then my parent's grief to sustain him."

I scowl. "That doesn't make sense. What do you mean by fed?"

"It's hard to explain and that's why I wanted to show you." The song changes and techno music blares through the room. The neon lights shift to blacklight and Cameron points. "The blacklight allows you to see what they're doing."

I gaze out into the crowd, unsure what I'm supposed to be looking for.

"Whatever they are, they're real and they're even more dangerous than vampires. They hide their true selves easily, blending right in with humans, but they feed on us, too. The day I decided to turn on our group of hunters was the day I found out Leslie Tate is one of them."

TWENTY-FIVE

I blink rapidly, realizing the implications of this information. Tate is immune to vampire compulsion. Tate can erase memories. All this time I've been obsessing over the vampire threat when maybe I should have been questioning my leader. "Leslie Tate is one of... *what now*?" I ask for clarity. I still have no idea what Cameron is on about and he's starting to sound a wee bit delusional.

"He's one of the vampire's mortal enemies, the demons, or whatever they are. I'm still not sure. In my mind, I call them demons."

"I always thought werewolves were the vampire's enemies." I lean back against the wall and keep staring out into the crowd of dancers. Sure, they're lit up with the blacklight, a sea of blue and white, but there's nothing strange going on that I can see. Certainly no *demons*.

"The werewolves were enemies with vampires but they were hunted to extinction hundreds of years ago. It's whatever *these things* are that are the bigger problem." He points again.

"Cameron, I'm so confused. I don't see anything."

"Look harder," he growls. "Look! Don't you see? They feed off of us. There are some doing it right now. Use your eyes, Eva, and you'll understand why I'm done being a weak and pathetic human."

I'm starting to think this guy is on drugs and never listened to his DARE officer.

"Kelli knows what I'm talking about. It's how she got me to be her fledgling. And once I'm turned and she can trust me, she's going to tell me everything."

"Talking about Kelli isn't going to help your case," I say. "She hates me."

"Adrian then. Ask Adrian."

I close my eyes and gather a breath deep into my lungs, trying to focus. I push away the fear bubbling just under the surface—Cam is really starting to scare me—and open my eyes again. I blink out into the room of dancers, looking for a change, anything at all.

And that's when I see it.

Most of the people here are the same.

But some are not.

Their features are the same as ours. They laugh and dance and kiss and are clearly here to have fun—just like us. But there's something different about them. There's something lacking. I don't even know what it is exactly.

"Okay, I think I see them."

He laughs with relief.

"But how are they sinister?"

"Look closer," he whispers against my ear. "See the energy?"

I squint and catch on to what he's talking about. It's so subtle I didn't notice it at first. The humans have light glowing around them. The others—whatever they are—do not. "Are you talking about the glow around the humans?"

"Those are auras," Cam says. "All humans have them. They're supposed to be all different colors but we can't see all that. We *can* see the outline of the aura in the blacklight. And we can see the ones who are being fed on."

I rub my eyes and look again. Still there. "This is so weird."

He leans back against the wall and for the first time tonight, his vibe isn't so frantic. "Tell me about it. I never thought that woo-woo shit was real. Kelli says it's the human's soul energy. Suckers don't have auras, which makes sense considering they already died. And whatever the demon things are, they don't have them either. And do you see what they're doing to the humans?"

He nods toward a tall man who is dancing close to a human girl. He smiles down on her like she's the only person in the room. She's beaming, and her energy is clinging to him like a magnet. Not just that, but some of it flows from her and into him. "You're right. He's feeding off of her energy."

"Yes. Exactly that. He is sucking away her life force. I believe this is what makes humans weak. This is why we get sick and why we're frail. These things are everywhere and they feed on us all the time. I wish I could carry a blacklight everywhere I go so I can spot them. One of these things came to feed off of my brother while he was on his deathbed, and then came back to feed off of my parents in their grief."

"What happened to him, this demon thing?"

He releases a long sigh. "My dad killed it and then he went to prison."

My mouth falls open. I have no idea what to say.

"And this, Eva, is exactly why humans are going to lose in the end. We don't stand a chance."

"Are there a lot of them?" In this room of hundreds, I can spot six, but it's hard to tell because they don't look much different than humans except for the no aura thing. The music changes and the blacklight switches back to the neon. Everything appears as it was before.

"Yeah, I come here every weekend and count. There's always at least ten by the end of the night and it's usually different ones, too. That tells me there are a lot. The vampires and these demons are fighting a war over their food source and guess what, babe? That's us. One feeds on our blood, the other on our energy. Since it's impossible for me to become whatever this is," he motions toward the dancers, "I'm going to become a vampire. I'm done being at the mercy of more powerful creatures. If you can't beat them, join them, right?"

"Right," I mumble once and then say again louder.

What Cameron is saying makes sense, and I need him to think that I agree. But to betray his team—his friends—in order to become part of the evil he claims to hate? That's dead wrong.

The next night as I'm riding home on the bus, I try to stay awake despite feeling as if I've been run over by a herd of elephants. This morning I had to drag my butt into training super early and then had a long dinner shift at Pops. Exhaustion paws at me like a demanding toddler. I haven't slept well at all during the three nights I've been staying at the casino, and I have *at least* one more to go. I'm stressed out about Mom who still hasn't answered my calls even though she has the freaking mafia after her. And the cherry—or rather cherries—on top is all this fledgling crap, the blood vow, and now everything going on with Cameron Scout. I know what I saw, but I still have a hard time believing him. I need concrete proof of what he's claiming and that there's actually a war going on. I mean, sure, he calls them demons, but he doesn't know what they are.

I scroll through the rental ads on my phone, but there's just nothing in my price range. Putting on my big girl pants, I send a group text to Seth, Kenton, and Felix.

Hey guys. This hotel situation sucks. Can you ask around to see if anyone you know has a room for rent?

Kenton replies immediately, **You got it. I know people.**

Seth pops in with the all annoying, **K**

And Felix adds an, **We will find you something by tomorrow. Hang tight.**

I smile. It feels good to let someone else help me for a change. I'm so used to doing things myself and being Miss Independent that I sometimes forget that there are people out there who care about me. I slip my phone into my pocket and get off at my stop. If the guys come through, and knowing them they will, then this really will be my last night at The Alabaster. I just hope that Adrian is right and Brisa forgets all about me. I don't want to get my hopes up, but I can't help it. That place is toxic. Those people are toxic. All the things I regret lately are things I've done there, things that have involved them.

I have to walk a block to get to the hotel, which isn't normally a big deal, but it's later than usual and much, much quieter. This area is tourist central, but right now there isn't a soul in sight. Vampires are probably nearby. I won't be able to hear them coming—they're too silent—and I don't have a stake on me. It's colder than normal for September, so maybe that's why I feel weird. Maybe I'm just imagining things and freaking myself out for no reason. Goosebumps crawl across my skin. The streetlight above me flickers and goes dark. I walk faster.

Arms grab me from behind, one around my waist and one over my mouth. My scream is muffled. A man drags me into an alleyway and shoves me up against the wall. The back of my head cracks against the bricks. Tears fill my eyes as I fight, clawing and kicking, but he's twice my size and my efforts are worthless. He keeps his hand pressed against my mouth.

I don't know him, but he looks like a mafia thug. He's human. Middle-aged and balding, the man is dressed in all black except for the gold chain around his beefy neck. It's like he's trying to live up to a henchman stereotype. "Listen closely, Princess." His voice is that deep thunder that comes before a storm and I'm suddenly very, very afraid. "You tell your mother that if she doesn't give Armondo his money, then not only will we find her and kill her, but we'll kill you right in front of her first."

Tears blur my vision.

He slams me against the wall again. "You got that?"

I nod against his hand and he smiles like this is any other business transaction. "That's great, Princess. Get it done."

My knees give out when he releases me, and I drop to the filthy concrete as he disappears into the night.

My head throbs. I reach around and gently press my fingertips to the back of my scalp. I wince at the pain, fingers coming away wet. My mind swims through mud as I try to process what just happened. The guys after my mother know where I am. I was just assaulted by one of them. I'm wounded. Bloody. And I'm sitting outside of the building where over a hundred thirsty vampires live.

TWENTY-SIX

Why am I always the poster child for what not to do around the vamps? I need to make some better life choices. I hiss as I try to hold back the tears. And now I have to get inside and upstairs to the room so I can take care of this. That's if I don't get eaten first.

I stumble out of the alleyway and around the corner, up the long set of stairs, and through the double vestibules. I keep my hand pressed to the back of my head the entire time even though I can feel the blood dripping. I'll be fine once I'm alone. Head wounds are bloody. Everybody knows that. I just have to keep going and get to safety. One foot in front of the other. Head down. Move quickly. Adrian's private elevator to the penthouse floor will help as long as I don't run into Hugo.

Blood splashes onto the marble floor.

Well, it's a blood casino, right? It's not like people don't bleed in here all the time. *It's fine. I'll be fine,* I tell myself, simply because thinking of the alternative is terrifying.

Across the lobby, Kelli sits behind her receptionist desk. She watches me carefully, her nostrils flared, but doesn't say anything. She tilts her head, inhales deeply, and then picks up her phone. I make it to the elevator bank and press the button for the one I need. There are four more elevators here that go to the other hotel floors. The one next to mine dings and opens; a young man steps out. He's pale, vampire-beautiful, and looking right at me with unimaginable hunger.

"You're bleeding," he speaks each word slowly, like they're the punchline to a joke.

"Yeah, I'll be fine. No big deal." My voice is shaking. He wouldn't attack me, would he? It's not allowed. We're in public. I know that the vampire hierarchy is a definite thing after yesterday, and, for whatever reason, the higher ups don't want humans to have their venom in us under any circumstances unless we're going to be turned or going to die. That's why the whole blood bag thing even exists in the first place. Sure, they'll kill us when they can get away with it, but otherwise they need us alive. We're no good to them dead.

Where is my elevator? I uselessly press the button again and blood smears against that, too.

"You smell good." The young man circles me like a shark.

"Uh—thanks." I press my hand harder against my skull, but

that just makes it worse. "The blood bank is back that way if you need a meal." I nod toward the casino.

Footsteps echo through the lobby. "Tray, what's going on here?" Hugo approaches, and for once I'm actually happy to see the guy.

"She's bleeding. Doesn't she smell amazing?" Tray's voice sounds far away. "I've never had the pleasure of virgin blood before."

Hugo stares at me. He steps forward, runs a finger along my cheek, and then licks the blood clean. His eyes go dark. "You," is all he says. One word—it obliterates my confidence.

Tray pounces.

He's so fast I don't even register what is happening until I'm on the floor and the guy is on top of me. He holds my arms down as his fangs extend. Hugo rips him off and throws him clear across the room. He crashes into a couch, breaking it in half, but rebounds lightning fast. He comes running back at top speed, diving for me with outstretched arms. His fangs glint under the golden lights.

I'm dead.

But I'm not going down without a fight. I ready my stance, prepared to defend myself to the bitter end, when the elevator dings. A flash of white and black flies out. Adrian Teresi is on Tray, ripping his head from his body, the blood splattering across Adrian's crisp white shirt. Tray disintegrates into a cloud of dust.

"I had it under control," Hugo screams at his brother.

"Clearly you didn't," Adrian roars back.

"He was my child, I would have been able to get him to stop. You can't kill what belongs to me. Brisa will—"

"You won't speak of this to Brisa! You have no case with her considering your protégé tried to sink his fangs into my fledgling."

Hugo growls, "I could have stopped him. I could have saved them both."

"Not since his bloodlust was so strong." Adrians voice lowers. "This is exactly why you can't take on too many protégés. They're weak and they make you weak."

Hugo points at me. "It's her fault. She's bleeding. And she's—"

"Enough!" Adrian sneers. He grabs me and flies us into the elevator. My vision blurs again. As the elevator is closing, I catch the bitter end of Hugo's glare.

As we rise, I finally find my breath as I sink into Adrian.

"Are you okay, Angel?" He turns me around and hisses at the mess of my bloody hair. "You shouldn't have come here like this. What happened?"

"I was jumped outside of the casino. I didn't have anywhere else to go."

"Who did this to you?"

"Whoever works for Armondo." I grimace as I turn back around, catching Adrian's confused look. "Remember? The whole reason I'm staying here is because my gambling addicted mother got herself mixed up with the mafia."

He sighs and runs a hand through his hair. A little bit of my blood sticks to the curls, turning them pink. "I shouldn't have let you stay here. It's too dangerous."

I laugh bitterly. "You think!" I press myself to the far side of the elevator; we are in a small space, I am covered in blood and need distance between us.

"You asked to come here. I did you a favor."

"And what did I get for it? You're no better than the rest of them. You used me to gain favor with your queen, just like all vampires use all humans. I'm leaving tomorrow. My friends are finding me a safer place to stay."

And at this point, I can't be around here anyway. Mafia. Vampires. It's all too much.

His face is a mask. "Good."

When the elevator doors open, I walk ahead of him to the penthouse and head straight into the bathroom. The blood is starting to clot now, but it's worse than I thought. I'm practically covered. I'll need to shower, but first I've got to get this wound sealed. Where's duct tape when you need it, huh? Adrian knocks on the door.

"Kelli is sending up one of the nurses. You need stitches."

I don't have it in me to say thank you to him, so instead, I sit down on the cold floor and wait. The nurse arrives quickly and stitches me right up as if she's done this a million times before. Adrian watches her like a hawk, asking question after question. If my blood is bothering him, he doesn't show it. He almost seems normal, and for a minute, I forget what he is, then immediately chastise myself for the slip up.

After the nurse finishes, I send them out so I can take a warm shower. I finish off with a tall glass of water and an extra strength Tylenol. I go right for the bed, too tired to care about pajamas. When I slip into the sheets sans clothing, the cool fabric feels like heaven against my aching body. To be all clean and unencumbered like this is a treat.

A light knock on the door is quickly followed by Adrian letting himself into the room. He has changed into a clean shirt and looks like he's ready to get back to business as usual. Good thing I'm neatly tucked in already—a minute earlier and he'd have walked in on me naked. Nothing he hasn't seen, I'm certain, but my heart races anyway. He needs to get out of here and let me have my privacy.

"Do you need anything else before I head out?" he asks curtly.

"Sleep." I reach toward the lamp, knowing I'm exposing my bare shoulder enough for him to realize I'm naked, but I don't care anymore. I turn it off the light. My eyes flutter shut and I bury myself into the blankets. My racing heart begins to slow and I release a long, slow breath. I'm so drained, I can hardly think straight. What must it be like to be Adrian and never sleep? It's all I want in this moment and I can't imagine an eternity without the peace it offers. "Goodbye, Adrian," I mumble. I don't say goodnight. I say goodbye, and I mean it.

He doesn't reply, but he does leave, closing the door behind him with a soft thud.

The next morning, I pack my things and move out.

If a girl leaving a college party house early on a weekday morning is considered the "walk of shame" then is me showing up here the reverse of that? 'Cause I feel like a total loser, but I'm fresh out of options. I even checked my bank account balance this morning just to be sure I couldn't swing my own place, and yup, I'm still broke as a joke. It's barely sunrise and Felix and the guys should be out any minute to head to the gym. I sit down on the lawn next to my duffle bag and shoot them a group text.

Look who's outside. . .

A minute later, Felix comes through the front door. His expression blossoms into pleasure when he spots me. "Eva, is that you?"

I wave. "Hey, good morning."

"What are you doing here?" Concern etches his tone and I hate that I put that there. I hate being vulnerable or seen as needy. I want to be strong, maybe even admired, but maybe that's not practical. Life is messy.

I sigh. "Let's just say I had a bad night at the hotel. I needed to get out of that place. Can I get a ride to the bank vault?"

His lip quirks. "The bank vault?"

"Yeah, sorry, I know Tate doesn't want it to have a name but that's what I call it in my head. We're the Bank Vault Vampire Hunters." I wink and he chuckles.

"Sure. You didn't want to meet us there?"

I pat the duffle bag. "Too proud to let everyone at the gym know I'm officially homeless." That and I have Cameron Scout to consider. He doesn't need to know any more of my business. "Can I keep my stuff in your car while we're there?"

"You're not homeless. I found a room for you with some girls who live off campus."

"Oh, thank you!" I pump my fist and we both laugh.

Felix lifts the bag over his shoulder and helps me up. When our hands touch, warmth spreads through my entire body. I inhale his minty rain scent and long to get lost in it, despite my goal to quit wanting him. He doesn't let me go but actually tugs me closer. Hope swells in my chest.

"I've been really worried, Eva. And I've been thinking about you a lot." His voice is gravelly, his eyes liquid.

I inch closer until there's no space left between us, *screw my goal.* "Have you?"

He nods once, running his warm palms up my arms, over my

shoulders, and finally cupping my face and tilting it upward. He doesn't know about the stitches, and I have to force myself not to wince. Luckily, he must not notice them. They are pretty small. He towers over me and I lift onto my toes while he leans down. *Finally.*

TWENTY-SEVEN

"Eva!" Kenton appears, bounding up the front steps. "How's my girl?"

Felix and I both shoot him a scathing look. He holds up his hands. "What?" His fraternity house is only a few blocks from here so I guess it makes sense that he'd walk over to catch a ride, but his timing sure sucks.

The house door bangs open and Seth comes out with a sour expression on his face. He points at me and Felix. "Don't even think about it. We're a team, remember? There's no room for error, which means there's no place for romance or friends with benefits or whatever you two are doing."

Kenton's eyes go round. "Oh snap! Did I just cockblock you guys? My bad."

I want to sink into the lawn and die, but then I wouldn't be able to kiss Felix, which I am going to do at the next possible opportunity.

"Let's get coffee on the way in," Seth adds, strolling past us. "My treat."

Felix snorts. "Doesn't make up for the interruption." He gives me a wink and a bright smile; I relax instantly. Okay fine, we can't hook up right now, but if Felix wants me after all, then I'm in. This is what I've been waiting for, and no way is Seth going to get in the way of that. I don't care if he's our team leader. He's not the relationship police. I've always known I was meant to be with Felix—he's been my crush for years. I've pushed every other possible love interest away in favor of this man. It's finally time to make Felix + Eva a reality.

"Luckily there's no lacrosse practice so I'm skipping class today to help you," Felix announces after dropping the others off at campus after training. "Jasmine and Olive have furniture already, but you need to bring your own bedding and towels and that kind of stuff. So let's go pick something out, and then I'll help you get settled."

I feign shock and fan my face. "A man going shopping? You're my hero, Felix Moreno."

"Hey, not all straight men hate shopping." He laughs. He's so macho and broody most of the time that it's fun to see this side of him.

"So. . .Jasmine and Olive, huh? Are they nice?"

"They're great. They're good friends of mine. Don't worry, you'll like them."

I hope he's right, but at least these girls are human. If only I could room with Ayla, then my life would be made, but that's impossible. I'm happy for her and hope she's having fun. Last I checked, she's still hiding out in her dorm room between classes, but I think she's starting to chill out again. Thanksgiving break can't come fast enough. I need my Ayla-time. Hopefully she doesn't murder me for what's about to happen between me and her brother.

During the next hour of shopping, I can't keep the grin off my face. With Felix, my troubles fade into the background, and even the stinging reminder on the back of my head doesn't bother me too much. I worked out this morning but didn't spar, and my high ponytail has kept everything safely hidden under a mound of messy black hair. The nurse had to put seven little stitches in and said they can come out next week.

Lucky number seven, yeah right.

But considering I had no signs of a concussion, maybe I am lucky. I could have died last night. Being alive and with Felix only solidifies what's most important to me. I'm not going to let this chance pass me by.

It takes a while to find parking close to the apartment, but since I don't have a car that's not a deal breaker. Felix and I carry everything a few blocks over to the building. It's not super close to the college campus but that's no problem for me. As we walk up to the historic row house central to almost everything in downtown New Orleans, a smile stretches across my cheeks. This building has been engineered from old gray stone blocks with black metal ironwork along the windows and an iron staircase leading to the front door. Ivy climbs up one side of the entire building, giving the place a total gothic vibe.

It's love at first sight.

"Pretty cool, huh?"

"This is what I love about this city," I sigh. "This building is amazing. How did your friends land an apartment here?"

"The building is actually super old and needs some work, plus they're on the ground level so when hurricanes come they always have to evacuate. A lot of renters don't like ground levels."

"Hey, I'm no stranger to hurricane season." In fact, we're in it now, but luckily we haven't had any come our way this year. "Whatever this place lacks in renovation, it makes up for in charm. I'm already obsessed."

We go inside to find a little mailroom, laundry room, and a staircase that leads to the other three floors of apartments. Under the staircase is a shiny black door and a welcome mat. Felix knocks.

The tiny girl who opens it has candy apple red hair and the palest skin I've seen on a human. At least she's human. If I never see another vampire again I will die a happy woman. Not likely.

"You must be Eva. I'm Olive." She hugs me right away, bouncing up and down on the balls of her feet. I can already tell this girl is the definition of extrovert. She instantly reminds me of Ayla.

"Hi, Olive." I beam. "Thanks so much for taking me on short notice."

"No prob, you're doing us a favor too. Our third roommate ditched us after only a month for a spot in some stupid sorority house. Ew, sororities, am I right? I wouldn't be caught dead in one." I chuckle because I'm not sure how else to respond. I don't care either way. I'm not the type to go for something like that but I don't begrudge those who are, though ditching your roommates with a lease hanging over their heads is pretty messed up. "She didn't even give notice. Anyway, let me show you to your room."

We follow her into the apartment. The kitchen, living, and dining spaces are all squished in together and about the size of my old bedroom. The walls are painted deep purple, and the furniture is a hodgepodge of styles that somehow works to create an eclectic design.

"What you see is what you get," she says, "we're pretty busy, so we're not here as much as we'd like, but we're proud of our little home."

"It looks great. Very thrift store chic. I love how all of these pieces don't match but still somehow look perfect together." And it's true. I'm going to have to send some pictures to Ayla.

Olive smiles knowingly at Felix. "Okay, you're right, I like her."

"I told you." When he smiles, my day gets even better.

"The bathroom's back here and so are the bedrooms. Rent is six hundred dollars a month and includes utilities and wifi. You'll pay me by the end of the month so I can pay the landlord on the first. Does that work?"

It's a tad more expensive than I was hoping, but definitely less than anything I could swing on my own, so I say yes. I haven't even seen my new bedroom, but I already know I'm going to love it because at least it's my own. Finally, I feel like I haven't been left behind by all my peers anymore. I'm a grown-ass woman who can take care of herself.

"Jasmine's a pre-med student and studies at the library all the time so you'll probably barely see her. I'm an art major so I come and go depending on what's going on at the studio. You work nights, right?"

She leads me into one of the bedrooms. I take it all in with a smile. It's got a four-poster queen-sized bed tucked into the corner with a matching black dresser. The walls are painted the same deep purple as the rest of the apartment, which I can definitely work with. Sure it's tiny, and the window is barred and faces a brick wall, but it's got a great energy about it. It feels safe. Welcoming. *Mine.*

"Yeah, I'm a server at Pops at night and am in an internship with Felix in the mornings, so I'm pretty busy too. But I'm not a student. You Tulane kids are way too smart for me. I hope that's okay with you guys."

"We don't care," she hands me a key, "so long as you're reliable and supply us with free Pops sometimes." She winks her huge fake eyelashes playfully, and I can't help but admire her makeup skills. Maybe she'll teach me her ways. "That place is the best. But Jasmine's a vegetarian so maybe bring her pie or something."

"That I can do."

"See, I like her." She raises her eyebrows at Felix and leaves us to it.

We make up the bed with my new white coverlet and hang the matching curtains. Tomorrow I'm going to find some cute throw pillows and a tie dye linen wall hanging to bring it all together. Ayla can give me advice on where to find the perfect things. I probably shouldn't spend any more money, but I want to, I need to. It's helping me take my mind off of everything, especially Mom. I've been trying to get ahold of her all day, but she's still missing. I'm starting to wonder if I should file a missing persons report, not that it would do me any good. And at the back of my mind is that mafia man's face from last night. I never want to see him again.

I unpack my clothes into the pocket closet while Felix sits on the bed, watching me lazily. Electricity fills the little room with him in it, and all I can think about is our almost-kiss this morning. I finish up and turn to look at him, instantly knowing he's thinking about the same thing.

"Hi."

"Hi." He grins.

This is the part where I hope he stands up and pulls me to him and kisses me, but he doesn't. He continues to sit there as the tension grows thicker. He knows what to do, I know he's capable of making a move. He's always had girls orbiting him and never shied away from them as far as I could tell. If we stay in the friend zone, before long it's going to get too awkward, and I can't let that happen.

"You know what, Felix?" It only takes three steps to go from standing by the closet to standing between his legs. He's so tall that I'm only a head taller even though he's sitting down on the edge of the bed.

"What?" He peers up at me. The dark lashes frame his yummy brown eyes, and from this close I can see the gold specks around his pupil. I get the answer I need in those eyes. He wants this too.

"I'm just gonna go for it." And I do—I lean down and press my lips to his. His response is instant, opening his mouth to mine. I can't help but moan. He wraps his hands around my waist and tugs me closer. It's not close enough for me, so I end up sitting in his lap. Much better.

I'm careful to keep his hands away from my scalp, not that he minds. They tend to travel lower anyway. Our kiss becomes an epic makeout session that lasts at least twenty minutes before my phone buzzes and ruins the fun. I groan and peel myself off him. "Ugh, no. . ."

"What's wrong?"

"I have to get ready for work."

"It's fine. I've got to go study anyway." He presses one final kiss to my lips and I walk him to the door.

I don't know what any of this means, but I'm not going to ruin it with questions or labels. I finally know what it feels like to have butterflies in my chest. It's as cliché as anything, but it's the perfect descriptor for how he makes me feel. For the first time in ages, I'm happy. I can't stop smiling.

He leaves, and not even a minute later someone knocks on the door. Assuming Felix forgot something, I open it. I want another kiss, too!

But there's nobody there.

At my feet rests a black box tied with a velvet red ribbon. Only thirty seconds ago this hallway was completely empty and now this? An inner warning bell wipes the smile off my face. I pick up the box to find a little white envelope tucked under the ribbon *Evangeline* scrawled in elegant handwriting across the front.

TWENTY-EIGHT

Everything about this box screams vampire. Who else would be dropping off presents in black boxes all tied up with red ribbon? It might be daytime, but they have plenty of humans to do their bidding, like delivering mysterious packages to unsuspecting women. I haven't even lived here for a day and they already know where I landed. I groan and bring the box inside. I don't have time to deal with this. I need to get ready for my shift, but I know myself—if I don't open it now, I'll go crazy thinking about it.

I take the box into my room and open the card first. The handwriting is unfamiliar and perfect, but it's the words that make me sick.

I have your mother. If you ever want to see her again, wear this dress to the riverboat casino tonight. Be there by eight.

There's no signature.

I scream in frustration and tear open the box. Inside is a black and gold flapper-style beaded party dress and shoes in my size. There's even jewelry to match. The only person who's ever done anything like this is Adrian-freaking-Teresi! I don't want to believe he'd take my mom but that makes me a fool. Of course he would. I'm still not sure why but there's got to be a reason. He told me he'll always do what's best for him and not for me. He warned me. I should have listened the first time. There's no time to debate this though. I'm going to have to save my mom—story of my life—so I pick up the phone and call Pops.

"This is Eddie."

I take a deep breath and try to steady my voice so it's not as frantic as I feel. "Hi, Eddie. It's Eva. I'm so sorry, but I can't come to work tonight. I'm having a family emergency."

He takes a long pause and suddenly I'm all too aware that even though he likes me, and even though he's had my back at work, he's my boss and he has a job to do here. "Are you sure you can't come?"

"I promise to make it up to you. I have no choice."

"You're putting me in a bad position here, Eva. Cami is out on maternity leave and Tennison is on vacation. If you don't show up I'll be understaffed."

"I'm so sorry." My voice cracks and tears burst from my eyes. Pops is always busy—being understaffed is a nightmare. I hate to disappoint anyone.

"Alright," his tone is unreadable. "Come in early for your next shift so we can talk about this face to face."

He hangs up, and as much as I'm worried about my only source of income and that I might have just lost my job, that is not my biggest problem. With shaky hands, I wipe away the tears and change into the dress.

The pier is crowded tonight. A sleek banner hangs across the ferry indicating it's been specially booked for a Roaring Twenties themed fundraising event. Who books a vampire casino boat for an event? Our city's mayor, Robyn Cox, that's who. All of the government is in bed with the vampires, they can't even help it, and the whole thing makes me want to scream. But I don't. I smile like a good little girl and give the person checking names at the door mine. She lets me right in without asking about my age. The laws are a joke anyway. The vamps already had the drinking age dropped. It's only a matter of time until the gambling age is lowered, too. It's been the big push during the last election cycle and nobody will be surprised when it happens.

The Roaring Twenties theme is carried throughout the boat to the max. All the decor is in metallic gold and inky black, reminding me of The Alabaster Heart's design. People are dressed up in gorgeous vintage frocks and suits and it's as if we've been transported back in time. My own dress hangs loosely just below my knees, the gold and black beads sparkling under the lights. I hate that I fit right in with the decor, like a prop. A full band plays lively big-band music and part of the casino floor has been cleared out for dancing. Waitstaff amble through the crowds with trays of hors d'oeuvres and glasses of bubbly champagne.

It's still a little light out so the vampires haven't arrived yet, but the pier isn't far from The Alabaster Heart and I know they'll be here soon. I want to find my mom and get us out of here, but I don't have much time to do that since the boat will be disembarking soon. And anyway, she's probably going to show up with Adrian.

I circle the room, avoiding making eye contact with anyone because I'm not in the mood for conversation and I shouldn't even be here. It's not like the mayor invited me. I'm not the least bit tempted by alcohol or gambling, unlike all of the adults. Quite a few of the young women hang off of older men, and I wonder if they're paid call girls. I wouldn't be surprised. Vampires have their fingers in everything seedy along with constantly meddling with the law, politics, and real estate to gain more control.

I spot the mayor standing at one of the craps tables. Wearing a sophisticated black dress, she blows on dice, throwing them to the table. She's not even playing, she's the "good luck" girl. Everyone screams and raises their hands—of course she just secured a win. I've never seen her in person before, only in political campaigns that I've barely paid attention to. I think I had better start paying attention. These people are going to ruin New Orleans even more than they already have.

The sunset finally gives way to darkness and we're joined by a procession of vampires. They're welcomed with open arms. Most people swarm them. I know that many want to be close to their enigmatic force, it's a pull the vampires have to their prey. They may look like us, but they aren't us, and to lose sight of that is deadly. To see vampires and humans mixing so easily makes my toes curl.

I stay far back and watch for my mother.

Adrian Teresi descends on the boat like some kind of God and I want to go slap him. It's impossible to leave a red mark on a vamp but I'm mad enough that I think I may be able to be the first. Kelli trails close behind her boss, and the mayor rushes over to them like they're all old friends. He smiles in his wicked way that is unique to him, and the two chat it up. Should I go over there and confront him? I'm not sure that's a good idea, and I don't see my mother anyway. So where is she? Is he hiding her somewhere? Kelli must feel my eyes boring into them because she spots me and her face goes slack. She whispers something in Adrian's ear. He looks up, and when he catches my gaze, I can feel him like an electrical energy pulse. A flash of confusion crosses his features. He seems upset that I'm here, which is odd considering he sent the note.

Didn't he?

My body goes cold as I realize Adrian isn't behind Mom's kidnapping. As if on cue, Hugo glides into the room with an older red-headed woman perched on his arm. She's classically beautiful and completely enamoured by the man. She's also human. And my mother.

The world tilts off its axis. What is he doing with her? How does he even know who she is? He leans down and kisses her gently on the mouth. My mother, kissing a vampire. I never thought I'd see the day. But then, I don't really know her like I thought I did. And that's a dull knife right into my heart.

I can't move. I can't breathe. All I can do is watch in horror.

The crowd thickens and I lose sight of them. The engines rumble to life. The boat starts to move away from the dock. Someone walks onto the little stage with the band and speaks into the microphone to introduce the mayor. Like a true politician, Robyn Cox glides up onto the stage as if it's the most comfortable place on earth for her to be. She smiles down at us, her perfectly styled short black hair and brown eyes shining under the lights.

"Thank you all for coming!" Everyone cheers, and she jumps into an impassioned speech about improving the city and the importance of vampire-human relations. This is a fundraiser event for her own campaign, so of course everyone here already supports her and is eating it up like a kid with a bucket full of Halloween candy. "And I'm excited to announce that the bill to lower the gambling age will be taken to Capitol Hill during the next session and all our projections indicate it will pass." More cheers. My cheeks burn at that. She's supposed to be helping her constituents, not feeding them to the vampires! When she points to the police commissioner and he cheerily holds up a glass of champagne to acknowledge her, I've had enough.

I edge my way along the crowd, trying to get closer to Hugo and my mom. The mayor says something about him and he leaves my mother standing by the side of the stage to go speak into the microphone. I still don't understand why Hugo would want me here. What's he going to do to Mom? My mind flashes to the quick and ruthless way he murdered that woman the other night and how Adrian sucked up the mess. Bile burns my throat with the hateful words I'm dying to scream.

"Thank you, Robyn." His cruel energy blankets the room. Or maybe I'm the only one who thinks he's cruel? Others look up at Hugo like he's some kind of savior. "As the co-chair of the VEC and the head of the government relationships board on behalf of the North American vampires, I've had a lot of experience on these matters. Now, more than ever, it is critical that we keep our lines of communication open. The last thing anyone wants is a war." He winks and the crowd quiets. His tone is all business, but his words are a threat. Do they see it now? Do they sense his cruelty like I do? "We need each other. This is a two-way relationship," he continues his speech. "And my brother and I will stop at nothing to ensure the best quality of life for vampires *and* humans."

I'm only a few paces from Mom. She's gazing adoringly up at Hugo like he's the sun in winter. Shouldn't she be hiding from the mafia right now? I clasp her hand in mine and whisper in her ear. "Hey, Mom, can you come with me?"

She turns and blinks at me, her eyes confused. "Evangeline, what are you doing here?"

I shake my head and tug her backward. Luckily, for once in her stubborn life, she follows. We move to the farthest edge of the room so that we can whisper without drawing attention from Hugo's speech. Every once in a while his eyes flick over to us. He's not mad that I've found her. Triumph sparkles in his eyes. This is all a game to him—one I don't know the rules to.

"What are you doing here with Hugo? He's a vampire."

She blinks at me, confused. "Umm—no, he's not. Hugo's my date."

"How do you know him?"

"Umm—" More confusion. "We met at—umm—I know him from—" Her voice trails off. She doesn't know because she's clearly been compelled to believe something that doesn't exist. She's not afraid, she's still sending adoring looks in Hugo's direction, but it's obvious he's brought her here as bait for me. She's a pawn and she doesn't even know it.

"Aren't you supposed to be hiding from the mafia?" I whisper-hiss. "I've been trying to get ahold of you for days. They're going to hurt me if you don't pay Armondo."

She blinks rapidly and a knot seems to untangle in her mind. "Oh, I'd forgotten." Fear mars her features and her hand presses against her chest. "I can't believe I forgot. I don't know how I could have. I'm so sorry, Evangeline. I'm working on it. I almost got the money, I swear." She opens the little purse on her shoulder. There's a wad of cash shoved inside. "See, I used what was left of the sock-money and got someone else to lend me some more and I just need to take some of this and win a few hands and we'll be free and clear."

I blink at her. "*You* took that money from my room? And now you think gambling it away is a good idea right now?"

"You don't understand. I'm out of time. I'm desperate."

Oh, I think I understand desperation.

Hugo finishes his speech, the crowd cheers, and then everyone disperses to chat or play or dance or whatever people do at these things. Meanwhile, Adrian stays centered in the room, connecting with acquaintances, but his bright blue eyes never stray from me for long. The last time I was on this boat with him, he also used my mother as a pawn. And then he killed a man. I can't forget it. I've been too lax around him since the blood vow, but I need to remember who he really is. What he really is.

Hugo appears. I can smell the blood on him from here. My stomach knots. I hope he hasn't been feeding on my mother. She doesn't have any bite marks and that would be illegal. "I see you got my invitation."

"Unfortunately. What are you doing with my mother? Do you even know her?"

He runs a finger across her cheek. "She was easy to find. I have contacts everywhere."

She peers up at him adoringly, but with a question in her eyes. "You found me?"

He chuckles low. "Sorry, doll, I don't actually know you. We're not together. A little compulsion to get you here was all I needed." She goes rigid, and he stares at her with a little smile on his lips. "Don't be afraid." His voice sounds different. Deeper. Certain.

Wrong.

She instantly relaxes, the fear melting like butter. To see how quickly and powerfully his compulsion works is unlike anything I've witnessed before. I step back, terrified for my mother, for every human on this boat.

"So what's really going on here, Hugo?"

"I'll explain it all in time, don't worry." He ushers my mom toward the gaming tables, and I follow. "First, there's someone else here that I think we need to have a little talk with."

We approach the roulette table. The wheel spins, the little white ball dancing across the numbers. Around the table, gamblers are busy placing their bets. The ones who want to take the biggest risk but possibly gain the biggest reward bet on the numbers. The ones who want to play it safe bet on the outside edges, on the even and odds, and mainly black or red.

A middle aged gentleman in a pinstripe suit and bowler hat turns to us and addresses Hugo. "You delivered the goods."

"I always do. I hope we can call this even for what my brother did to your man, Paulo."

That name rings in my ear. Paulo. Who's Paulo? Then I remember he's the gambler Adrian killed right in front of me. Apparently, he was also a mobster.

Mom stumbles back.

"Uh oh," Hugo chuckles, "care to introduce our mutual friend to your daughter?"

Mom shakes her head, and her eyes go round as marbles.

"I can introduce myself," the man says. When he smiles, an old scar on his left eyebrow cuts deep into his face. He's a large guy with a sinister energy and a depth to his eyes made by years of corruption. He sticks out a thick hand with a big gold ring on one of the fingers. "I'm pleased to finally meet you, Eva. I'm Armondo."

TWENTY-NINE

"Your mother loves to gamble, doesn't she Eva?" Armondo continues. "So why don't we play a little game?"

"What do you want?" I rush. "She's got the money on her. She can pay you back right now."

Armando laughs bitterly but offers his hand. Mom shoves the purse at him and he peers inside, greedy eyes assessing. "This might be half of what you owe me, Virginia."

"I can get more."

"Time's up."

I always thought it would be the blood loss that would be my mom's ruin, but it's not, it's the gambling. It's what that *need* to play—the addiction—has led her to do. It's this man who has no qualms about hurting her, maybe killing her, maybe killing me too. Hugo grips Mom's upper arm and she winces.

Armondo goes on, "How about your daughter makes a bet

for you. Beginner's luck, right?" He chuckles. "If she wins, I'll take the money and we'll call it even. If she loses. . ."

"What?" Mom's voice is barely a whisper.

"Then you both die."

Hugo shakes his head adamantly. "You can't touch the girl. She belongs to the vampires now. She's ours."

Panicked, Mom shoots me a questioning look that I can't answer.

Armondo leans back and curls his lip before taking a long drink of his liquor. He sets the drink back down and assesses the three of us. "Fine. Virginia's life then."

"I won't do it." I shake my head and plead. "Please, I can't do this. Don't make me do this." I'm not a gambler, I hate it, and to have to gamble my mother's life is out of the question. It's so loud in here, so busy and lively, that nobody seems to notice our little group conversation. If they did, would they care?

"If you don't place a bet, then I'll kill her. This is her only chance." He means it. I have the wound on the back of my head as proof. His henchman was just a taste of what he's capable of and to think that he'll hurt my mom sends me over the edge. I lock my knees so I don't weaken and glare daggers at the man.

Hugo raises an eyebrow at me. "Sweetheart, you better do what the man says."

The next bet has come and gone and the little white ball is spinning around the wheel again. I watch it, my stomach going hollow. It slows and lands on the green double zero. Everyone around the table groans as the winnings are swooped up by the dealer. This is the fail-safe for the casino, the assurance that more often than not, the house wins.

"It's a simple game of odds," Mom whispers to me, her eyes pleading with me to give her this chance. "Make the safest bet."

Hugo shoves her against the table and she cries out. "No more talking."

Is there such a thing as a "safe bet"? I don't think so. The whole point is the risk. But I take the rolled wad of money and set it on the table. The dealer calls something out and the pit boss zips over. It's the same vampire from my first run-in weeks ago. His eyes light with recognition, but this time he doesn't tell me to leave. He nods to the dealer who counts out the cash and replaces it with a stack of pink chips.

"Double the money," Armondo says. "You have options. You can put it on a number and if you win, the payout is thirty-five to one. I'll let you keep the extra. Doesn't that sound nice? You'd be a wealthy woman. Or you could play the outside thirds, giving yourself a third share of the spoils if you win there. That's a lot of money too."

"Or I can play it safe and take the two to one odds." I move the pile onto the red rectangle. It reminds me of blood and vampires and all the reasons why we're here tonight. At the last second, I switch it to black.

"Black it is," Armondo says.

Hugo smirks. "Not much for gambling?"

"No." I fold my arms and glare.

By now we've attracted a crowd of onlookers. There's got to be at least ten thousand dollars on that single bet, and people are excited to see the result. I spot Adrian and Kelli standing not too far off. Adrians face is an unreadable mask. I can't tell if he's happy to see me or wishes I were dead. It could go either way, and I wouldn't want to bet on that, either.

Mom levels me with a hard look. "Eva, whatever happens, I want you to know this isn't your fault." But it feels like it. If I win, I double the money and get Armondo off our backs. I don't even want to think about what will happen if I lose.

The dealer spins the wheel and the little ball goes *plop, plop, plop* with no concern for what its movements mean for the future. It slows and slows, until finally lands on thirty-six, red. My heart plummets. At the last second, it bounces once more, and lands solidly in number eleven.

Black.

I crumple to my knees as the crowd explodes in cheers. I've never been so relieved in my life, every ounce of anxiety leaving my body in that moment. Mom crouches and wraps her arms around me. "I'm so sorry, baby. . .so sorry," she whispers over and over. She promises to get better, promises things will be different. But I know nothing will change unless Adrian comes through with the compulsion and gets her to stop.

We stand, and I wipe away tears.

"It's your lucky day." Armondo sounds disappointed, but he's a man of his word, collecting his winnings and moving on to another table.

"That money isn't much to him," Hugo says, pulling me up to standing. "He'll blow it by the end of the night. If only you'd made a better bet you could have pocketed some of that for yourself."

Like I care about that right now.

"Then why did he do it? Just to punish my mom?"

"In part, but mostly to prove a point to me. The vampires and the mob have been at odds in this city for years. This wasn't about the money so much as it was about honor and asserting dominance in front of vampires. He knows he'll never have what we have." His fang extends and he sips from a glass of blood. My stomach churns. "Immortality."

"When does this thing dock? I'm ready to go home."

"The party is just getting started." He retrieves his wallet and hands my mother five crisp one hundred dollar bills. "Go have fun, Virginia. I have business to attend to with your daughter."

I expect her to tell him off, to insist that she's had enough excitement for tonight. Once again, my expectations break my own heart. Mom takes the money. Avoiding eye contact with me, she heads in the direction of the Texas Hold'em table. I see her sit down and place her first bet, then rub her hands together as if she's preparing for a fun night ahead. If my heart was broken before, now it's in absolute shatters. I can't believe it. And yet, I can. And lying to myself is the worst part. *She took the money from my room.* My eyes burn with tears—I force them back.

"Come. . ." Hugo places a hand on my lower back and leads me toward the dance floor. "Let me cheer you up. Aren't you happy to have that mafia trouble behind you?"

I can't answer that.

My body follows even though my mind is back with Mom, begging her to reconsider. It doesn't matter that she is now gambling with Hugo's money. Soon it will be hers again. She's been in hiding for days, and now she's back to doing the thing that landed her there in the first place.

We end up on the dance floor where the music is a loud noxious riot of instruments. I can't keep up as he swings me to and fro like a paper doll. I have no idea what I'm doing and I don't want to be here. "Can I go home now? I don't want to dance."

"This isn't about what you want, Eva, it's about what I know." He laughs. "Don't you realize that by now?" I try to leave but his hands hold me back, fingers biting into my flesh. He's too strong. I'm confused by his statement, what he knows. It doesn't make sense.

The music slows, and a silky voice brushes across the back of my exposed neck. "May I cut in?"

"You're so predictable, Adrianos." But Hugo hands me over to Adrian and takes Kelli in his arms. "Let me guess, you were responsible for what happened back there at the roulette table?"

Adrian doesn't say anything. The music is a slow sultry tune and he pulls me against him, the steps taking us farther and farther away from Hugo and Kelli.

"I didn't expect to see you here," he says at last.

"I didn't expect to be here. Hugo threatened my mother, so I came." I look up into his blue eyes. They're so reflective in the golden light that I can see myself staring back. "What did he mean about the roulette table?"

"It was nothing."

"Please just tell me," I sigh. "I don't think I can handle any more deception in one night."

"Then you've come to the wrong place." Emotion shifts through his irises and they're no longer blocked. Suddenly, I can see into the oceanic depths of them. I could get lost there if I'm not careful. I would drown and it would not be pleasant. At least, I don't think it would be. I wouldn't want it to be. What if it was?

"I'm the only vampire in North America who can fly," Adrian relents. "I'm also the only vampire in North America with telekinesis."

The reality of what happened sinks in and my mouth pops open in awe. "You saved her. You moved the ball at the last second to black. Thank you." I can't help it. I hug him. I never thought I would be grateful to a vampire but I am. I misjudged him.

Adrian freezes and doesn't hug me back.

"That's enough." He dislodges himself. "Let's go find out why Hugo really brought you here. I'm growing tired of his little game."

"What do you mean? It was all to appease the mafia guy."

"Trust me. I know my brother; we've been at odds for centuries. The only person Hugo cares to appease is himself." He slips his hand into mine and tugs. "Now come on."

"Centuries. . ." I swallow, once again questioning his age.

Adrian catches the question in my expression and tilts his head at me, his eyes narrowing. "As far as I know, Brisa is the oldest vampire alive and I'm her oldest son, Angel. I'll let you guess what that means for my age." But I can't even wrap my mind around that kind of eternity. How many wars, how much pain and suffering, and how much technological advancement has this man experienced?

When we make it back through the dancers to Kelli and Hugo, Hugo looks at our clasped hands and smiles with glee. "This is going to be fun."

THIRTY

"Let's go down to the VIP room and discuss a few things, shall we?" Hugo leads us through the maze of people and to the back of the boat. Along the way, we're stopped several times by eager humans. Adrian and Hugo shmooze them over like it's nothing, like we're not on some important walk to discuss *whatever*. These guys really know how to turn on the charm, and it seems to take forever to shake off all the humans. All the while my mind is buzzing with thoughts of what could be coming next. Truth is, I haven't a clue. I feel like all my cards are showing and none of them are aces.

We finally make it to a tiny stairwell that descends into the bowels of the ship. Kelli isn't anywhere to be found. It's just me, Adrian, and Hugo. I follow them down the stairs because there's no other choice. What am I going to do, run away? Jump into the river? I can't tell these creatures no. Their power is on another level.

We walk down a long thin hallway with little metal doors on either side. Some have words inscribed on them with "restricted" or "crew only." One says VIP in gold lettering. That's our target. The room is small, the lights are low, and we're not the only ones in here.

A woman with shiny black hair is pressed up against a man in a police uniform. Her dress is hiked up around her waist and his hands roam her backside. She groans and shifts closer just as I realize who they are. Mayor Cox and the police commissioner! To walk in on them engaging in an affair is so stereotypical that I almost laugh. Both have wedding rings on their fingers. Both have spouses upstairs.

"Get out," Adrian deadpans like he doesn't have the time for this.

The two jump apart and offer their apologies. Hugo smiles with even more glee than before, and all I can think is that this juicy piece of information is going to help him in his quest to control the city.

They scamper out of the room.

"And then there were three," Hugo says.

I take in the small polished space and try to relax. The windows are the waterproof bolted-in kind, typical on boats. Outside, the top of the water laps against the bottom rims. The river is black and sparkling under the moon. On the near distant shore, the city lights crawl past. The room itself is wallpapered in deep maroon with black foil accents. There's a minibar in one corner, a flat screen television on the wall, with two black leather chairs and a couch evenly spaced out.

Hugo closes the door and motions for us to take a seat. I sit next to Adrian on the couch and Hugo sits across from us in a chair. He lounges back and smiles. "I don't think I've had this much fun at a party in a hundred years. You remember that time when we—"

"Why are we here, brother?" Adrian cuts in. "Get to the point."

"You know, Ardrianos, for someone who's lived as long as you have, you'd think you would have learned patience by now."

Adrian's eyes narrow. There's hatred for his brother in those eyes. It's clear as day. "Believe me. I'm patient," he says, "I'm more patient than I ever planned on."

Hugo snickers and slaps the arm of his chair, then stands and crosses to the minibar. He pours two bourbons. "Would you like something, child?" he asks me. "What's your drink?"

I'm parched, I could use water, but I don't want to take a thing from Hugo. After the way he toyed with my mother, he's my new favorite fanger to hate. "No." My voice is clipped.

He smirks and hands the glass to Adrian, sits back down, and the two drink. I knew vampires could drink but it seems pointless. "It's one human thing that we can still have," Hugo says when he catches me looking. "Not that the alcohol affects us. It doesn't do anything to our blood but it's a different taste and it doesn't make us ill. I'll admit, I prefer my alcohol mixed with blood but sometimes it's fun to switch things up every now and then." Hugo smirks at me, lazilly swirling the amber liquor in his right hand before taking another sip.

"Vampires don't eat food or drink water. Alcohol is a luxury, and blood is a necessity," Adrian adds. "What's your point, brother?"

Hugo raises an eyebrow in my direction. "Are you prepared for that, Eva? Are you truly willing to give up your humanity?"

My body goes hard. He's calling my bluff.

I'm not going to become a vampire. I never had any intention of doing so, and it's the last thing I want. I'd rather die than feed off of other's blood and abuse their addictions so that I can survive. But this is a floating casino and I came prepared to lie and cheat and game my way out of here. "Of course." I smile happily at Adrian and take his hand in mine. He flinches. "I trust you. From what I understand, I'll be bound to you and unable to defy you." I bat my eyelashes. "But I know you'll take good care of me."

"Lucky me." He frowns, peels his hand away, and takes a sip from his drink.

Hugo laughs. "It will be a lucky man who has the opportunity to break a strong-willed woman such as yourself, Evangeline.

It's unfortunate for my brother, but that man won't be him."

I shake my head, confused. Adrian freezes.

"Do I have your attention now?" Hugo's face turns stony. "Good. Listen closely. I take a new protégé every year as my queen allows. There's a reason I've lost five of my protégés in a single month and that my queen won't grant me more children, and that reason is you, Eva."

A weight crushes down on me and I try not to sink under the pressure. How much does he know?

"What are you talking about?" Adrian asks sharply. "Do not waste any more of our time. Explain yourself."

"First was my newest child, Roxy. She didn't even make it past the graveyard. Hunters got her. Or the sun. Then I lost three more a few weeks later; those men definitely weren't killed by the sun. And of course we know about what happened in the lobby with my bloodthirsty child whom you killed without consulting me." He counts them off his fingers. "All deaths that were caused by Eva, here."

The two exchange heated glares before turning them both on me. The pressure is too much. My hands are shaking. My heart is racing. I don't know what to do.

"The lobby wasn't my fledgling's fault," Adrian spits. "And the others have nothing to do with her. Do not make false accusations or I will see that you are punished. You have no proof."

Hugo laughs gleefully. "Ah, but you're wrong. I figured it out in the lobby when her blood was spilled. She's connected to my line, but yet she's human. So how can that be?" He leans closer to me and his voice goes low. "There is only one way a human can connect into a vampiric line and that is through venom. If our venom enters your human bloodstream it makes you able to feel, sense, and track the vampires within the family of the vampire who bit you. It also makes us far more attracted to you and your blood more desirable."

"This is forbidden information!" Adrian growls. "Brisa has only allowed you to speak of this to Eva because you've made up lies. My fledgling is no hunter."

"This is why you don't drink directly from human flesh unless you intend to kill or turn," I whisper breathily.

"Indeed it is one of the reasons," Hugo confirms. "I knew it the second I smelled your fresh blood in the lobby, and I confirmed it when I tasted it for myself. So tell us, Evangeline, how long have you been a vampire hunter, and which one of my children bit you before you killed them?"

Time stills. Everything slows. I don't know how to lie my way out of this.

Adrian watches me closely. I expect him to defend me or keep denying this, but he does neither. Hurt crosses his features, then anger. He turns on me with a sneer, "Answer him!"

"I—I was defending myself." Fear prickles over every inch of my body. "I followed a friend to the cemetery because I suspected he was a hunter, and then this new vampire attacked me and I staked her with one of his stakes. Her fang barely grazed my arm. I thought it was nothing. I didn't know." My voice comes out shaky. I hope they don't think it's because I'm lying. Surely, they hear the adrenaline racing through my veins and the pounding of my heart.

"And what of my other children?" Hugo snarls. "You were connected to them. You must have killed them."

"That wasn't my fault! We were at a party. Vampires came. I think they were following me. They had no place showing up at a human college party, but they were there and they attacked my friend. We were defending ourselves and—"

"It is not easy to kill vampires!" Hugo stands and flies at me. Adrian lets him. In two seconds I'm slammed up against the wall and choking under his stony hands. They grip my throat and squeeze. "They were following you because I ordered them to, I had suspicions about you from the beginning. You are a hunter! Admit it!"

Tears stream down my face. My vision blacks at the edges. There's no choice. Either way I'm going to die.

"Tell the truth or I'll kill your mother and then I'll kill you!"

"Yes," I mouth.

"Do you confess it?"

I try to nod but it's hard. "Yes," my voice is strained under his death-grip.

He drops me to the floor and my lungs burn as I gasp for breath. Adrian stands rock still and peers down at me like I'm a bug in need of squashing.

"So here's what we're going to do," Hugo continues. "You've already been approved by the queen to be a fledgling." I look over his shoulder at Adrian. "She knows of my suspicions and said that if I can get a confession, then I can have Eva for myself."

"And what do you intend to do with her?" Adrian raises an eyebrow. He stands back with his arms over his chest. Anger rolls off him in waves, filling every crevice of the small room. "Because I don't care anymore, brother. I am tired of family drama. This is why I never want to take any children. They are a liability, not an asset, and I am done."

He's done. The words feel like a battle axe to my chest.

But wait… why is Adrian pretending not to know who I really am? He already knew I was a hunter. And why is he so quick to hand me over to the brother he so obviously hates? There's something more going on here. With my eyes alone, I will him to save me, to intervene, to do something, because he's my only hope. But he does nothing. He turns away, appearing well and truly done with me. Maybe this is it. Maybe he'd rather turn me over to his brother than deal with me any longer.

Hugo peers down his nose and his fangs extend. They're like two little daggers—two little promises of pain to come. "I intend to turn her. Tonight."

THIRTY-ONE

Everything happens in a blur of blind panic. Hugo binds my hands and feet and mouth with thick black fabric and Adrian carries me off the floating casino and onto a speed boat that has been tied to the side of the ferry. My oversized flapper-style dress hangs around my knees and I pray that it stays that way. My life depends on it.

Adrian drops me on the floor and I lay there curled up in the fetal position as the boat flies down the river. I try to maneuver through the bindings at my wrists and ankles but it's useless. I start to cry. My tears blur the stars, the moon, and the rare glimpses of city and freedom. Even though it should barely register on my list of worries, I'm cold and starting to shiver. Before long it consumes my thoughts. I let it, at least it's something to focus on that doesn't terrify me. My dress is loose enough and long enough that I can tuck my legs up into it. I make sure to stay on my left side even though it's extra painful to lie this way. The beads of the dress bite into my flesh, many of them probably cracking where I lie on them. I can't believe this stupid gown is what I'm going to be wearing to my death. That's if I don't find a way to get out of becoming a vampire. I'm going to fight to the death. But if they win, if I rise up as Hugo's new child, I will join the sunrise. I don't know if that's possible, if the thirst will overpower me, but I vow to try to die before I hurt someone.

Vow—the word shocks me back to the present. I look at Adrian. He's driving the boat. The wind blows his dark blond hair behind him and his biceps flex when he makes a turn. I have vowed to help him, haven't I? Not Hugo. Maybe that's why Adrian is going along with this. Maybe the blood we already exchanged will somehow bind me to him instead of his brother. He might be playing the both of us. What if I wake up as Adrian's child, after all?

My stomach hardens. If I had food in my belly, I'd throw up. These brothers are truly evil. I'm nothing but a toy for them to fight over.

After a while, the boat slows, and Adrian drives it to the shore. Hugo picks me up like I weigh nothing and I grit my teeth when his arm gets too close to my upper thigh. He smells of expensive cologne and alcohol and blood. I don't want to smell him, I'd rather smell the water and the dirt and the cold air. He carries me off the boat and into a wooded graveyard. There are no underground graves here this close to the water. The tombs are above ground, ranging from dark gray stone to cream limestone, with inscriptions too old and weathered to read. Moss covers many of them. The moon is bright enough to see by, but the vampires have no issues either way. They can see in the dark. Soon I will too. The thought makes me whimper.

"Have you already prepared the grave?" Adrian asks. It's the first I've heard from him even though he trails behind us like a dark shadow. I meet his eyes. They glow like two little blue orbs in the darkness. I murmur pleas for help against the fabric gagging my mouth, but he only watches.

"I have," Hugo replies. "Why are you not fighting this? It wasn't long ago that you were defending your little Angel." He snickers. "Yes, I've heard your pet name for the girl. Maybe I'll call her the same."

Adrian rolls his eyes. "You know I don't like to take children. I thought I wanted Eva but she betrayed us. There's no way I would turn a hunter into my child. I'm surprised you're willing to after she killed some of your family. If I were in your shoes, she'd be dead already."

Hugo tightens his arms around me. "Then I guess that's where you and I differ. I will always take a new child. My family bond is stronger than most. She will be loyal after the change."

"Because she'll have to be," Adrian challenges. "But won't you always wonder if she'll hate you?"

"She'll love me," Hugo snaps. "Children always love their fathers, even when they hate them. Now come on, it's this way. I had to get farther from the river to find a place I could dig."

Hugo moves like liquid smoke through the crowded graveyard and I'm carried along with him. Adrian levitates and flies above. I wonder if it's a talent that makes Hugo jealous. I would be. We arrive at a spot with a pile of disturbed dirt. Hugo walks me right up to the hole and tilts me so I can look inside. There's a coffin at the bottom. The lid is already open and a white silk lining glistens up at me.

I shake my head and try to yell through the fabric but it's useless.

He sets me down on the cool grass and unbinds my limbs. "You need to be able to claw yourself out of the coffin or it won't work."

He stares into my eyes and says, "If I remove this and you scream, I'll be forced to put it back on." He unties the gag from my mouth and I cough, sucking in the foggy air. I don't scream. Nobody would hear me anyway. "After I bite you, you will have my venom in your bloodstream. It might hurt at first but it will feel good soon after, so don't be afraid. After that we will exchange blood, and then I will bury you. In three nights you will rise as my child and I will be here to greet you."

I shake my head. *No. Please, no.*

"Shh—don't worry, child. Once it's all done, you will be thanking me." He runs a calloused finger down my face and wipes away a tear. I bristle under his touch. "And you will love me."

What does that mean? Love? Does it mean I will want to be around him like a daughter and father, or that I will want to be with him like a lover? He's older and scary and awful, and this can't be happening. It can't.

Adrian hovers above us, viewing the dreadful scene like a voyeur, like it's nothing he hasn't seen a million times before. He almost looks bored. I hate him for that look, maybe even more than Hugo.

"Let's begin." Hugo's fangs extend once again, but this time he lunges for me and they sink into my neck. I do scream, I can't help it. The pain is blinding and white hot, but my eyes flutter closed and it soon transforms into utter and complete ecstasy. The warmth of it washes through me like a salve to a wound. I've never done drugs, but perhaps this is why people get addicted. I could get lost in this. Forever. It's a cruel kind of beauty and I want more, more, more...

Hugo releases me and sucks in a greedy breath. Vamps don't even need to breathe but he does it for show. "Virgin blood. Mmm, it's been a while since I've had some as sweet as yours." He licks his lips. "I must be careful or I'll kill you." He wipes the red from his face and turns to Adrian. "I would offer you a taste but we can't have her blood bond confused with the wrong master. Sorry."

He's not sorry. It's a taunt. Adrian may have exchanged blood with me, but he never bit me, so my earlier theory is out. This really is happening with Hugo.

"I would never give my venom to a traitor," Adrian says nonchalantly, but I can see the crazed look in his glowing eyes and wonder if it's from a thirst to taste my blood or something else.

I start to cry again. "Shh—Eva. It will be okay." Adrian's voice is smooth and easy. "Sometimes you lose when you play a game of high stakes."

There it is. That word. Stakes. *He knows.*

Adrian lands on the grass a few feet from us and sits back on his heels. "Are you going to get this show on the road or are we going to be here all night?"

Using his fangs, Hugo rips into the pale flesh of his wrist. Crimson liquid gushes down his arm. "I have to admit, it may make me a sick bastard, but this is my favorite part of the process. I love knowing part of me will always be with you."

He extends his wrist toward my mouth and his eyes move heavenward. This is my chance, what I've been waiting for, and what Adrian alluded to with his comment.

Adrian's bluff.

My ace.

I gather my courage, tap into weeks of training, and slip my hand under the fold of my dress. The long thin wooden stake I've had strapped to my upper thigh has been waiting for me this whole time. Adrian always warned me not to bring this around the vampires, always said they'd kill me if they found it. He demanded I stop. Good thing I didn't listen.

The stake is cool salvation in my palm and I grip it with all my might. I spring forward and sink it directly into Hugo's chest. It slices through the ribcage and into his spongy heart. He gasps and looks down at me, shock seizing his body. He never expected to be bested, not by me. But it's not just me, it's Adrian. He knew the stake was there the whole time, his satisfied smile says it all.

"No. . ." Blood seeps from Hugo's mouth.

"You should have known this could happen, *Father*. I am a hunter after all." I'm a sarcastic bitch. Adrian laughs. I push Hugo off of me, and he crumbles into ash.

It's over.

I stand and brush myself off. The pile of Hugo-dust blows away with a gust of wind and I watch it go with relief. My legs are shaking. His venom is still racing through my body. It makes me feel stronger, more powerful, *better*, but I want it gone. I imagine it racing through my veins like a dirty virus and hope my body can fight it off soon. I press my fingers to the bite on my neck. There's blood but the wound has already healed over thanks to the venom, sealing away that last shred of Hugo into my body.

Adrian hovers above me and that damned satisfied smile plays on his face. "See, my brother was wrong. I am rather patient."

"You're sick, too."

He doesn't care. He's barely even listening. "I've wanted to do that for ages, but I couldn't. My maker forbids us from killing our siblings or ordering our progeny to do it." He laughs. "It does make me sick, I know, but I thank God you walked into my casino. You *are* my Angel."

I glare. "How dare you speak of God. You're vile."

He stills and his eyes narrow. "You have no idea."

"You wanted him dead and risked my life in the process. You allowed him to bring me here and get this far so that I could kill him for you." I'm boiling over with anger and have nowhere to direct it but at Adrian. "You played me. I almost died!"

"You're alive. Don't be so dramatic." He nods toward the stake, his demeanor returning to business-as-usual. "Please, let's dispose of that. It's evidence and I'd rather not have it around, though I admit I would love to keep it as a souvenir of Hugo's demise. It would be my most-prized possession."

I scoff. I don't want to get rid of the only weapon on me, but if Adrian was going to kill me, he would have done so already, not to mention, what if one of the vamps was able to smell Hugo's blood on it? I shouldn't have the murder weapon on me, that's like Crime 101. So I do as Adrian wishes and walk back to the river and toss the stake in. "Can we go home now? I'm so done with vampires."

"Hmm, does that mean you're going to give up hunting?"

"Yes," I bark out. I would be happy to never see another bloodsucker in my life. But even as I say it, I don't know if I can give up hunting or abandon my friends.

"You're such a liar."

"Takes one to know one."

He laughs and lands gracefully in the boat as I climb inside. I sit in the chair across from the driver's seat, the same one Hugo just occupied. It's cold and I'm still shaking. I tuck my legs up into my dress again and try to banish Hugo from my memory.

Adrian drives us back to the city slow enough that we can hear each other over the engine. The story he plans to tell the queen and the others is that when we arrived at the graveyard, hunters showed up and killed Hugo while we escaped. He will insist that I am not a hunter myself, that Hugo wasn't able to prove anything or get me to admit to anything. He'll say that he was going to gift me to Hugo out of pity for all his recent losses and because he'd decided he didn't want to take a child after all. But since Hugo died, Adrian invited me to continue on as his fledgling.

"As if I would agree," I snap.

"Well, wait," he continues. "I haven't gotten to the best part.

You see, after such a terrible ordeal, you were spooked by the hunters, and decided to go on living your life as a human. And I, in all my infinite mercy, decided to grant your wish."

I scoff. "Good. Consider this the end of our relationship."

It's a great story, but this is the oldest vampire on earth we're talking about, and I'm a little skeptical our story is going to land. "And you think Queen Brisa is going to buy that? What if she orders you not to lie?"

"You let me worry about Brisa." He sighs happily and rakes his hand through his hair. "She's busy with other matters and Hugo has been out of her favor for quite some time. The vampire court is full of problems, and this will mean little to any of them. She'll be upset about Hugo's death because it's one less child for her, but that anger will be directed toward the hunters and not us."

"Oh great," I scoff, "so just send her after my friends. Wonderful."

"She doesn't know about your little gym under the bank. I'm the only one who does and I won't be telling her."

"I hope you're right. I still think she'll just order you not to lie to her. If I were her, I'd do that all the time."

His fingers dance over the steering wheel as he looks at me for a long moment. "Oh, and do you want to be the vampire queen, now, Angel?"

"Ew. Never."

He nods. "You're right, she can order us about, and she does it quite often, but I've built a tolerance to her over the years. My words are very easy for me to control. It's actions against her will that are hard to take, especially something as final as killing one of her other children when she's told me I couldn't."

I fold my arms and sit back. "Interesting."

"What's interesting?" His pale face glows under the moonlight. "You'll forgive me, but I've been around too long to find much interesting anymore."

"Your worldview is truly sad." I deflect the question. "It's a wonderful world if you know where to look. It would be even better without vampires, no offense."

"I've lived long enough to know with certainty that this world is rather bleak." He narrows his eyes. "Now tell me, what's interesting?"

"Just that you hate your maker even more than you hated Hugo."

He leans back. "Ah—that. Yes. I love her and I hate her. It's a rather complicated relationship that mostly errs on the side of loathing."

"For her or yourself?"

He stills in that vampiric way of his and doesn't answer. I change tactics. "You called me on my bluff back there. You knew that even though I said I'd stop bringing stakes around vampires that I would still do it. I think it's time I call you on a bluff, Adrian."

"Oh? And what's that?"

"We don't actually have a blood vow."

"Hmm. . . what makes you think so?"

"You wanted me to believe it was real so I would spy for you, but I haven't done a thing we agreed upon and nothing has happened to me. I'm supposed to take your word for the blood vow, that it will somehow kill me if I don't comply." I sit up straighter. "But I believe it was all a fabrication."

"Hmm. . ."

"What are you thinking? Am I correct?"

"I'm thinking that Hugo was right, you would make an excellent vampire. It's too bad you hate us so much, not that I blame you." He sighs and shakes his head. "I'm also thinking that you are smarter than most humans I've met because you're right. There never was a blood vow. Bonds forged in blood only exist between vampires themselves."

"I knew it." I pump my fist. "I can't believe you played me like that. Wait, scratch that, I totally can."

"The deal still stands if you want it. You give me information about Leslie Tate and what's going on in his organization, and I'll break your mother free of her gambling addiction."

I go quiet and think about the offer the rest of the boat ride home. I consider it from all angles. "What is Leslie Tate?" I finally ask. "Cameron is convinced he's some kind of demon."

"Hmm, if we work together, maybe I'll tell you."

Should I work with him? There's reasons to do it, plenty of reasons. But when we get to the dock and see the ferry with all the people still on there, still partying and reluctant to leave, I know my answer. I never want to be in bed with vampires, literally or figuratively.

"I'm out," I say at last. "I can't betray my friends for my mother, as much as I want to. I just can't be that person."

"And why not?"

He ties the boat to a post and we climb onto the dock. I'm a bloody mess, but it's dark and there's nobody else out here. They're all still on the boat, gambling their souls away. I stop and turn, taking in his beautiful face and hoping it's the last time I see it. "Because I want to be better than vampires. Not physically, not mentally, I'm talking about morally, Adrian. I want to be a good person."

"And vampires can't be good?"

"You know they can't." Even the times he's tried to help me, the times he's brought feelings out in me, or been on my side, he's still used me in his games.

Hurt cracks through his hard exterior. It's nothing I've seen on his face before. "You're right. I'm a lost cause. Best to stay away from me." And then he levitates into the moonlit sky and flies away.

THIRTY-TWO

In the days since Hugo bit me, I've become a different woman. All of my senses are heightened in the best possible way. I feel invincible and so, so alive. If this is what vampire venom can do for a human then I'm certain people would do just about anything to get their hands on it. It's no wonder the vamps are so adamant to keep this a secret. Every day this week I've woken up thinking the venom will have dispersed but every day I feel as invincible as the day before.

I stroll through City Park, marveling at the enhanced colors, the cleaner scents, and the brighter and warmer sun. It's as if I was wearing a filter over my senses all these years and now that it's been taken off, I don't ever want to go back.

This is my favorite park in New Orleans. It's filled with tree-lined paths, grassy knolls, ponds, bridges, and artistic statues. The place attracts tourists, families, photographers, sunbathers, and just about anyone looking for some peace and calm in an otherwise lively city. The Spanish moss trees here are my favorite, and it's one of those that I'm heading over to now. I chose this sundrenched area in a public spot and picked a time in broad daylight to have this meeting with my friends. I can't risk any vampires or their human minions overhearing. There's no way a vamp could be out here and a human wouldn't be able to get close without notice.

All week at our practices I've been avoiding talking to them and it's eating me up inside. I can't do it anymore. I have to be honest and explain everything from start to finish if I'm going to lose some of this guilt and hopefully get the guys' help. They might hate me after what I'm about to confess. Part of me fully expects that they'll never speak with me again and the idea of losing Felix is killing me the very most.

I spread out the pale blue picnic blanket that I borrowed from Olive and set down the sack of food in the center. Maybe another girl would have brought along a basket of bite-sized cucumber sandwiches, pita bread and hummus, fancy olives, crackers, cured meats, and expensive cheeses. But not me. I picked up cheeseburgers and fries on the way over. I have no place spending my money on other people's meals, especially considering Eddie's still mad at me, but I need a win with my team. I'm hoping greasy food will do that for me.

"Well well well, what have we here?" Kenton is the first to

arrive. He runs over and plops down on the blanket, quick to dig into his burger. From afar, I spot Seth and Felix strolling across the field, chatting like old friends. Felix's eyes dance with flirtation when they lock with mine. We share a delicious secret, definitely yummier than anything I could have brought to the picnic. My thoughts fill with memories of our time kissing earlier this week. I want to do it again. I'm certain he does, too, because we have plans to meet up tomorrow—just us.

What will it feel like to kiss him now that I've got vampire venom in my veins? The thought excites me way more than it should considering the guy might never talk to me again. Another kiss isn't guaranteed.

Felix purposely doesn't sit close to me, but his lingering gaze says it all. He wants to keep our relationship private between us until we can work out how to explain it to the others, especially Seth who thinks he's got some kind of say in it as our team leader. Keeping quiet is probably a good idea, what with the bomb I'm about to drop.

"Is this a bribe?" Seth questions, ever the observant one. He's the last to sit down. He skips the burger, going right for the fries instead. My smile falters into a slight grimace and that's all it takes. He knows. "What is it, Eva? Spit it out."

"You're good at reading people, you know that? You should play poker," I say. He bites into a long fry and raises his dark eyebrows. "Except don't because you'd be corrupted by the vampires."

"And how much do you know about that?" he questions, pointing the fry in my direction. The little dab of ketchup on the end reminds me of blood.

I lean back on my hands and summon my courage. My heart is racing and I'm certain my face is betraying my every thought. I've never been good at disappointing people. "I have to tell you guys a story, but I need you to let me tell it from beginning to end before you interrupt me."

I've got their full attention now. Everyone but Kenton puts down their food.

"Agreed?"

They exchanged worried glances but they each nod.

"Alright, so you know Adrian Teresi?"

"Everyone knows *of* Adrian," Seth says slowly, his hackles obviously rising. Kenton blinks at me and Felix stiffens.

"Well, I *know him* know him." Here goes nothing. "I was working for him."

"You were what?" Kenton sputters, nearly choking on his food. He coughs and I hand him a water bottle. The color has drained from Felix's face, and mistrust ignites in Seth's eyes. I get it. I'd feel the same way.

I hold up my hands in surrender. "You agreed to let me tell the story from beginning to end, so please let me."

They don't say yes, they don't say no, they don't say anything.

I start from the beginning and don't hold a word of it back. I explain it all. The problems with my mom, getting nicked by that fang that night I followed them, and how the tiniest bit of venom connected me into Hugo's bloodline without my knowing. The worst of it is the blood vow with Adrian. As I tell them how it all unfolded, shame slices me up into a million guilty pieces. I'm not proud of what I did, but I am proud that I didn't follow through for Adrian in the end. I'm super lucky it wasn't a real vow and that I was able to call Adrian on his bluff. When I tell them about Hugo's toying with me and the eventual staking in the graveyard, I can tell they're impressed but don't want to show it cause they're also pissed. And I finish it all off with why Leslie Tate is so interesting to the vampires, because whatever he is, he's something that feeds on humans too, and how Cameron Scout is a two-faced twerp gunning for eternal death.

"Okay." I pick a piece of tiny lint from my shorts and stare at my knees. "I know there's a lot to unpack there. So, do you have any questions?"

I'm met with a wall of guarded expressions. Nobody utters a word.

"Umm—okay. Well, I think I need your help," I say at last. "Cameron is going to screw us over and there's still the issue of Tate being MIA and—"

"Eva," Felix stops me. "Why didn't you come to us before? I'm not happy about any of this, but mostly I'm hurt that you didn't think you could trust me."

"Yeah," Kenton adds, "we would've helped you."

"Really?" I never thought they'd understand, let alone want to help me.

"Yes," the two say in unison.

"I guess I was worried you wouldn't believe me or if you did you would hate me." I peer over at Seth who's being awfully quiet. "And what about you?"

He considers me for a long moment. "I am partially responsible here. Had I welcomed you into our team like I should have from the start, you might have felt more comfortable telling us the truth in the beginning."

I want to ask him why he didn't welcome me, but I decide to leave that conversation for later. I have a feeling it has something to do with my crush on Felix, like maybe I'm not the only one who has feelings for our mutual friend. I don't know if it's true, but if it is, it's not my place to bring it up now.

A gust of wind rustles past us and takes the weight of my secrets away with it. I smile. The back of my eyes burn with tears and I want to kick myself for that—I am not a crier—but it feels good to have people who care about me. I've been so alone. Hugo was right all those nights ago when he called me out as being lonely, but my isolation was only because I was the one not letting others in, not the other way around.

"So will you guys help me?"

"Of course we'll help you," Seth says, "we're a team. But this isn't just about Cameron and Tate. Don't you see the opportunity you have here?"

I blink at him. I'm not sure where he's going with this.

"You need to go back to Adrian and take him up on his offer. We'll figure out how to stall on the Tate stuff, but this is your opportunity to learn secrets about the vampires"—his eyes gleam ruthlessly—"and take that bastard down."

"You can't ask her to do that," Felix hisses. "It's too dangerous."

Kenton stays quiet. He's become far more pensive than usual. "It's up to you, Eva," he says finally. "I'll support either decision."

"Are you nuts?" Felix isn't thinking clearly. He's thinking about me romantically, not about me as a vampire hunter, a member of this team, and someone who does have an edge that no other hunters have.

Seth is right.

I never wanted to go back to the casino or see Adrianos Teresi again. As much as I want to hate Adrian, as much as I try to convince myself that I do, I don't. He's helped me and I've developed a bit of a soft spot for the man. It makes me weak and part of why I've wanted this whole thing to be over. But I also want to save the humans from the vampires, even if that means besting Adrian. It's not everyday I'll get a chance like this. This idea is a crazy gamble, one that might cost my life, but the payout could change everything.

My heart picks up speed and against my better judgement, I decide to take the chance. "I'm in."

I haven't seen my mom since she chose Hugo's money over me. My heart is broken over what's happened to her, but she's not the person she once was, and I don't think there's anything I can do to save her. Of course, there's always a chance now that I'm going back to tell Adrian we've got a deal, but I'm not going to get my hopes up again when it comes to Virginia Blackwood. The let down is too painful. Too much damage has been done. I need to move on and let it go.

My job is still on shaky ground, but luckily Eddie is a total sweetheart and is letting me keep it as long as I promise not to leave him in a lurch again. I'm thinking about my lunchtime picnic and walking to work for my next shift. It's a nice evening, the sunset is casting everything in a golden light, and it's not too far to walk from my new apartment so I choose to forgo the bus.

"It's now or never, Eva. Just do it," I mutter to myself. I slip my phone from my pocket, call the casino, and ask the customer service rep to direct me to Kelli.

"How may I assist you?" Her voice is polished indifference.

"Hey, Kelli, it's Eva Blackwood, I'm wondering if I can have a meeting with Adrian sometime tomorrow or Monday. Is he available?"

She sighs heavily. "Haven't you had enough?"

"Apparently not."

She smacks her lips. "Can't say I blame you. The man is a force of nature." I can hear her fingernails clicking against her keyboard. "I'm only giving you a meeting because he's told me I have to look out for you, and I can't disobey my master. But just so we're clear," she adds in a sing-song tone, "I still hate you."

I can't help but laugh. I don't love Kelli either, but I'm starting to warm up to her, which says a lot. "I wouldn't have it any other way, Kelli."

"Tomorrow at noon. Don't be late. There's something Adrian would like to discuss with you, too."

I wasn't expecting that, and part of me wants to take it all back and cancel. Who knows what's going to happen when I step foot in The Alabaster if Adrian wants to "discuss something" with me. I've never had a positive outcome in the past, that's for sure. But I take the appointment and end the call. I have to get my stitches out anyway, so I'll kill two birds with one stone when I go to the casino tomorrow.

I round the corner and stop short when I see who's leaning against the wall of Pops. I don't know where she's been staying or what she's been up to, and seeing her here catches me off guard. I nearly trip over my own feet.

"Evangeline." My mother rushes forward and wraps me in a

tight hug. Her familiar rose scent hits me like a slap to the face. It's usually mixed with a tinge of cigarette smoke and booze from being in the casino, but today she smells fresh from a shower. I want to hug her back, want to instantly forgive and forget the events of the past month, but I can't. "I'm so sorry, Angel," she whispers against my cheek. "But I'm all better now."

I sigh and remove her arms, stepping back. "No, Mom, it's okay. You're an addict and the vampires only make it worse. That's what they do. To everyone. But you are who you are too, and I need to accept that and love you and stop holding it against you." Now for the hard part. My voice shakes. "But I'm also done trying to save you. And I can't be a big part of your life when you're like this. Sorry, Mom, but I have to save myself."

"You're right." Her eyes shine. "You're absolutely right. And I'm proud of you for saying that, I know it was hard, and I am ashamed for what I've done. But, honey, I mean it, I'm better now. I'm clean."

My heart clenches and I sidestep her. "I have to get to work."

She grabs my hand. "Please hear me out." Her voice goes low and she whispers excitedly. "Last night I was at The Alabaster and something incredible happened."

"Let me guess, you won big."

"No, that vampire guy, Adrian something, he took me up to his office and compelled me to give up gambling."

"What?" I gasp. I blink at her in confusion. Why would he

help her? I backed out of the deal.

"I know! I couldn't believe it either! I have no idea why he would bother. I asked, but he wouldn't say." She smiles brightly, looking a good ten years younger. "It's not just gambling either. I'm free of any unhealthy addiction for the rest of my life. And it worked. I have absolutely no desire to do anything like that again. Just the thought of that awful casino makes me upset."

"I'm really happy for you, Mom. I don't even know what to say."

She whispers. "And what's more, he said I couldn't tell anyone this but you, but he also compelled me to be free of other vampire's compulsion. Nobody will ever be able to get in here ever again." She taps her forehead.

I'm floored. It's as if everything I thought I knew about the world was a lie—it all tilts to reveal something brand new. "He can do that?" And also, how can I get in on it? I've never heard of such a thing. The very idea of it offers the freedom I've been searching for. This is *everything*.

"I mean, I don't know, but I guess so?" She laughs and her Southern accent grows thick. "It's not like I'm dumb enough to go test it, but he was pretty confident about what he was doing."

She hugs me again and I can't help it, a million emotions overwhelm me and for the first time in ages, I let myself cry over my mother. She shushes me and pats my back, and I let her do that, too. I bury my face into her shoulder and let it all out, years of frustration and sadness, and that newfound bright spark that Adrian has given me. He gave me my mom back. Why would he do this?

I don't know what's going to happen with him tomorrow. I no longer have a deal to strike since he's already given me what I wanted. I will need to think of something else he'll believe, some other reason why I would agree to be his little spy. But I also want to thank him, and maybe that's the craziest part of this whole messed up situation. Never in my life did I think I would be thanking a vampire, but Mom always said never say never, and it turns out she was right.

He *saved* her.

He didn't have to do that, and yet he did. For me.

There's got to be a reason besides the kindness of his heart. Adrian's heart doesn't even beat. He kills. He lives his eternal life—or death—from drinking our blood. He runs the city and deals in addiction and plays dangerous games with his ruthless queen. No, this move with my mother is a play for something bigger, and I intend to find out his endgame before it's too late.

The next day, I march into The Alabaster Heart at exactly twelve-noon, with my head held high, and what I hope is a brilliant plan up my sleeve—one that had better work or we're all dead.

DEAR READER,

Thank you for taking a chance on *Blood Casino*. I've been dreaming of this world for over three years, so to finally have it in your hands feels a bit lucky and surreal. If you liked it, please leave a quick written review on Amazon and Goodreads, and please tell your friends. Word of mouth is to an indie author, what blood is to a vampire—seriously, I can't do this without you. Speaking of vampires, would you like to read the blood vow kissing scene from Adrian's point of view? You can get that bonus chapter and other fun goodies by joining my Facebook reader group called "Nina's Reading Party" or by signing up for my newsletter on my website at **www.ninawalkerbooks.com**. I appreciate all you do and can't wait to share the rest of this series with you. Happy reading!

Much Love,
 Nina Walker

EVANGELINE BLACKWOOD

ASPIRING VAMPIRE HUNTER

HARD ON THE OUTSIDE BUT A SOFTIE ON THE INSIDE

VIRGO WITH SCORPIO RISING = WILL CUT YOU

IF YOU MESS WITH HER

ALWAYS TRYING TO DO THE RIGHT THING

EVEN WHEN THE WORLD SUCKS

LIFE MOTTO: WHEN SOMEONE SAYS YOU CAN'T DO IT,

DO IT TWICE AND TAKE PICTURES

ACKNOWLEDGEMENTS

Thanks to the readers; I couldn't do this without you. Thank you to my husband Travis for your continued support and inspiration. Of course, I have to thank my awesome mother for her support and her casino wisdom, not to mention the dream I had about her that inspired this entire world to begin with. Huge thanks goes out to my incredible cover designer Clarissa Yeo and her 3D artist collaborator KH. Thanks so much for agreeing to take on the *Vampires & Vices* covers and for rocking them beyond my wildest imaginings. Thanks to Molly Phipps for formatting the hard copies; there's nobody else I'd rather hire because your formatting is the best. Thanks to Melissa Stevens for the amazing book trailer. There are no words for how well you knocked that out of the park. A big thanks goes out to my lovely editor Ailene Kubricky—you're an absolute star! And to my proofreaders Sarah Mostaghel and Kate Anderson for helping me find those pesky typos with each and every book. Thanks to my many author friends who championed *Blood Casino*, from listening to me gush about the idea, to reading the early copies, to writing editorial reviews, and giving me loads of amazing advice. You know who you are and you ladies mean the world to me.

ABOUT THE AUTHOR

NINA WALKER writes young adult paranormal romance, urban fantasy, dystopian fantasy and more. *Blood Casino* is her eleventh published book and the first in the *Vampires & Vices* series. She lives in Southern Utah with her sweetheart, two kids, and three pets. She loves to spend as much time outdoors exploring the real world as she does spending time exploring other authors' brilliant imaginations. She's recently started narrating audiobooks, including some of her own. You can learn more about Nina and her books by going to www. ninwalkerbooks.com or by following her on social media. Her Facebook reader group is called "Nina's Reading Party" and her Instagram and TikTok handles are @NinaBelievesInMagic.

CPSIA information can be obtained
at www.ICGtesting.com
Printed in the USA
LVHW02014928082I
696290LV00018B/1541